"BETTER OFF DEAD"

Best wishes

John Paul Carinci

"BETTER OFF DEAD"

By

John Paul Carinci

1stBooks - rev. 8/2/00

Chapter One

"Hi, this is Frank Granstino from the Financial Life Insurance Company, how are you today?"

"Okay," the woman said hesitantly.

"Well, that's good! The reason I'm calling," I said with a smile, "is, I'm helping all the homeowners in your neighborhood with their life insurance needs. I'll be in your area Tuesday and Thursday. Which night would be better for me to drop by and introduce myself?"

"Neither! Why don't you get a real job, and stop bothering people!" she screamed as she slammed the phone down.

I proceeded to cross her name off my list so hard that the pen ripped the page. All in a day's work, I thought, as I closed my prospecting list.

Earlier, another woman - she must've been elderly - blew a whistle into the phone. She blew it so loud that I had to switch ears on the next call. Maybe she thought I was a pervert or a weirdo. But that's the trouble with the phone book, you never can tell who you're going to reach.

Prospecting for new sales is tough. So far, my first six months in the business has been murder.

The district manager, Tom Somi, reminds me: "Hey sport, you're only twenty-seven years old. Give the business a chance."

"Enough of this!" I said, "I already have an earache!" As I packed my briefcase, with calls still to be made. After I take a break for lunch, I'll drop in on some businesses in the area and leave my cards.

The district office was pretty quiet for a Monday, especially for a bright and sunny April day. As the experts say, "You're in business for yourself, your time is your own."

Now our manager, Tom Somi, is a tough man who screams a lot. Tom only wants to know, each week, total premiums and how many policies were sold by each of the forty sales representatives. He's a bottom-line type of guy, that no one wants to go up against.

Just this morning at our district meeting, Tom fired an agent. George Flayer had been with the company for two years. His first year was good, but his last six months were terrible. No sales, coupled with cancellations brought him down.

Of course Somi capitalized on the firing. He made George come in for the district meeting. Then right after our meeting he fires him, making George clean his desk out in front of everyone. Tom really is pond scum.

"Somi, that 'potato head', let me go!"

That's all George could say to me as he packed up his files.

With my legs up on my desk, leaning back in the chair, I realized that this business can be brutal.

Insurance sales is difficult because we're selling a piece of paper. The one thing that keeps me in this business is that I truly believe in what I'm selling.

I reminisced about my last job, working for a major bank in Manhattan, as a general accounting clerk. All I had to do was show up, sit at my desk till five, with no real work, no challenge. Slowly, I was getting melt-down of the brain.

After I left my dead-end job, I vowed to be productive somewhere. When I started selling insurance a little over six months ago, it was very difficult. Since I have few relatives, and only a couple of close friends, I was very reluctant to try to sell any of them life insurance - at least in the beginning.

I wasn't like most agents, who rely totally on friends and relatives. And after a few months fail out of the business. I relied solely on strangers and referrals. That's why I didn't start off with a bang and was just barely able to pay my bills each month.

I drive a 1972 Buick Century and live in a modest 2 room apartment in Bensonhurst, Brooklyn. At 27 I was still able to chase away any thoughts of marriage.

As my phone rang, it startled me back to reality. I've always been somewhat of a dreamer.

"Hello, Frank Granstino here."

"Frankie, it's me, how're doing? I caught a couple of minutes before lunch."

"Pauly, how are you, you got my message a couple of nights ago?"

"Yeah, I didn't get a chance to call. So what did you think about the Knicks game last night?"

"Aw, they stink! Do you believe they blew a twelve point lead? Sometimes that Starks really does stink."

"I know, he gets carried away trying to make those three-point shots. Maybe they'll win tonight. Toronto hasn't been winning lately. Frankie, I'll catch you later, over the weekend. Let's get together. Gotta run!

"Okay Paul, I'll catch the game tonight on re-run. Later, bro!" I said, as I hung up.

Paul was my best and oldest friend; we went back almost twenty years. There wasn't anything I wouldn't do for Paul, or he wouldn't do for me. For the longest time we lived only two blocks from each other, so we saw each other every day. Even our parents became friends. We were so close-knit they had no choice.

"Time to get moving," I said, as I packed up some forms, and realized the time. "Time to blow this joint!"

After lunch, and some prospecting of the business area on foot, I went home to hang out. We make our money in front of clients, not in the office. Since I had an appointment this evening at 7:30, I took an afternoon nap.

The business is lucrative though. It's possible to earn up to two thousand dollars for one large sale. Not bad for a couple of hours of work. This business has its highs and lows. The lows are terrible, when sales are bad.

My older sister Candice helps me keep it all in prospective. Ever since our dad died tragically a couple of years ago, from a car accident, Candice and I became even closer.

She always tells me, "Don't worry about the clowns that don't want to buy, it's their loss!"

At times she's better than a psychotherapist.

My appointment was with a guy named Jimmy Lanski. Jim is married and has two children; the perfect prospect. With children his need for protection would be great.

At the time I made the appointment I found out that Jim worked off the books, had no life insurance and was interested. "This should be an easy sale tonight," I thought, as I dozed off.

3

Chapter Two

It was 7:20 pm when I reached Jim Lanski's home. I like to be early. The Lanskis and I hit it off great. There was an immediate rapport between Jill, Jim's wife, Jim and me.

The Lanskis knew that they needed life insurance. They had no problem with the ninety dollars a month premium, for the five hundred thousand dollars of protection on each of them.

They were so happy with my needs analysis that they willingly gave me a few referrals. Which was great. Referrals are the life blood of the business. With referrals, you at least have a chance to succeed.

The Lanskis told me to call their cousin, and their uncle. The Uncle is Jim's mother's brother. It really was a great night! I thought as I drove slowly back home, savoring the moment of sweet success.

Bright and early on Friday, I was back in the district sales office. Fridays are our reporting days, and the time when the agents tally up their sales and report them to management.

The office reminds me of the old West that I've seen in the movies. Each week we have many agents coming and going through the doors like the swinging doors of a Western saloon. All the new agents come into the business like they own the world - tough and confident.

In my short career so far with Financial Life, I've met some real characters. There are agents that sit through district training meetings, reviewing the horse racing form, pretending to be listening intently, while secretly itching to get out of the office to bet the ponies.

That's the biggest reason Harry never amounted to anything. Harry has a bad gambling problem, and unfortunately he keeps forgetting which is his money, and which is his client's money for premiums.

Then there's wild Audrey. Audrey is a fairly new agent with the company, and one of only two women of the twenty three agents in the district.

Audrey thinks she's beautiful, when in fact, she's as ugly as sin. So to compensate for her looks she resorts to showing some extra skin. This tactic seems to be working quite well with all the guys. One day she'll wear a real short dress and no underwear, at least that's what Ben, the district's only black agent, claims.

Ben looks like a pro wrestler. He's a big guy, with broad shoulders and a big fat neck and head, much like a football player or a weight lifter. Definitely not someone you'd want to mess with.

Well, the way Ben tells it, Audrey, during a Friday agency meeting, kept lifting her dress up, ever so slowly, until as Ben once said, "You didn't have to use your imagination anymore." All I know is, that all through the meeting, Ben's eyes were getting bigger and whiter than we've ever seen.

Then there's good old Freddy. Freddy's always in the bathroom, and when he does come out he's always sniffing like crazy. His eyes are always bloodshot. He usually looks spaced out. Audrey said one day, "It doesn't take much imagination to figure out what 'coke-head Fred' has been doing!"

It comes down to the bottom line. Some agents get away with murder.

There's also Mel Flaine. Mel is the office rummy. He just plain stinks like a bar rag. Rumor has it, old man Mel can only stay sober long enough to get through the weekly Friday meeting just to get his paycheck.

One day Mel came in the office drunk, tripped over a chair and almost killed himself. The office was almost empty, so only the secretary saw him.

Mel's the veteran of the office. He's been with the company for nearly thirty years. So they just leave him alone, even though he doesn't sell too much any more. It makes you wonder just what the pressures of selling can do to some people.

The last character of the office is Louie Remi. Now, Louie is fifty-five years old, divorced and not all there. Louie is at rock bottom in the insurance industry. Even though he's been selling for some twenty years, he doesn't earn more than a clerk in K-Mart.

Louie is neurotic. He's on a powerful anti-depressant medication. One day he'll come over and hug you, and tell the whole world how terrific you are. The next day he'll curse you out.

Louie always was weird. He has even been known to threaten peoples' lives, then blame it on his medication. One time he threatened to kill another agent because he thought the agent stole a lead off his desk. Five minutes later Louie found it under his phone and tried to apologize.

Louie's also notorious for spreading wild rumors about people throughout the office, especially when he gets jealous of the top sales people. His personality is like Jeckyll and Hyde. It's really a pisser though, to watch the reactions of the new agents Louie comes in contact with. I learned right away that the best thing to do is stay far away from crazy Louie. With all the strange and wild personalities we have, they should re-name our agency: The Outer Limits.

There's just too much pressure to write business each day. To make matters worse, the company threatens to fire you every thirteen weeks, if your numbers don't exceed their minimums.

"The Enforcer", as he's sometimes referred to, is the district's manager Tom Somi. Tom is a tough manager. Even his appearance is intimidating. Tom is fifty five, about five foot ten, big, maybe 250 pounds and bald. He looks tough, like he could take on three guys at once in a bar room brawl.

I'm sure he was in the Army for a while. He's comical though. Every time Tom gets mad, the whole top of his bald head gets beet-red, along with his face and his ears. His whole head gets so red you expect his head to burst any second - a hot tamale ready to blow. Most of the agents try not to get him excited. But not me. I guess I always get on peoples' nerves. After all, I know I can run faster than him.

It is really funny when he gets all red in the face, except when it's you that he's glaring at. Maybe it's been my low-production, but lately Tom's head always seems much redder when he's around me.

The most frequently asked questions from Tom are: "So what have you got so far for the week?" and "How much in premiums did you sell?" Then he always seems to turn red. So I try to avoid him every chance I get. I usually wait for him to go to the bathroom, so I can slip out quickly past his office and through the back door.

Since it was our Friday report day, I submitted my three new applications. Two of them being the Lanski sales. The total annual premium came to fifteen hundred dollars. Not bad for the week. But since I went blank the previous two weeks, I was trying to keep a low-profile, and I definitely wanted to avoid Tom. Quietly and slowly, I slipped smoothly past his door, and into the hallway. Thinking that I made it past the big-guy, I smiled, until I heard a booming voice: "Not so fast Granstino!"

Slithering back I said: "Who me?"

"No your mother," he barked. "So you think you had a good week, do you? You want to cut out of here at 11:30?"

"No, Tom, I wanted to drop in on some people."

"Why don't you just drop back into that seat there," he said, pointing to the chair, "and tell me how you're going to replace the two prospects you no longer have now, Frank?"

I had to admit, the big guy had a point. I had sold two different families this week, so I had two less prospects now. "Tom, I've got new names, I've got referrals!" I said boasting.

"Oh you do, do you? Maybe you think that by keeping them in your briefcase there, they'll multiply like humping rabbits?" he asked sarcastically.

"No sir!" I snapped back.

His head and ears were beet-red again, he smiled sarcastically again and said; "Why don't you make some more calls before the weekend, so maybe we'll all be able to eat again next week!"

"Good idea boss!" I said, as I exited his office by backing out into the agents' room. I knew I wasn't going to win this fight, not with this red-faced gorilla.

I was holding five good-quality referrals, like they were maturing savings bonds. I didn't want to use them. Maybe I was scared that I couldn't convert the referred leads into appointments.

Sometimes agents don't have a single lead to call, and must resort to making cold calls from the phone book. And sometimes, when they do have some quality leads they're somewhat reluctant to use them, for fear of using up their ammunition.

I waited for the big gorilla to go to the bathroom and I quickly slipped out. I'll call my leads when I want to! I thought, as I drove my car into the start of my long anticipated weekend.

Chapter Three

The weekend was fairly quiet. I'd recently broken off my engagement with Lisa DeVoe. Lisa and I were going together for about two years. And, as is the case in many relationships, it was much better in the beginning. But amazingly, as soon as we announced our engagement the relationship started to sour to such a point that I felt trapped. Like I'd lost my freedom and the ability to do the things that I wanted to do.

Then, one day about two months ago we just blew up at each other. The fight was so intense that we realized it was far better to split up than to possibly kill each other.

Lisa was a beautiful woman. She had long auburn hair, sparkling green eyes, and long legs. She stood about five foot nine and looked like one of those fashion models, tall and slim. Lisa was two years younger than me, and very smart. Maybe too smart.

I realize now, that beauty alone doesn't guarantee a happy life together. There has to be much more than looks; something magical and special. A spark that will last forever.

I did miss Lisa though, I wasn't really sure which part I missed the most. The physical relationship, or just the comfort and security in knowing that I had a girlfriend who cared for me and that I wasn't alone.

On the weekends I try to forget about the insurance business completely. This weekend I took in a couple of good movies on cable. I also watched some baseball on TV, and went out to a club with my friend Paul.

On Sunday, I went to see my mother in Staten Island. Of course I stayed for dinner. Mom made my favorite: lasagna. No one makes it better. Paul couldn't make it Sunday at my mother's, but he has a standing invitation for dinner any time.

My sister Candice was there too along with my niece, Michele. Candice is thirty five years old. Michele is so sweet, she always gives me a big hug and kiss. She looks up to me, ever since her father ran off years ago.

It'd been a couple of weeks since I had dinner over Mom's place. I love my mother, and my family very much, I only wish I could see everyone more often. Life today though is very fast paced. Before you know it a month slips by.

By Sunday night, the pangs of loneliness set in once again. Lisa entered my mind, while I was straightening up the apartment.

Bright and early Monday morning, I was in the office sitting at my desk, planning my week. I was the first one in the office. It was good, there was no one to distract me, no small-talk to waste my time.

As I sat with a large container of coffee, along with all my notes and prospecting names scattered over the top of my desk. I thought, who should I call first? Which ones were my best prospects? I put the hottest ones at the top. It was time to make some quality appointments and keep Tom off my rear end.

By 10:00 I had made a top 50 list. Then, the prospects I've been calling for weeks now, and unable to secure appointments with, were put toward the bottom.

Alright then, number one: Tony Vongemi, Jimmy and Jill's referral, looked real good. Tony is Jimmy's boss and uncle. By far, this was the best lead I had.

I remembered that Jimmy said there was no medical insurance on the job. There were 10 employees that worked there, and it was a family-owned restaurant. The name of the restaurant was: Little Part Of Italy. It was on 86th Street in the Bay Ridge section of Brooklyn. The time was 10:20 am, time to call the restaurant.

"Tony please," I said,

"Hold on!" snapped a deep and powerful voice. After about a minute I heard, "Yeah what is it!" With a smile in my voice I said, "Hi Tony, it's Frank Granstino, from Financial Life Insurance, a friend of Jimmy & Jill Lanski's. They suggested I call to speak with you about medical insurance. I'd like to make an appointment to drop by and see you."

"A friend of Jimmy's, sure, come by tonight at 7:00. I got to run, good-bye!" he said this so fast, I almost didn't catch it, as I heard the phone slam down.

On my way out of the office, Tom stood in my way blocking my exit. "Anything good setup for the week?" he asked.

"How about a ten man group at a restaurant?" I boasted.

"It's about time Granstino!" he said sarcastically as he moved out of my way.

As I walked past him, all I could think to myself was: Watch it, go bother someone else!

My friend, Paul Luggi, worked in the city for Trelane, a large accounting firm. Like most New York City workers, he worked nine to five. I called him a prisoner, because he could never leave.

"Oh yeah, at least I don't have to beg people for a sale, like you, so I can eat each week," he'd always say.

Although he had a point I still felt free, and "freedom does have its price." I keep reminding myself. I knew Paul would be at work, so I called him.

"Hi Paul it's Frank. What do you know about a restaurant called: A Little Part Of Italy, I've got an appointment with the owner tonight?"

All I heard was laughing, then he said, "Don't you know?"

"No I don't know, what's the joke?"

"I think that place is run by the Mafia! Frank, you'd better watch yourself, pal! I'll talk to you later, I've got to run," he said, while laughing hysterically.

That's all everyone knows how to say, I said to myself, Mafia this, Mafia that. Everyone in Brooklyn can't be in the Mafia, not every store and restaurant at least.

Chapter Four

It was ten minutes to seven, as I circled around the block for the third time passing the restaurant, looking for a parking spot. I didn't want to park in their parking lot, at least not on my first visit. I'm funny like that.

Another five minutes passed before I caught an available parking spot not far from the restaurant. It's times like these, that I really hate Brooklyn.

The place was beautiful. It had an all-stone exterior with hand-carved solid-wood double doors, which were stained in a rich walnut finish. Inside the restaurant there were shining marble floors with white, fluted wood columns throughout. The hardwood floors were walnut with elegant heavy trim gracing all the ceilings at the top of the beautiful walnut-planked walls.

The tables were of solid marble, with black wrought-iron chairs that had lush red-velvet cushions. All this was topped off with soft Italian music. "Talk about ambiance," I thought. It gave me a feeling like I was actually in an elegant cafe in Italy. It was by far the most spectacular restaurant I had ever seen.

A maitre'd, dressed in a white tuxedo, smiled, and asked, "How may I help you?"

"I'm here to see Tony," I said cautiously.

"Is he expecting you?"

"Yes," I said, I have an appointment, just tell him Frank, from Financial Life."

Still in awe of the place, I patiently waited. A short time later the maitre'd returned and motioned me to follow him to a back room.

Seated at a table towards the rear of the room, was a man in his late fifties. I knew it was Tony Vongemi, because the only other people in the room were two big and bulky-looking guys in their late 20's. They were hanging around one on each side of the doorway.

Tony was impeccably dressed, his suit was perfectly tailored, his salt and pepper hair was styled and neat. He had expensive looking diamond rings, but not too flashy. I could tell Tony Vongemi had class.

I introduced myself. He was very cordial. We spoke about his nephew Jimmy, my client and his head waiter. "Jimmy is a good boy," he said. "We also like Jill."

We also talked about the Yankees and the Knicks which, we were both fans of. "I miss Don Mattingly. He was a worker. Really committed to the task at hand. I respect that. We look for hard workers in my line of work. Those are the kind that get ahead."

"I know exactly what you mean, Tony. Mattingly was my favorite Yankee too."

I guess we hit it off well. So well in fact, that Tony had given me two tickets for Sunday's basketball game. The Knicks were playing the New Jersey Nets at the Meadowlands. I was thrilled to death, I just loved the Knicks.

"You're going to the game on me, my friend. Wait till you see the reserved seats we have this season. You've never been this close to the action. You're going to feel like the players are going to pass the ball right to you!"

Tony wouldn't let me talk about business until I had dinner with him, as his guest. Feeling very much at ease, I had the seafood special and a couple of glasses of fine white wine. After a fabulous dinner Tony offered me an imported cigar, which I politely refused. While I watched him smoke we had a couple of cups of espresso, with Sambuca on the side, while we talked business.

"Okay, talk to me. I want to take care of my workers. They're good people. They do anything for me. What can I do to show them I appreciate their respect and dedication?"

"Well, you could start a medical group plan, and pay for some, or all of the premiums," I said.

I then showed Tony a few different quotes for group medical insurance.

"Do it, just start the ball rolling. Let me know what the damage is, and it's a done deal. Okay with you Frankie?"

"That's a good move, your employees will appreciate it," I said.

16

"Yeah, a little respect goes a long way. At least that's the way I see it," he said.

Then, Tony asked, "How about life insurance for me? That's a good idea. What would three hundred thou cost?"

"About $6,000 per year."

"That sounds good Frankie, sign me up! You know, I like you Granpino.."

"That's Granstino, Tony, but you can call me Harry, if you want."

"You're a funny guy too! I like that. Just make sure you do the right thing!" he said, as he reached for his checkbook and proceeded to write out a check for a thousand dollars.

Tony handed the check to me as he said, "I'll give you the other five thou, in cash, when you drop the policy off to me."

When I asked Tony for referrals, he told me that he'd be calling me next week with some leads. All in all it was a great night. I made my quota for the month in just hours.

I was thrilled and somewhat relieved that the constant sales pressure I was feeling, from low-production, was finally lifted. On the way home I stopped at Dunkin Donuts and celebrated. Three donuts and a couple of cups of coffee later, I headed home a very happy man. This business is great when the sales are coming in. It's keeping it going that's tough.

Chapter Five

It took only two weeks to get Tony Vongemi's policy issued. He was approved as a preferred non-smoker even though he smoked cigars. The company allows for cigar smoking by the insured as long as no cigarettes are smoked.

Tony's blood tests all came back favorable and his blood pressure readings were excellent. Not bad for a 59 year old man. My friend Paul couldn't believe that I sold Tony Vongemi a policy.

I told Paul how friendly Tony was, but all he did was laugh. Paul said, "Frank, you're the most gullible guy around. I checked it out. Don't you know that the Mafia owns The Little Part of Italy restaurant, and that Tony Vongemi's whole family is in the mob. Frank, Tony's brother, Bobby 'The Bull Dog', is a captain in one of the most powerful families in organized crime."

Shaking my head I said, "No, Tony Vongemi is a legitimate business owner. I met the man, he's a nice guy. He's got class. I don't care what his family does, Paul, besides, I've got to make a living. I can't be scared to sell to everyone I come across. Anyway, how can I get into any trouble just selling life insurance?"

"I don't know yet," Paul said, while in deep thought, "but you better be above board in everything you do!"

"Frankie, how've you been?" asked Tony Vongemi as he hugged me when I entered the back room of the restaurant. Reluctantly, I put my arms around him.

"Great!" I said, "Nice to see you again Tony."

"Carlo, get Frankie a drink and whatever he wants to eat!" he shouted at one of the guards standing watch at the doorway. The man jumped, as if he'd been stuck with a needle.

I quickly turned my attention back to my business. After all, I was there to deliver his policy and get the rest of a six thousand dollar premium, which was my biggest sale ever.

While placing the policy in front of Tony, I said, "Congratulations Tony, you've been approved for three hundred thousand dollars worth of life insurance!"

"What do I owe you?" he asked.

"It comes to five thousand one hundred fifty dollars." I said confidently.

"Benny, get me the money from the safe, and hurry up!" he barked.

Again somebody jumped and ran, all I could think of as I watched was, Boy these guys move pretty fast. Especially for guys that look bigger than football players.

"How did you like that Knick game, Frankie?"

"Tony, it was great! Thanks for those tickets. I was so glad they won that night, it was really a close game."

"Yeah" he said, "I had a thousand on that game!"

Benny returned carrying all crisp new one hundred dollar bills, and proceeded to count them out for me.

"Tony, thanks for allowing me to help you with your insurance needs. I'd now like to help some of your friends."

"You want some names Frankie Boy?"

"Yeah, sure!" I said, confidently, "if you like the job I've done for you, Tony."

"Well Frankie, I've been thinking for a while now, since I saw you a few weeks ago. I'm going to make a list for you of some of my Paisans to call on, because I like you Frankie," he said, as he reached over and pinched my cheek quite hard. "You're not pushy. Not all sales, you're okay!"

"Thanks-Tony. So when do you want me to pick up the names?"

"Drop by tomorrow after lunch," he said. "Just remember, Frankie, do the right thing! You take care of me, I take care of you," he said, while staring at me.

As I looked into Tony's eyes, I knew, that I definitely would do the right thing.

The next day, at the restaurant, I picked up the sealed envelope with names that Tony had left for me. It was about 1:30 in the afternoon. He left it with the bartender. I was told, Tony wasn't available, so I stayed for one glass of white wine then left.

As I drove back to my office, I kept wondering how many referrals Tony had given me. After all, getting quality referrals is the hardest part of the job.

Once I reached my office, I settled in at my desk. I quickly gathered up all of my office mail and put it on the side as I opened Tony's referred-leads envelope. Inside the envelope, it looked like a gift from heaven. Not only were there names, but so much more. Tony wrote out the occupation, salary, marital status, number of children of each of the prospects and more. From what I could tell, Tony only gave me his friends and workers, no relatives.

Then, what was very interesting, were the instructions Tony put next to each person's data: how much premium to charge each family, and approximately what amount insurance I should sell each person. He explained, it was his estimate, based on his knowledge of each person's income.

Most importantly though, I was instructed to tell each referral that Tony Vongemi wants them to buy the insurance only from me. This type of thing just doesn't happen to life insurance agents.

For what must've been twenty minutes, I sat staring aimlessly at the list in front of me. There were thirty different referrals, all listed with complete notes.

There was no doubt about it; Tony Vongemi was my most important insurance connection. In sales we call them "center of influences." With his solid leads, I could easily meet all my quotas, and finally stop begging people to buy policies from me.

Over the next three weeks, I was able to sell eighteen new policies to twelve of the Vongemi referrals, for annual premiums of almost nineteen thousand dollars. Selling policies on these leads was quite honestly the easiest sales I've made since I started my selling career. They anxiously wanted to buy as soon as I mentioned Tony Vongemi.

All I'd do, was mention his name and like magic they'd do anything for me. It was turning out to be a real gold mine. I had finally found the pot of gold at the end of the rainbow. I wasn't going to do anything to jeopardize the gold mine now.

Not only was I selling Tony's people, but I was also getting referrals from them too. Sales were so good, that I sent Tony a giant basket of gourmet fruit, and imported cheeses.

Tony was so happy with my gift, that he mailed me another thirty names. I was on top of the world. Enclosed, once again, was full information on each referral. Including their income, along with the amounts of Insurance he suggested that I insure them for, and what he felt they could afford.

When I told my friend, Paul, just how many leads Tony had given me, and how much money I was making, he cautioned me again. Paul said, "Frankie, be careful buddy, watch your back!" Then he asked, "Frankie do you know how to swim?"

"Of course, Paul, don't be silly!"

Then Paul said sarcastically, "You'd better learn how to swim with concrete shoes!"

"Nice talk Pauly! Why don't you just get my casket ready. You're always so scared of everybody!" I said, somewhat pissed off.

"Don't say I didn't warn you Frank!" he said in a completely serious tone of voice.

All I cared about was making money, and keeping the sales manager, Tom, off my back. For a change, actually for the first time since I started, I was doing extremely well.

After these two most recent months now, I had sold thirty five of Tony's leads. I felt ecstatic. Things were going great for me.

Every few days I'd call to thank Tony and he'd give me more leads and also give me free tickets for basketball and hockey games. It was almost as if I was doing him a favor. But in reality, he had already put almost thirty thousand dollars of commissions in my pocket, and he was responsible for making me the number one agent in my district.

Even Tom the manager, told me to keep up the good work. For a change he'd lightened up. Now, he didn't care if I missed meetings or reporting days, as long as I had plenty of business. For once he was a happy man.

Everything had turned around for me. My pay check was so large now I couldn't spend it all. I was socking most of it away each week. For the first time in years, I'd built up a nice bank account. Financially I was happy. But I had no girlfriend, it was lonely. But time was moving fast. All the leads were keeping me so busy, selling and delivering polices, that I didn't have much time for anything else.

For once in my life though, I felt no real pressure. My bills were all paid up, and I even bought a brand new car, a ruby red Cadillac Eldorado. I had always wanted a Cadillac. My whole life, all I ever drove were bombs. Finally, I owned a car that didn't bang and rattle as I drove.

Frank Granstino had finally arrived. I'd finally achieved success. The entire office showed me respect. I even started smoking expensive cigars which Tony had gotten me started on. He even gave me my first several Cuban cigars. "If you're going to smoke, go in style," Tony said, when he handed me my first 'real cigars'. The cigars I now smoke, at least are affordable. But they still make me feel like a big shot.

For the first time, I purchased a real gold bracelet, and a sapphire and diamond pinky ring. Then there was the big screen television set, a forty inch job. When Paul saw the television, he flipped. "What do you think, you're a movie star now. Sure it's great, especially for the basketball games, just don't get carried away buddy!" he said.

"Aw, don't worry, easy come, easy go!"

Chapter Six

It was Monday morning and I was dragging a little. I arrived at the office a little late, while outside, the temperature was 93 degrees, and it was only 9:30 in the morning.

The weather report predicted that it would break one hundred degrees once again for the fifth day in a row. Much too hot to work, I thought, as I slowly and lazily drifted into the office and sat at my desk.

The telephone message stared at me from the top of my desk. It was marked: "9:01 am. Monday: Urgent, call Mr. V. at home."

I knew instantly who it was, but why he called worried me. Tony, had never before asked me to call him at home. Let me wake up first, I thought as I poured a fresh cup of coffee.

As I dialed his number, I sipped my coffee trying to come alive. "Hello Tony?"

"Yeah, what is it!" he snapped, in his usual rough sounding voice.

"Tony, it's Frankie G, from Financial Life, how are you?"

"Oh it's you Frankie. How've you been?" he asked, as his voice softened up considerably.

"I'm great Tony, what's up?"

"Oh yeah, Jo Jo's dead," he said so abruptly, that I couldn't answer. "Frankie did you hear me!" he snapped.

"Huh, oh y-yes," I stammered, still stunned from shock. "When, what, ah, what happened?"

"Heart attack. Over the weekend. He went in his sleep. Didn't feel a thing. You know Frankie, that's the way to go. Quiet-like," Tony said.

"Tony, he was only 33 years old and in perfect condition. He passed his insurance physical with flying colors," I said feeling totally flabbergasted. "He had small children. Tony this is terrible," I said, as a tremendous feeling of sadness overcame me.

"Yeah, these things happen. So, what do we - what does the wife have to do to collect Frankie? The body's already in the morgue"

The way he said it was so cold, so matter-of-fact-like. All I could tell him, was that I would call him back later.

Then I asked about the wake and the funeral. Tony told me that everything would be done from Italy, where that morning they were flying the body back to.

I knew Jo-Jo came from Italy, so I didn't think much of it. All I could do was feel very sad for his three little children and his lovely wife, Caterina.

Somewhat in a daze, I sat at my desk deep in thought, oblivious to all the office noise and activity. The sales office was packed for a Monday morning, with all its urging phones and sales stories being shared by many agents.

I was troubled for the moment, contemplating. My mind was racing, deep in thought. Thinking about the loss of my first client. My first death claim, since becoming an agent. I never thought it would happen so soon. I even remembered the smile on Jo-Jo's face, when I spoke of the possibility of dying.

No one ever thinks that it could happen to them. Death is a distant thought for most people. I remembered sitting at the kitchen table in his apartment, together with his wife, Caterina and his three children, I remember thinking, How loving and respectful these children are.

I remember seeing the sparkle of admiration in Caterina's eyes, as I spoke about her husband. Especially, as I asked all the questions on the application, including the type of work he did.

What'll happen to the family - now? It just depressed me, thinking about it. Especially when Jo-Jo's face was so vivid in my mind. As much as I talk to everyone about the possibility of dying, I still never want to accept the fact that one of my clients will ever die. Especially when there are children involved. I hate this part of the job, I thought, while staring into space.

After speaking with Tom, the manager, I called Tony back. I told him that all we need is an original death certificate and an obituary clipping from the local newspaper. Tony said he'd get the requirements needed. Even though I told him that I'd gladly visit the wife to pick it up.

"He was a Paisan, he worked for the Family, so I'll take care of everything, Frankie, You understand," he said. "We're also paying for the funeral," he said with pride.

Of course, I immediately backed off, knowing I wouldn't get my way. I said, "Fine, Tony, I'm always here if you need me"

"I need you only to pay the death benefit," he said, as I heard the click of the phone, after he abruptly hung up.

I filed his attitude away in my mind. Tony did have a tough way about him. No doubt because of the Mafia family association, or maybe just his own unique personality.

Still, all I could hear was my friend Paul's words, "Watch your rear end Frank," and the one about learning how to swim, "wearing your concrete shoes."

Maybe I was overreacting. Maybe, I was blowing it all out of proportion. Still I couldn't help wondering; What did I get myself into with this Vongemi Family?

The Financial Life Insurance Company paid out the death benefit of five hundred thousand dollars, to Caterina. Surprisingly, it took only six weeks of investigation to settle the claim.

I was feeling a little guilty. After all, I had sold only a fair amount of policies so far for the company. Less than two hundred thousand dollars in new premiums, and already I was responsible for sticking them with a half-million dollar death claim.

Feeling somewhat self conscious, I didn't want to show my face around the office, at least for a few days. Again I felt sad and disappointed, mostly over losing a young client.

I was, however, doing a great job with new sales for the office. For the year so far, I was currently the number one agent in the district. Most of my recent sales though were from Tony Vongemi's leads. Ever since meeting Tony, I had sold more than thirty of his referred leads, and was currently making a great deal of money.

27

Chapter Seven

Tony was very pleased with my handling of Jo-Jo's death claim. After the insurance death claim check was mailed, Tony invited me to be his special guest at dinner. Of course, I accepted. Maybe he had more referred leads for me.

With sales going so well I dared not jeopardize my relationship with Tony. I enjoyed being the number one agent in the district. And I loved the fact that I was stock - piling money in the bank. I had been broke for so long, that I didn't want go backwards ever again.

Once I arrived at the restaurant for dinner, Tony told me how professional I was, and what a good job I was doing with the leads he'd been giving me.

Tony reminded me, "one hand washes the other, Frankie. You take care of me, I take care of you. Understand?"

"Yes Tony, absolutely!"

And Tony did take care of me. We had the biggest lobster tails I'd ever seen, along with a fancy white wine called: Pouilly Fousse. When Tony was happy he didn't spare any expense. And on this night he was ecstatic.

But I was slowly learning more and more about Tony Vongemi, the man. I kept telling myself not to get too close to him. I guess I was starting to wise up. For the first time, I realized that there was something more to Tony. Something more than a classy restaurant owner. Every time I felt myself really liking Tony Vongemi, the person, I kept telling myself, how I like my kneecaps. I especially like that my knees bend, whenever I want them to and I'd like it to stay that way.

Another month had passed until I heard from Tony again. This time another client of mine died, it was also someone given to me by Tony.

This time I was told that Liborio Tiullo had died, from an accident while crossing the street. I couldn't believe it, I had lost another client, and now the insurance company was faced with another claim. This one was also five hundred thousand dollars.

Now I was really starting to suspect something. Especially when I found out that Liborio's family had moved to Italy just two months ago, and that this wake would also be in Italy.

I was beginning to seriously wonder about Tony Vongemi, the man that I'd thought was nothing more than a shrewd businessman.

A few days later I received a call from Tony. He asked me to come to the restaurant that evening. Tony told me he had just received Liborio Tiullo's death certificate.

I didn't want to speak to Tony. Not at this time. Even though I was selling so much insurance, the company was talking about giving me my own detached office, along with a secretary of my own.

I knew that I owed my new found success for the year to Tony. But I had no desire to be any part of, nor have anything to do with any kind of fraud - or the Mafia. Still, I knew that you just didn't say no to Tony Vongemi.

It was almost 7:30 pm when I entered Tony's restaurant. This time Benny and Carlo, Tony's heavies, were both waiting for me. They were sitting at the bar.

As soon as they saw me they jumped up and rushed over to me. Carlo said: "The boss is waiting for you in the back room. Let's go, Bub."

I looked at Carlo, then at Benny. My first instinct was to run back outside, but casually I strolled along. After all, Tony liked me, I told myself as I felt my hands starting to sweat. These guys are looking more and more like gorillas, I thought to myself as we kept walking slowly to the back room.

Tony was waiting for me. As soon as I walked in the room he jumped up to greet me, and of course there was the usual hugging. This time though, he kissed me on both cheeks. I hate when grown men hug, and now we'd progressed to kissing, I don't understand it. My ears must've turned red, because they felt hot all of a sudden.

"Tony, my friend, how've you been," I said, as if I had actually missed him.

"Great Frankie, my boy. And how are you?"

30

"Oh, I'm just fantastic," I said, as he slapped me on the back just hard enough to remind me, that he was the man.

"Come, sit with me, we'll drink and eat. You spend a few hours with me my friend. Frankie, you don't mind do you? You've got nothing to do, do you?"

"No, of course not!" I said, as I thought, I'd rather have a fist fight with the heavyweight champ, than be around these mugs. I smiled as I casually looked at Carlo and Benny, who took their usual spots standing guard near the door. They just stared straight ahead.

Tony waved his arm, "Have the cook start preparing our meal!" he shouted at Carlo. Tony smiled at me, with a twinkle in his eyes, and said, "The chef is preparing us something extraordinary. Peking duck, it's one of his specialties."

"Great Tony, I've never had it, but I've heard that it's very good," I smiled.

One of the waiters ran through the doorway and asked us what we wanted to drink. Tony abruptly stopped him by waving his hand in his face and said, "Bring us the Cristall champagne and make sure it keeps flowing!"

All I could do was smile, feeling a little like I was Tony's personal date for the night. That stuff is expensive, I thought to myself. I was so glad I wasn't a girl, or Tony would surly be expecting sex tonight, I thought. Then I looked closer at him and thought. Thank goodness he's not funny, or I'd really be in trouble!

"So, how's business Frankie? You still leading the office in sales?"

"Yes, thanks to your referrals. Thank you again Tony," I said.

"Good. You're a good boy, Frankie. You stay that way. Don't ever change!" he said, cautioning me with his finger in my face. "You're a good boy. You don't do any drugs, I can tell, you know!"

"No, Tony, I would never touch the stuff. Women are my only vice," I said, smiling from ear to ear.

"Yeah, me too, Frankie," he said, with a little wink.

He waved at Benny now, and put up two fingers. Benny just shook his head and left the room.

"Boy, this man has some power!" I thought.

The champagne was smoother than anything I ever had. We started a third bottle of Cristall, as our dinner was almost over. What a magnificent meal, and great champagne! I thought, You'd think it was my last meal, it was so good.

"Tony, thank you for dinner. It was great. I'm stuffed!" I said, before I realized that I really didn't want to use those words, in front of this man.

"Yes, me too, Frankie. It wasn't bad"

Why was Tony being so nice to me? I was scared to approach him about the two dead clients he referred to me. It was too much of a coincidence. I refrained from mentioning it, as much as it bothered me. Especially when he told me, "You know Frankie, I think of you as one of us. One of the good guys, don't ever become a rat. We hate rats!"

At that instant Benny entered with two gorgeous women, one on each side. One was a blonde blue-eyed bombshell, the other a brunette with green eyes.

Tony got up from the table and introduced the girls. The blonde's name was Alice, the other girl was Susan. I couldn't take my eyes off of Susan; it was those beautiful green eyes.

Tony announced: "Alice and Susan will join us for dessert."

With a light buzzing in my head from the champagne, I was ready for anything.

My eyes lit up, as Susan sat next to me, she touched my arm and said, "Well, hello, handsome!"

I must've melted. After all it had been months since a beautiful woman was this close to me. Her perfume was enticing, but not overpowering. All I could do was smile. Tony had our waiter bring us various bottles of after dinner liquors. I was feeling no pain.

After about an hour of chit-chat, Susan stood me up and started dancing slow, as she pulled me up to join her. Right there next to the table, as we danced close, Susan whispered little suggestions to me and blew softly in my ear. Well, that was all I needed, I held her closer than before. The warmth of her body against mine, felt magical and gave me goosebumps.

At this point she winked at Tony and Alice, Susan led me to Tony's private office. It was like a dream come true. I was there being seduced by a beautiful woman. We quickly changed the convertible couch to the bed, and the rest of the night made wild passionate love.

All I could think as I wobbled up the steps to my apartment was, What a night! What a spectacular girl! This guy Tony is alright! And then I caught myself. Wait a minute, if he's dirty, then someone's collected one million dollars, and I'm the guy writing up the polices!

Not only that, but at this point, I must've written fifty or more of Tony's leads. What the heck is going to happen? How many more young people are going to die? I called Tony the next day. "Thanks Tony, last night was great. I can't get over the ladies, they were awesome!"

"No problem, Frankie. You're like family now. By the way, stop by later, I've got twenty more leads for you buddy!"

"Alright, thank you again Tony," I said, but I really felt like running. Now he considered me; "like family"

Great! Just what I needed, I was now a part of the Vongemi Mafia Family. All I could think of was the movie, The Godfather, where everyone was getting killed off.

With the Mafia, no one was ever safe, no matter how important. What's going to happen now? I thought, as I shook my head from side to side. I knew that I was in too deep. Just thinking about my situation scared me. I had to continue to be friendly, but I didn't want to be buddy-buddy. Not with Tony, or any of his friends. All this thinking made my head throb.

Chapter Eight

It'd been three weeks since my night of delight with Tony Vongemi, and of course Susan. Then, just when I was starting to forget, the call came in at the office. It was Tony.

He sounded nonchalant, as he said, "Frankie, Anthony Probine is dead, they think it was his heart. Too bad for Anthony, huh, Frankie!"

"Yes, Tony, I can't believe Anthony's gone. He was so young. Tony, I'll drop the papers off at the restaurant, so we can begin working on the death claim." It was a call I'd been expecting. My worst suspicion was true. Something stunk in Brooklyn, and it wasn't cheese.

What was worse, was that I had insured Anthony for a one million dollar life insurance policy. That made two million dollars in claims, so far. All of them, Tony Vongemi's personal recommendations.

All of a sudden I felt like throwing up. I wanted to tell Tony Vongemi exactly what I thought of him.

It was then that I realized for the first time ever, I was bringing home over three thousand dollars a week, all because of Tony's leads.

What was I going to do? I couldn't tell the insurance company. I couldn't tell my manager, Tom. I couldn't even tell my friend Paul. I'd only be putting other people, good people, in terrible danger. No, I had to keep it all to myself. As hard as that seemed, I had to try to come up with some idea on my own. Maybe I needed a break, a change of routine for a while. A change of scenery, maybe I'd take a vacation to Paradise Island, in the Bahamas. I had plenty of money now.

There's enough of sales commissions coming in and I've got vacation time coming. I said, trying to convince myself. That's what I'll do. As soon as I submit the latest death claim on Anthony Probine, I'll just take off for a two week vacation.

It was 3 o'clock in the afternoon when I walked through the entrance of the Little Part of Italy restaurant. I purposely showed up at that time so no customers would be around.

After seeing Tony sitting at the bar, I walked over to him. He gave me the customary hugs and kiss that I hated so much.

Not wanting to be there at all, I handed Tony the death claim forms for Anthony Probine's claim and informed him that as soon as he had them completed, I'd submit them to the company for payment.

Then I told him about my sudden vacation plans. He looked a little annoyed as he said, "Why so sudden Frankie? Are you running from someone?"

"No Tony, I just need a break, a change of scenery."

"What about my claim? I mean the Probine's claim?" he snapped.

"Oh don't worry, Tony I'll be back way before the company is through with their claims process. It'll be alright."

"You know Frankie, that's a lot of money. One million dollars. A real lot of money. Nothing better go wrong!"

As I drove away from the restaurant, all I could hear over and over again, was Tony, with his tough Brooklyn accent, saying; "Nothing better go wrong! Nothing better go wrong!"

Feeling edgy, I pulled into the first bar I saw. A place called The Cool Splash and ordered a couple of glasses of white wine. I was starting to feel a little nervous.

My hands were cold and clammy. Maybe it was all the claims, or maybe it was just Tony Vongemi, and my fear of the Mafia. I had three drinks in ten minutes.

Once again I heard the threat, "Nothing better go wrong!" What had I gotten myself into? Here I was, a young man just starting my business career, and already I was in trouble.

Already my career was in jeopardy. But, more importantly I was now part of some kind of conspiracy with the mob. Feeling trapped, like I was in deep trouble now, I didn't know what to do.

I knew one thing for certain though, I must keep my mouth shut, and not panic. I've got to play along. After all, I thought, I'm only twenty seven years old.

Chapter Nine

There's something magical about flying above and through the clouds. The plane was a TWA 747, a big roomy and comfortable plane. It looked brand new to me. It even smelled new. It'd only been a week earlier that I made my reservation.

The bigger the plane, the safer I feel. Flying for me has always been a nerve-wracking experience, although I've recently learned to relax and finally try to enjoy it.

This flight was extremely relaxing, especially since I was going in style. First-class all the way. Why not. That's what I said to the travel agent when she asked if I wanted first-class. After all I'd been through I might as well go in style. Because you never know when you're going! It was only yesterday that I booked the first class trip. Never really a regimented person, I don't like to plan anything way in advance. I'm a spur-of-the-moment type of guy. After all it was right now that I needed a break. I needed to go somewhere, sit in the sun and forget.

To me, a vacation is seeing nothing or anyone that you know at all. Nothing to remind you of home, and going to a remote place where the sun is always shining and the drinks are always flowing.

I've always been partial to the ocean. There's nothing that can match the natural sounds of mother nature, as she sends the waves onto the sand from the deep seas.

It's so soothing and relaxing to sit on the balcony and take in the ocean. With it's hypnotic waves and sounds, as I smoke a fine cigar, read a book, or eat breakfast out in the open air.

When Tony Vongemi heard me talk of vacation, he suggested the Diamond Palace in the Bahamas. I immediately fell in love with the resort from the travel brochures, changed my plans and took the next available flight out. Tony told me to call a fellow by the name of Jeremy Roberts. "Jeremy is good people," Tony boasted, "He'll take good care of you!"

Tony instructed me to tell Jeremy to give me the finest suite available, and bill it to Tony Vongemi's personal account. Not wanting to get involved any further, I tried to refuse, but after

Tony became slightly suspicious, I quickly, and happily accepted.

"Tony, it would be an honor to accept your generosity," I added, with respect.

You just don't argue with Tony Vongemi! You go along. You give him what he wants, or he'll just take it. I've learned that much, so far, by being around him. Just make sure to show your appreciation or watch out.

So I gave in. And in return I got what I wanted; a fabulous vacation away from Tony "The Tiger" Vongemi and the whole stinking mess I was into. Tony told me again: "Don't worry, Jeremy will take good care of you in the Bahamas, he's a Goomba!" Now I was worried. That's exactly what I was afraid of - someone taking care of me!

I made the arrangements with Mr. Roberts. As soon as I mentioned Tony Vongemi, his whole attitude changed. He couldn't have been more helpful. And he had assured me, as he put it - "I promise you, your stay will be a most pleasurable one!"

When we landed at the airport I was prepared to take a taxi to the hotel, but waiting, right outside the gate, was a young black man carrying a sign with my name on it. I couldn't believe it, but he led me right to a silver Mercedes Benz limousine, which I later found out belonged to the Diamond Palace Hotel. It was only used for VIP's, politicians and special guests.

We arrived at the resort hotel in only about twenty minutes. The ride from the airport was comfortable and scenic, I told myself; I already like this place!

Jeremy Roberts, was waiting for me when I walked through the large bright entrance of the hotel. There were floral arrangements throughout the lobby, along with elaborate, colorful Persian rugs, covering solid walnut floors.

Jeremy was a tall, slim, elegant looking black man with a goatee, and a French accent. Jeremy, as he wished to be called, ushered me over to the concierge desk and handed me an envelope.

"You don't need to check in, Mr. Granstino, I've taken the liberty to do it for you. In fact, I've taken care of everything Mr Granstino! We want your stay to be extraordinary.

"Enclosed sir, you'll find a set of keys to insert in the elevator, so that you can access the private and exclusive penthouse suite floors. You'll also see another set of keys for the room. One is to gain access to the foyer area, and the other is for the front door of your suite.

"There's also a voucher, Mr. Granstino, for complimentary chips for use in the casino, and feel free to charge all your meals to your suite, which of course is totally complimentary.

"Now, James will show you to your room. And Mr. Granstino, I'm only a call away. Your stay with us is most important. Anything you need, anything, will of course be provided for you Mr. Granstino, we want you to tell Mr. Vongemi only good things about us!"

I thought to myself, Vongemi's got these guys jumping too.

The suite on the 33rd floor was simply spectacular: Marble floors, large white columns, mirrored walls, plush white rugs, and an exquisite circular fireplace right in the middle of the room.

There was a fully stocked bar with all quality label brands. Over to the left, were two steps which led to a platform and a room with a Jacuzzi along with a complete steam room. Then, over to the right was a sunken six foot deep pool, which was heated to a comfortable eighty-five degrees.

Still in awe, I sat at the bar and opened the chilled champagne which was waiting for me. As I slowly sipped the very expensive and quite dry champagne, I took in the more intricate details of this magnificent room.

Leaning back, I opened the envelope Mr. Roberts gave me, and found that the chip voucher inside was for one thousand dollars of complimentary chips.

Once again, I realized, Tony was buying me. He was slowly and meticulously sucking me into the wonderful and extravagant world of the Mafia.

In my wildest dreams, I never thought I'd ever even know someone in the mob no less be a part of it! I've finally arrived, I thought.

Now, would I be able to live. Or, would I be the next body washed ashore, with no face, no name and no identification? Another John Doe that the city finds and buries in Potters Field?

With a glass of champagne in hand, I strolled all through the elaborate penthouse suite, past the large fresh flower arrangement in the living room and into the master bedroom.

The room was rich with beautiful cherry wood dressers and an armoire. The floor was a rich dark stained oak, and deep pile expensive carpet. There was a huge twelve-foot round bed with silk lavender sheets and huge pillows. This elaborate suite was much more than I could've imagined.

Lying back on the large, firm bed, I seemed to disappear as I sipped my champagne and tried to relax. Feeling like I was in another world, I wasn't going to think about anyone or anything.

I just wanted to chill out and calm myself down. I felt so relaxed, that before I knew it I fell off to a dead sleep. Maybe it was the sweet calypso music coming from CD system.

By the time I woke up, I guessed that three hours had passed. Even though I was on vacation, I didn't care that that much time had just slipped away.

There's a price for everything in life, and for now relaxation was what I needed. For the first time in months, I'd started to calm down and it felt great.

But now I was starving. One of the restaurants was on the first floor. It was called The Shipwreck Bounty, a seafood place.

The lobster was great, as were the jumbo shrimp. There was no doubt in my mind why they were rated a five-star restaurant, as the hotel brochure claimed.

After watching two pay-per-view movies in my room, which I knew would be free, I took a relaxing dip in the Jacuzzi. With the gentle streams of water to relax me, I drank a half a bottle of white wine then went back to bed.

Tomorrow's another day, I thought, as I drifted off to sleep. After all, I have a couple of weeks here. No need to rush things.

Chapter Ten

It was 8:02 am when I woke. It's amazing how the human mind knows what time is. Even on vacation, the mind is conditioned to wake a person up precisely at a given time.

Well, this time I wasn't budging. I'm not getting up until 10:00 I thought, as I closed my eyes again. I don't care how nice it is outside, it feels good to sleep. I turned over.

Sometimes I'm lazy. I remember as a child I could easily sleep all day, and still want to sleep some more. It only seemed like a split second later, but it was 10:05. I was awake and it was time to get up.

The shower I took was invigorating, much better than at home. This shower had a dial for the pulsating rate you desired. I set it to the maximum for the greatest massaging effect. Slowly, I was falling in love with this long-needed vacation, as I wondered if I'd ever want to go home.

I was starving by the time I grabbed a quick breakfast of pancakes and eggs, and a bowl of fresh fruit. The Bahamas is known for fabulous fruit, and I knew that I'd be getting my fair share of it everyday.

Between the fabulous fruit and fresh fish, I'd be gaining weight quickly, unless I did a lot of swimming. So I rushed back to the room, put on my bathing suit and headed to one of the hotel's pools. The Diamond Palace Resort had three gigantic pools spread throughout the complex. I chose the biggest pool in the resort.

Slowly I walked out to the pool with the huge waterfall on one end, and a barbecue grill with a swim-up bar area right in the center. As I walked, I absorbed the beautiful sights of this fabulous area. This pool looked like five Olympic-sized pools in one.

It was almost 11:30 by the time I reached the pool. The sign that hung near the pool area, already showed the temperature at 83 degrees with a sunburn ratio of seven. The sun was very strong, and a high-rated sun block lotion was recommended.

41

Nothing changed, not even in paradise. As usual, I wasn't prepared and had to purchase the sun block lotion at poolside.

The resort was very accommodating though, by providing anything from lotions, to hats and sun visors. I paid nineteen dollars for a small bottle of number twenty sun block.

After rubbing the sun block all over, I settled down in my chaise lounge and opened my new paperback book. It was a best seller, by the award winning author, Og Mandino, one of my favorites.

The name of this paperback was The Choice. There wasn't one of his books that I didn't love, starting from his first book. Mandino is considered an inspirational-religious writer, and his books are spellbinding to say the least.

It seemed like hours, but only forty minutes had passed, when I looked up from my book and saw a beautiful woman to my right. She said, "Is this chair free?"

"Sure," I said, happily, as I quickly looked her over. She looked to be approximately twenty-three years old. This gorgeous woman had silky dark-brown hair that hung just past her shoulders and beautiful, mesmerizing hazel eyes.

As she sat down, she quickly removed her top and shorts revealing a stunning, baby blue string bikini and a fantastic body. I almost bit my tongue off, while trying not to leer

Quickly I looked away and stared back into my book. Out of the corner of my eye, I could tell that she was now applying some sort of lotion. Continuing to read, I dared not look, even though I was dying to.

All of a sudden, she leaned over and asked, "Would you mind?" As she motioned to her back. Quite startled and with the dumbest look on my face I said, "Sure!" as I took the number 6 Coppertone suntan lotion from her.

While applying the lotion carefully, I made sure not to press too hard, or put too much on. I was a little nervous.

As I spread the lotion slowly, I couldn't help thinking to myself how fabulously soft her skin felt. Maybe it was the heat, maybe the resort, but I've never felt skin like hers before. I always thought that there's something sensual about a woman's neck, with soft pertruding shoulder blades and the gentle slope of the small of the back.

My mind was starting to drift, as I caught myself and said, "There you go!"

"Well, thank you very much! My name is Alicia," she said, while smiling with a twinkle in her eyes.

"Well, hi. I'm Frank, and anytime I can help!" I said with a big foolish looking smile.

Guys are real suckers, I thought to myself.

"This place is beautiful isn't it Frank?"

"It's just gorgeous Alicia, are you here for the week?"

"Yes, and you?"

"Maybe two weeks, maybe more, depending on when I feel like working again."

"That's great! Maybe we could spend some time together?"

After a slight pause, I said, "Absolutely!" Although I still couldn't believe what she'd just said, and doubted it would happen.

Alicia and I spoke about books, authors, everyday humdrum, and the fabulous pool. We took a few dips in the pool together, staying near the waterfall at the center. We had a few exotic drinks and a lot of great laughs. It felt like a dream, I couldn't believe my luck. Alicia was gorgeous. She was twenty seven years old, and single. She lived in Boston, and was an executive secretary in a Boston law firm.

Alicia was fairly tall, possibly five foot six, and she had long legs along with a nice body. As we spoke I tried not to stare at her body.

We were getting along great, like we knew each other for years. It felt so natural talking to Alicia, that I really did feel like I was in paradise.

That evening we met at 6:00 in the lobby. We took in the beauty of the spacious lobby for several moments. Our plan was to have a couple of drinks, then dine at the resort's spectacular Shipwreck Bounty restaurant, which I told Alicia all about. Since this was her first day here she followed my suggestion. After we had a few Passion Punches, the hotel's specialty, we moved on to the restaurant.

Alicia and I each ordered the house special, lobster and shrimp in a special wine sauce, which was simply fabulous. After a couple more Passion Punches, we were feeling no pain. I signed for everything, charging each bill to the penthouse suite. A person could get addicted to this kind of life.

The resort's premier club the Oasis, in the south wing tower, had entertainment every night except Mondays. So we danced away the evening to great live Caribbean music.

The place was jumping with excitement. Alicia was slowly putting me into a hypnotic love spell. As we were staring into each others eyes, she looked fabulous with her big hazel eyes, and her great smile. After a few minutes I was a goner. After all it doesn't take much to get a guy in the mood. At least not this guy. By one o'clock in the morning we found ourselves with our arms around each other, and wanting much more.

I suggested my gigantic penthouse suite, where I had a bottle of chilled champagne waiting. After all, I had a mob boss's suite, I was the big shot now.

I suggested that we sit on the huge, tropical - looking couch in the spacious living room, as I put on the big screen TV, and tuned into the local cable channel that plays non- stop Caribbean music videos.

It wasn't long before we were all over each other, kissing and hugging. After approximately fifteen minutes of this, Alicia stood, reached out a hand, smiled and led me to the master bedroom.

Of course I was prepared for sex, but I had no idea it would be so soon, and with someone right out of Vogue.

It must've been two solid hours of non-stop, passionate lovemaking before I fell asleep. And what a good sleep it was. I was dead to the world, and couldn't have cared if the world ended there and then.

Chapter Eleven

It was 6:00AM when my eyes opened only slightly. It was much too early for me. Maybe because of all the activity from the night before, or maybe because I thought that it all might've been a dream. This was definitely not a dream. Not with this headache.

But when my eyes finally did focus I realized that I had a hangover. A tremendous hangover. And that's when I saw her.

She was absolutely beautiful, lying only a few feet away with her eyes closed. Alicia, the girl I barely knew looked like an angel, with her hair tossed widely around her lovely face, so innocently.

No, this was no dream. She was here with me. Not able to sleep I lay there staring at the ceiling. Thinking, wondering why me? And just savoring the memories. I replayed the whole scene again in my mind, slowly, frame-by-frame, as if it were a movie. From the moment we met at poolside, through the wonderful, magical evening till now.

After several minutes of deep thought, I realized that something was wrong. I looked over at Alicia, my angel of love, who was sleeping like a baby. Then it hit me. I'm a confident guy, I feel that I'm good looking, but I know I'm not knock down handsome. Even though I'm not bad looking, I've never attracted a woman this easily, not to mention a gorgeous woman like Alicia.

Yes, something was going on, headache and all. I thought, while staring at the ceiling. While Alicia slept and looked beautiful I was trying to sort this thing out.

It was now 7:00AM and my mind was really in overdrive. Was this his way of watching me? Or maybe Tony Vongemi was just showing his appreciation by taking care of me. Somehow I strongly suspected that Vongemi was keeping me under close observation.

Perhaps Tony was hoping that I'd confide in the beautiful Alicia. Maybe I'd tell her my plans, my fears, my suspicions.

Maybe I'd tell her what I really thought about the Vongemi Family.

Well, I wasn't about to let on to anyone, here or back home that I knew anything. My game plan would be just to enjoy it. Take it for all it was worth; ride it till the end. After all, I could also be as sly as a fox if I wanted to.

If Tony wanted information, I'd give him information, I'd feed Alicia all the positive, happy-go-lucky information I could. I'd play his game, I thought as I closed my eyes and fell back to sleep alongside Alicia, the spy. But now, I, was a counterspy.

By the time I finally woke, it was 9:15, Alicia was still asleep. So I went out onto the balcony. The fresh-smelling morning air, along with the melodic sound of the singing morning tropical birds, told me it would be another beautiful day in paradise.

As I sat taking it all in, on the balcony, my mind returned to what had been troubling in Brooklyn. I was thinking, scheming, working on a plan. A plan, I felt would save my life. A plan to get me out from under Tony Vongemi's hold. Lately I felt as if I was in the Mafia, even though I was totally innocent and unaware that I had been sucked in.

It was almost 10am when Alicia finally opened her beautiful eyes. In the morning some women look washed out, their faces looked stripped, their eyes blank and bare. Alicia looked great.

Alicia had a naturally beautiful face, so even with no makeup she still looked beautiful. When Alicia smiled at me, with her perfect white teeth, my heart skipped a beat. No, I was definitely going to ride this thing to the end. It was almost like a honeymoon for us, even though I knew it would eventually all come to an abrupt end.

We each took separate showers, I shaved and we got ready for breakfast. It was a beautiful sunny morning as we reached the Garden Terrace restaurant.

The sky was the bluest I'd ever seen. The ocean waves were just a gentle ripple and the leaves of the palm trees moved just enough to convince me that it was all for real.

The Garden Terrace is where we had our breakfast, outside overlooking the perfectly manicured and flowered grounds of the resort.

While we were eating our breakfast, the birds sang their songs, sounded their ritual mating calls and playful chasing of one another. This truly is paradise, I thought, as I stared into Alicia's beautiful hazel eyes.

We feasted on omelettes made fresh for us at our table by a roving chef. There even was a fabulous fruit bar set up with all types of chilled fresh fruit, which I could eat all day.

Later on, we sat poolside once again, working on our tans. I felt like a piece of bacon sizzling in this hot Caribbean sun.

There was no way we could stay for long periods of time in the sun, without cooling off in the pool. The sun was so hot that the pool felt like bath water. Still, it was so refreshing I felt like falling asleep in it.

Not a bad way to spend one's life, I thought, as I picked up my book again, and entered still a different world.

After ten minutes or so, I made believe I was reading. It was actually planning, thinking, trying to analyze where I was, what I'd gotten myself sucked into, with Tony and the Family. My mind was working like a computer, non-stop, calculating each projected move with possible, ultimate outcomes.

Much like the moves of a chess match, I realized that each action on my part, would result in a specific reaction. And the frustrating part of it, was each time I played out potential actions I could take against the Family, the resulting reaction I always came up with was me being killed.

The Family could very easily silence me, make me fish food, or part of some building's concrete foundation.

I was getting more depressed by the minute. So I put my book down, and closed my eyes like Alicia had. I fell off to sleep on the lounge chair, with the sun warming my body right through to my bones. If only I was rich I could live like this everyday. What a life - the most fantastic woman, I've ever been with, and God's best climate-controlled island around.

"So Frank, how does it feel to be away from all the pressures of work?"

"Alicia, I never thought I could, but I'd trade it all in back home for a life right on this little island!"

"I know what you mean, I love it here. It's like a secret. Most people don't know this place exists. Frank, anything in particular back home bothering you?"

As I thought, I looked towards the sky. "Well, Alicia, I guess the biggest thing I need a break from is the pressure my sales position puts on me, each and every day."

"I hear you, I needed a break, a change of scenery too. This place is just perfect, isn't it?"

"Absolutely, like heaven on earth!" I looked closer into Alicia's eyes. Which drew me in.

After a half hour we awoke, took another long dip in the pool and ordered lunch. It was amazing, all we had to do in this paradise was raise a little red plastic flag on the back of our lounge chair. The poolside waiters and waitresses were all dressed in their exotic-colored shorts and T-shirt uniforms. When they saw a raised flag they'd practically run over, take your order and get you anything you desired. The only thing they didn't do for you in this garden of eden was carry you to the pool on their backs.

With our lunch, I felt like having a white wine, but changed my mind and joined Alicia, who'd ordered a pina colada.

Like a deep-seated splinter, Tony Vongemi was still bothering me, more on my vacation than when I was home. The way I figured it, the longer I knew Tony and his Mafia family, the more I understood his operation and dirty dealings.

Tony made it look like we were good friends, but I knew better. That's very common in the Mafia game: make them feel real comfortable, and when they least expect it - knock them off!

This little trip convinced me that sometime in the future I'd know just a little too much about the Vongemi Family. Too much knowledge for my own good. No matter how well liked I might be, I was still an outsider, a potential threat.

The potential threat, was that I could do too much permanent damage to the Vongemi Family just by talking. I knew now, full well that one day I'd outlive my usefulness to the Family. After all, Tony wouldn't risk jail time over me.

Not when he could make one simple phone call, and the pest, the little Frankie headache, would go away quickly, quietly and harmlessly. Then the Family would go on undisturbed, to find some other sucker.

I realized I'd have to keep thinking of a phenomenal plan. One that could be carried out to masterful perfection. Anything less wouldn't be acceptable. It had to work. It had to be perfect. And perfection took time and plenty of patience, neither of which were my specialties. I kept it up though. My mind just kept working, planning and thinking. Even when I wasn't aware of thinking, my subconscious mind was, while it worked overtime.

Chapter Twelve

Who was this man? I said to myself. I've seen him now for the last three days. He was standing out from all the other vacationers I saw. There was something intimidating, tough-looking about him. Maybe it was his size, or his face, but why is he constantly watching me?

I looked closer. He was about six-foot-three, about twenty-seven, and a very in-shape 250 pounds. He had his hair cut real short, flat-top style. His face was badly pot- marked. Clearly someone you'd never forget.

Then there were his eyes, which were cruel looking, piercing like the eyes of a madman. This guy was definitely not someone you'd want to bump into while he was eating an ice cream cone.

I realized that it must be Vongemi's man. A tail, a stooge. Someone to report my every move. That's great, I'm being monitored by a gorgeous girl and a gorilla. Maybe he was going to try to knock me off here. No, that wouldn't be good, I tried to assure myself.

The Mob does it better than that, and not at a vacation resort with thousands of tourists as witnesses. No, it wasn't my time. But it scared the heck out of me. So much so that I had to pee. So I casually excused myself, and left Alicia sun-bathing at poolside.

Feeling very curious at this point, I had to see if this goon was actually following my every move. First I quickly rushed through the hotel entrance and ran to the nearest bathroom.

Then I swiftly walked out the side door at the end of the hallway, and stood around the corner of the hotel. I was just in time to see the big jerk come running out the hall exit. Looking all around in panic. Much like a child who'd just lost their mother.

Just as I thought, it was Tony's man. Probably with strict orders, no doubt not to let me out of his sight. Did the Vongemi Family think that I was running away?

Or maybe, that I'd be doing something strange in the Bahamas? Maybe they were just trying to play it safe? Well they got caught with their pants down. This jerk with the flat top head wasn't very good at being inconspicuous.

I thought to myself, I'm not a hero, I'll let him see me again. After all, I don't want to raise any suspicion in Tony's mind. He can't know that I'm on to him. Alicia, also mustn't get the slightest indication that I suspect anything with her.

This is supposed to be my relaxing chilling-out vacation. I'm not going to push my luck with Tony. Why should I? Why rock the boat? I'm not going to show him anything but respect. I won't let on, that I know he's got my every move covered.

I'll try to enjoy the rest of my vacation. After all, the big man is paying for this beautiful paradise resort. The Vongemi-fear is a strange emotion, I don't want to give Tony a reason at this point, to think that I'd be better off dead.

Why worry? I'm going to lie back and enjoy the whole scene, as planned - especially, Alicia.

Alicia gives me the impression that she's very attracted to me. There's something happening when our eyes meet. When our lips touch, and the magical sensation begins, there's a certain kind of high, even if it's only for a short while. Making love to Alicia, convinces me that I'm truly capable of accomplishing anything. Meanwhile, I continued working on a solid, well-thought-out plan.

Alicia and I were totally exhausted from the fierce rays of the sun. So we went up to the suite for a nap. Of course we couldn't keep our hands off each other.

We made passionate love, then fell off to dead sleep. All the wine we had both drank, along with the sun and the sex, was better than the best sleeping pill. We didn't wake until 5:30 p.m., just in time to prepare ourselves for a busy evening of food, entertainment and of course, casino gambling.

We had a spectacular gourmet dinner which consisted of filet mignon, a freshly prepared Caesar salad, various vegetables and a fine aged dry red wine. The restaurant was very romantic along with candlelit tables, and a wonderful woman who played soft background music on the harp.

Alicia and I danced the night away to an eighteen piece big band orchestra in the main ballroom. I only wanted to dance slow and close... Very close.

The main event of the evening though, was the well- known casino. There were thousands of sparkling lights, many bells and various winners screaming.

All this suddenly greeted us as soon as we entered onto the casino floor. The place was packed. What I liked about the casinos in the Caribbean, was the way people dressed up.

There were people dressed in gowns and tuxedos, but almost everyone, in general, was dressed up. Most of the men wore sport jackets or suits, and the women wore colorful light dresses.

There was no doubt, it was much nicer than in Atlantic City. This casino was smaller than the ones in Las Vegas and Atlantic City. But in my opinion, this results in a much friendlier atmosphere with the dealers and the players.

We started at the slot machines, and they were truly one-armed bandits. Then we ended up at the tables. There was a game called Caribbean Stud Poker.

This was the first time that either of us saw or played this game. Caribbean Poker is a game where the players each play against the dealer, and whatever each player does, will in no way affect the other players' hand or wager at the table.

We were both quickly in the hole, losing about a hundred dollars each after a rough start. It was then that I was dealt a full house. The dealer was dealt a pair of fives.

With that winning hand, I had won a hundred and seventy five dollars. Not bad, but I knew better. That's why I quickly cashed out. I convinced Alicia to cash out, also and join me for a walk along the beach.

The moon was full, the sky pristine clear, and the air was cool, calm, with no wind. The stars were sparkling bright, like miniature light bulbs. It was then that I suddenly caught a glimpse of him out of the side of my vision.

It was Tony's goon. He was watching my every move. Did he really think that I couldn't see him spying on me? Or maybe he didn't care, and wanted me to see him. These tough guys just love to intimidate everyone.

Sometimes, the fear of something is far more important than the action. The Vongemi Family, loves to put the fear of what may happen to you if you don't watch out. It's very effective. It works with me. I was scared silly, at least for the moment.

Not wanting to look back, I paid extra-special attention to beautiful Alicia and the gorgeous sky above, with its millions of points of lighted stars. We walked as we gazed in awe at the spectacular, star strewn sky, clearer and more brilliant than either of us had ever seen. We continued hand- in-hand, taking in the sounds of the ocean and the surroundings.

As I looked deeply into Alicia's eyes, I felt myself leave the present world and enter a different one. A new and special world, with an invigorating sensation. A strange feeling came over me. This special feeling is something I've never felt before. It was a special high without any side effects - hypnotic.

I caught myself just in time. I told myself that this wasn't love. Not that special love one looks their whole life for. Alicia was put up to this little act.

I must keep things in perspective. She may be slightly attracted to me but I must control my feelings. I told myself again to enjoy the whole scene, and have a ball. Just as long as I realized that it would definitely end. And when it did I'd be by myself, alone again.

We walked for hours under the stars and we talked. We spoke about feelings, past loves and our jobs. I felt so comfortable around Alicia.

It felt natural to open up my feelings to her. I could talk to her about anything. Then again, I caught myself. But I asked myself which act Alicia was playing. Was she a well paid escort, or the real thing.

I shook my head, stopped thinking and continued to enjoy her company. No matter who she might be playing, I was going to stop analyzing and continue to enjoy the feeling.

Chapter Thirteen

With my arm around Alicia, we headed toward my suite. We wanted each other. Forget all the other emotions, this one emotion was real. We couldn't restrain ourselves, at least not me. Even though it was 4:00 am, we had to have each other. Especially after the spectacular, romantic, star- filled evening we'd just had together.

Once again, we made passionate love for what seemed like hours, but in reality, was only 25 minutes. Feeling totally exhausted, much more than usual, I fell soundly off to sleep.

My mind woke me at 8:30 AM sharp. Not today, I thought as I glanced over to the clock radio on the nightstand. Why can't I stay asleep on my so-called restful vacation?

It must be my subconscious mind working overtime. And for once, where I'd find my next prospect, was not one of my concerns.

Alicia was snoring very lightly. She looked like an innocent baby as she slept. A beautiful baby, even in the morning she looked great. She just had perfect beauty, and elegance about her.

Carefully, as not to wake her, I got out of bed and headed quietly for the balcony. There I could calmly stare out at the sea, and do some long awaited thinking.

The hypnotic sounds and sights of the ocean, along with the clean air has the most relaxing calming effect on me. It works almost like a tranquilizer. A great way to chill out.

There was a light breeze blowing in from the ocean. The air was full of fresh ocean air. The birds were already awake for hours and probably already working on their lunch.

As I stared out at the ocean, I couldn't help thinking that I saw only ocean as far as my eyes could see.

My problem was still here, bigger than ever. There was no fooling myself, I feared for my life. I knew that sooner or later Tony and the Family would grow tired of me.

I was convinced that when I'd outlived my usefulness, they'd come to the conclusion that I'd be better off dead. I became somewhat depressed, thinking about my own death.

But I had to admit, in some strange way, I was starting to feel less fear with each hour. Maybe it was all this thinking. Somehow the mind starts to toughen up when faced with severe problems.

Almost in a trance, I kept thinking, and listening to the waves. If they want me dead, then that's exactly what I'll give them, I convinced myself.

I stood on the balcony and looked all the way down to the ground. It was a long way down from my magnificent suite. No, I wasn't going to jump off the balcony now, but I was definitely going to plan my own death.

My mind finally came to a logical conclusion. The wheels were turning as I thought about my suicide, a planned fictitious suicide.

Maybe I'll make believe I jumped off a bridge. No, that's no good. The Family would never be satisfied that I was dead, without my body as proof.

Ok, so how do I give them my so-called "dead body", without of course, actually being dead? Then there was another problem: If I've got to give them a body, to convince them I'm really dead, then the body has to look like mine, or at least be unrecognizable, due to the suicide death.

That's it! I'll plan my so-called suicide as a jump off a tall building. So tall in fact, that no one will recognize the body. That's what I'll do. I'll plant all the proper identification and suicide letters at the site, on the body and again at my home. This way there'll be no mix up.

Still standing while looking out at the ocean, I was now smiling. It was starting to take form, this plan of mine. It of course, would need fine tuning. There must be no mistakes. Pure perfection. Nothing less would work!

The Vongemi Family wasn't stupid, and the plan must be believable enough, so my family wouldn't be harmed in any way. I was playing with the big boys now. If I screwed up it would be disastrous. I could, somehow accept my own death. Maybe, because the fear of it for so long, was slowly preparing me in a strange way to come to accept it.

I realized that it was inevitable, unless and until I did something truly dramatic, spectacular, and believable.

No, I wasn't that scared any longer. My intense fear had turned into a driving force, a determination to beat these cruel people at their own sadistic game.

Of course I realized that I still needed to work the fine details out. But one fact remained: If planned correctly, if the plan was meticulously carried out, I was truly better off dead.

Chapter Fourteen

It was early Saturday morning and our last full day together in paradise. Alicia and I discussed the day over a wonderful breakfast on our balcony. The sounds of the ocean and native birdsong were like mystical joyful music, as we enjoyed our bacon and eggs, and fresh fruit. There's a peace in listening and watching an ocean.

It beats all the stress there is in big-city living. If I could, I'd live permanently somewhere overlooking the ocean. Somewhere as beautiful as here in this paradise.

Relaxed, and bronzed with a great tan, the ten days away from Brooklyn were fabulous. Even with all my problems, they seemed less severe in this place.

Meeting Alicia was even better. No matter how set-up it was by Tony and the Family, the company was nice to have, the friendship great, and the intimacy of course was fabulous.

I can't remember ever having so much sex in a ten day period, even when I was in serious relationships.

Speaking at length about it, we both agreed to call each other regularly even though I knew I was setup, she was the informer, and not the true friend, she played.

I didn't expect Alicia to call. After all, her spectacular performance was over. She was good though. I must have acted extremely well also. Except, the lovemaking, on my part, was no act. I did wonder though, what Alicia felt, if anything.

"You're the most interesting person I've met in years," Alicia said.

"You're not half-bad yourself," I said with a big smile on my face.

"Yes, we do get along great, and that's very important," she said. "I want you to realize that I'm not this intimate with anyone, in such a short span of time. Frank, it's just that there was a special chemistry between us. I don't want you to get the wrong idea."

"Don't be silly, I felt the special chemistry also," I said, as sincerely as I could. But I still wondered to myself, Is she a professional call girl?

As we finished our breakfast, we decided to make the most of our time, and our last day together. We made arrangements to go horseback riding along the beach in the morning.

More than a few other vacationers told us they'd loved the horseback riding.

The stable, the Fun Time Corral, looked professionally run. They provide an experienced rider to accompany and control the group.

We both informed the people at the stables that we were novice riders, and so we were given gentle horses. With our riding helmets on, once we were up and aboard, we were on our way.

Alicia got a beautiful white horse with brown markings, called Spots. I was on a light brown horse, whose name was Dallas. We signed up for the hour-long deal.

Our group, on this morning, consisted of five guys and five girls, plus the leader. The horses were tame and they all stayed pretty much in line. After about fifteen minutes though, my horse took off on a wild out-of-control run. The horse ran as fast as it could and wasn't cooperating, while I tried as best as I could to slow it down.

Pulling back only seemed to aggravate the horse more. This horse was evidently pissed-off at something. The leader was trying to catch up, and had her horse running all-out, as she screamed at me to pull back on the reins. Not used to an out-of-control horse, I was slightly scared. I knew something was wrong.

I wasn't really a novice. I had ridden about twenty times before. But I always say it's my first time riding a horse, I seem to get much better horses that way.

In this instance something was really wrong, as the horse ran, and as I pulled harder, the whacky horse tried to throw me. This is a great way to break my neck! I thought, as I held on for dear life.

60

At first, I thought the horse was sick. I then realized later, that this was a running horse, that sometimes loved to run all out, and wasn't too concerned how or where it ran. It was definitely not a horse for beginners.

Even with not too much experience, I realized that I must take control, or I'll land on my head. I must show this horse that I was the boss. I took my heels and whacked them into the horse's flanks as hard as I could.

This normally makes a horse gallop. I waited a couple of seconds, since this crazy horse was already running at a full gallop. Then, all at once, I yanked firmly back, with even pressure on the reins. This time, for whatever reason, the horse reluctantly obeyed and stopped.

Maybe the horse was tiring, or maybe I did convince him that I was the boss, not him. No matter what, my little fiasco was finally over.

When the leader ultimately caught up, she was able to calm the crazy horse down. I'm sure the horse, by this time, was ready for his rest.

It was then that the leader, Jane, told me my horse's nickname was Rebel. That was perfect. I also learned that this was the last horse to give a novice, unless you didn't like them and wanted to have them thrown or killed.

I was totally convinced that someone switched my horse at the stable. By this time, I was definitely paranoid, especially with that big gorilla following me.

For the rest of my ride, the horse was as tame and polite as a pack mule. My hands were still shaking, and all the way back to the stable, my mind was racing. Alicia tried to talk to me, but I tuned even her out.

I dared not let on that I knew that someone was out to get me. I wanted Alicia, who I knew had nothing to do with this incident, to believe that I had no knowledge of her Vongemi Family connection.

The only suspect that continually came to mind was the big gorilla, Tony's goon. I had somehow, amazingly, put him out of my mind for the last few days. Ever since I convinced myself that the Vongemi Family was only monitoring my every move, cautiously watching me, in case I started to run, or talk.

No they wouldn't kill me, I told myself. Not yet. They still needed me. There were millions of dollars still to collect on their insurance scam. I was still useful to them, and only when I've outlived my usefulness, would they need to bury all the incriminating evidence, that tied the Vongemi name into the multi-million dollar insurance fraud.

Of course, I held the most crucial and incriminating evidence around. With me permanently out of the way, the Vongemi Family could go on with their everyday operations, untouched and millions of filthy dollars richer.

Yes, I'd convinced myself to ignore, for the time being, any threat from the mob. Now, this big jerk had changed my mind.

Oh, I knew he was still following me, but I paid no attention to him. I was able to consciously ignore him, besides, Alicia was enough to make me incoherent. But this goon watching was one thing. Trying to kill me, now that was something else.

He now had my full attention. In fact at this moment, I only wish I had a nice, heavy two by four beam to greet the back of his head with. But judging by the size of him, I'd rather use a four by four.

Chapter Fifteen

Maybe the Vongemi's weren't trying to kill me. Maybe they were just trying to send me a message - a warning of some kind. After all, I assured myself, the mob does a lot of warning or scaring of people.

In fact, they have a special knack in scaring people into doing what they want them to do. One especially popular scare-tactic is getting businesses to pay the mob so-called protection money. Unfortunately though, the only "protection" their money is buying is against the ones charging them the money.

But, of course, if you don't agree to pay the protection money, things mysteriously start to happen. So out of fear, businesses reluctantly agree to pay.

Convinced that the Family only wanted to put the fear of God in me, I left the stable for the hotel, along with Alicia. After all, we had only this last day to spend in our fairy tale romance, even if it was a fantasy romance that would end. If Tony was, in fact, paying her to romance and watch me, I'd make sure to get his money's worth of loving and living it up before the end.

Determined to move my fictitious suicide along, I put everything else out of my mind, there was plenty of time to be scared-silly when I got home to Brooklyn.

When we got back to the room, I convinced Alicia that we should take full advantage of our last day together. First, at noon we ordered room service. We called for a couple of bottles of their finest champagne, finger sandwiches, and a couple of shrimp platters.

When the food came we fired up the sunken Jacuzzi, and settled in-with the champagne and food. After an hour or so in the warm Jacuzzi, we relaxed, drank some more, made love again, drank some more and made more love. Tony definitely got his money's worth, with Frank Granstino. That was for sure.

Afterwards, we were both totally exhausted from our wild and crazy afternoon. We laid quietly in bed. Alicia had her head resting comfortably against my arm.

She then, quite suddenly, and out of desperation tried to ask some very pointed questions. Alicia, no doubt frustrated, must've wanted to go home with some worthwhile information for Tony. And when better, to ask than after mad passionate sex.

If Alicia went home empty of useful information, she'd be embarrassed - or worse. But I had been expecting some sort of pointed questioning for the past few days now. I was shocked it took her so long.

"So you're going to jump right back into your job when you get back?"

"Yes, I have to, I'll have so much waiting for me. So much to catch up on", I said.

"Was there anything back home that was bothering you Frank?"

"Alicia, in sales, especially life insurance, you constantly have to be aggressive. Sometimes you have to push people so you can convince them to buy the protection they desperately need.

"But, also every year, you need to take some time completely away from sales. It recharges your batteries, gives you back the energy you need. Do you understand? I just had to recharge myself"

"I guess I can understand the way you feel." she said, "You must get tired of selling at times."

"Well, after you've recharged your batteries, you actually look forward to getting in front of prospective buyers again.

"It gives me a natural high. Believe it or not, selling insurance is much like acting on a stage. Just like the actor or singer that needs to perform in front of a live audience. I also need to be in front of people and getting feedback, trying to help them, trying to give them advice. To lead them and encourage them to buy the insurance they need."

"Frank, I've never thought of it like that before, I'm just so glad that we met. You seem so different from all the other men I've ever known. There's something sweet about you. Non-threatning. Something sincere.

"We must stay in touch with each other. Maybe we can still date from a distance - it's not that far," she said with a twinkle in her eyes.

She sounded so sincere, so loving, but I knew it would never happen. "Alicia, I'd love to see you again. We'll stay in touch for sure!"

But I knew she wouldn't allow me to really get to know her. She couldn't, even if she really wanted to. Not since she worked for the mob, no matter in what capacity it might be in.

We fell asleep in each others arms, exhausted from a non-stop day. We still had one last big night to spend together. The magic I felt with Alicia was like poetry. She made me want to write special words of love and sing sweet love songs to her, I've never felt that way before.

I woke up well-rested, about a half hour later. Alicia was out like a light. Very carefully, I moved ever so slightly, as I inched slowly out of the bed. Being extra careful not to wake her, I went into the living room.

I had to know. I had to see right now. I couldn't wait any longer. Even if it was painful. Looking at the piece of paper, I had with Alicia's address and phone number. I touched the numbers on the phone, softly, as I waited, I looked at the address: Harbor Road in Boston.

The ringing was interrupted by an operator recorded message which stated; "The number you have dialed is not in service. Please check the number and try again." As I stared into space, the message played again. I quietly hung up the phone.

My strong suspicion was true. There was no such number, and definitely, not Alicia's phone number. The address apparently also was wrong. Now I knew I was set-up. What little hope I'd had, quickly disappeared. Still, I was actually relieved, although I was a little disappointed, I was glad. Knowing now, was better than wondering all the way home.

After I put the paper back in my wallet, I slipped carefully and ever so slowly, back, next to my lovely, gorgeous woman.

After a half hour Alicia woke up. We kissed each other, passionately, for what seemed like an hour more. It would be our last passionate kiss. Alicia claimed it wasn't, but I knew differently.

But still, I had no complaints. This by far was the very best vacation I'd ever had; big goon and all.

Chapter Sixteen

Our last kiss took place in the Bahamas airport, as Alicia went to her gate number and I to mine. We got to the airport at 8:00 AM on Sunday.

My time in paradise was coming to an end. Tomorrow it was back to work. Two weeks was a long time to be away from the office and there'd be plenty of work for me to catch up on.

Thinking back, I thought of all the easy sales I'd made with the Vongemi leads. The sales came much too easy. There was no resistance. I should've realized that these so called prospects were all buying whatever I suggested. Or maybe, I thought I was a fantastic salesman, all of a sudden.

We all want to be that good, but I should have realized that with only one year in the business I wasn't that good yet. I guess I still have a long way to go to reach that high level of salesmanship.

I knew that I'd have to continue working on Tony's leads. I'd have to act as if I'm on to nothing, just business as usual. Tony mustn't suspect that I was aware of the trailing and spying.

No, I'd need more time, to complete the stringent plans for my own demise. There was no way I could ask for, nor did I want, anyone's help.

So while I continued to work Tony's leads, I'd be diligently working toward my own main goal. The urgent goal to disappear permanently and convincingly. Somewhere where the mob would believe that I'm dead.

My friend Paul was waiting for me at Gate 34 of Newark airport, when I returned from vacation. It'd been over two weeks since I spoke to him.

Paul was always there for me whenever I needed something. Whether it was a ride to pick up my car from the gas station after it was repaired. Or just someone to hang out with. Or even when I needed to just talk. Paul was a true friend. He also was without a girlfriend at this time, so we both had a lot of time on our hands.

After we picked up my bags from the luggage carousel, we headed out to the local diner for a big breakfast. Although I felt like I'd gained ten pounds on my vacation, I still felt hungry at the moment.

I was in the mood for a Greek omelette. It'd been months since I'd had one.

In the last few weeks, I noticed that I've been eating a lot more that I used to. Maybe it was because I was scared of being blown away by the Vongemi Family. That would do it for sure.

Paul helped me to catch up on all current affairs, since I'd totally ignored the news on vacation. I usually do. Every time I go away I couldn't care less about world events and news. Why should I look at bad news when I'm trying to get away from all the everyday stress and tension?

"Frank, the Knicks are still in a slump, they now lost four straight games. They stink. And when you stink you deserve to lose. It's also rained for the past nine days with a record downfall and damaging winds. Our weather has been the pits!" Paul had a big smile on his face. "And you probably had fabulous weather didn't you?"

"How did you guess? It was gorgeous. Just look at my tan. And the food! Paul, you'd go crazy there."

Our food had finally come. I had just taken a big mouthful of my long awaited Greek omelette when Paul said, "Oh yeah, I almost forgot, there was a Mafia rub-out while you were gone."

I almost choked. After I took a big swallow of water, I realized just how casually Paul said it. "What about the rub out?" I asked, trying to be as nonchalant as possible.

"Oh it wasn't really a rub-out, not really. What it was, was the FBI was told by an informant, in the Witness Protection Program that the mob had killed a respected member of the district attorney's office.

"I think his name was Sean O'Donohue. He'd been murdered execution style about eight years ago. According to the newspapers, the snitch just told the FBI where to find the body."

We continued eating when I asked quite casually, "Where was the body?"

Paul started laughing, "You'll never guess, so I'll tell you." In between laughter he said, "You know the Jack In The Box hamburger drive-in on Staten Island?"

"Yes, sure," I said, "I've gone many times after going to the night clubs, in Staten Island, on Wednesday nights."

"Well," he continued, "they dug up the clown menu board, where you speak into to place your order. It seems that they found the body under the clown, beneath the concrete slab, from when they built the place."

"You've got to be kidding, Paul - under the clown?"

"I'm not making this stuff up, Frankie, I saved the article for you. There's a whole story," he said, while he laughed.

We both had a hearty laugh for about five minutes, Paul was laughing so hard he had tears in his eyes. Then I asked him, "So - Paul, who knocked him off?"

"Well, they claim that it was the Vongemi Family that ordered the hit. It was Willie Shoteri. He's known as Willie 'The Ears' Shoteri. That was the snitch. Willie claims that there are six more bodies he knows about."

My stomach took a sudden flop. "Paul, why do they call him Willie 'The Ears,' does he have ears?" I asked with a smirk on my face.

"Of course he's got ears. The papers said, that Willie got the nickname because his ears stick out like Dumbo. It's not a name Willie liked, I'm surprised he never got his ears shot off yet. I'm sure if they ever catch up with him, the Vongemi's will cut his throat, right before they blow his brains out."

By now, my food was backing right up into my throat, as I pushed the half-eaten omelette away. It was then that Paul asked me, "Frank, I told you about the Vongemi's once. Do you have any dealings with them now?"

"Not for a few months now." I said. "It all quieted down."

"That's good. Because they're evidently much worse than I told you, I had asked all around, you know. Frank, did you meet any hot babes down there?"

"Not really. I had a great time. There were some hot looking women, but I didn't luck out," I said, making sure not to let Paul know anything about Alicia.

"I'll bet, the babes down there had the best bodies, right Frank?

"You got that right, my eyes are still strained."

He never would've believed me, Paul knew me too well. If I told him how beautiful Alicia was and how we made love so many times he'd instantly know I was set up. I didn't want to go into my problems. He couldn't know.

As much as I liked Paul and I'd normally trust him with my life, I couldn't tell him about my continued involvement with the Vongemi Family. I couldn't tell Paul how the Vongemi's paid for my hotel suite and all the amenities.

No, I couldn't let on about beautiful Alicia or the two weeks of intense sexual romance, even though it was set up by the Family.

I also couldn't tell Paul about the Mafia goon. Or how I felt that someone tried to kill me. Or at least put the fear of the mob in me. If I did tell Paul any of it, I'd only be putting his life in danger. No one could know. Not even my own mother, as much as I loved her. I dared not risk anyone else's life. My life alone, was more than enough to risk.

All I kept feeding my mother was that I was doing very well, but I was working non-stop, prospecting almost five hours a day to come up with the sales leads.

No one could know about the so-called suicide plan of mine, and how I was going to disappear for good. As I thought carefully about this suicide scam of mine, tears filled my eyes.

I couldn't help it, my emotions took over. How do you say good-bye to everyone you love, especially your mother, without being able to properly say good-bye? Without saying: "I have to leave Mom!" Without saying: "Don't worry, I'm not really dying, I didn't really kill myself, it was all an act."

Visions of my childhood came to mind. I remember my mother taking me to the park, walking with me, explaining life as it revolved around us. My mother always took me to the playground, and on the swings and sliding pond. These memories never fade, they're what shapes our personalities. This is why our mothers will always be special to us.

70

I always dreadfully feared, as I was growing up that I'd lose my mother. I'd lie in bed as a small boy and cry, until I fell asleep. Just the thought of my mother possibly dying, or ever leaving me always started me crying. Now I was getting the same exact feeling again. Not because she was dying, but because I'd never see her or talk to her ever again.

More importantly I wouldn't be able to tell her that I was still alive. But, I had no choice. As much as I thought it out, this was the only way out. Any other way, would only put everyone I love in grave danger.

I even thought of turning Tony Vongemi in to the FBI. But, I quickly realized, no matter what happened to Tony, he'd still give the order to kill us all.

There was only one plan. One sure way to end it once and for all. One guaranteed way to get the mob to forget me, "I was better off dead!"

Chapter Seventeen

After our breakfast together, I asked Paul to drop me off at home, because I was tired. "Paul, we'll get together later to watch the Giants and Cowboys football game on TV. I'm exhausted, I think the whole two weeks finally caught up with me. I'll just take a nap for a while, then I'll be fine."

"Alright Frank, you look burned out anyway, buddy. It must be all those hot bikinis, you saw."

"That's it, I'm exhausted!"

When I got home, I laid down and had a good cry for myself. Obviously it was the fact that after my disappearance, I'd never see my family and friends, ever again.

After sobbing for about ten minutes I finally did fall off to sleep. I was totally exhausted and stressed out.

When I awoke I felt depressed. So I gave myself a talking to. Whenever I'm down, I repeat all the good and wonderful things I have going for me.

This self-help always seemed to work in cheering me up. What it actually does, is put things into crystal clear prospective. By repeating over and over again to myself all the good and positive things I had in my life, I'd be convincing myself that things really aren't as bad as I thought they were.

I'd repeat things such as, "I have two eyes, two ears, two arms and legs, and they all work very well. I have my most important asset - my mind - and I can speak."

"I feel that I'm fairly intelligent, and I can do almost anything I set my mind to do. I now have plenty of money in the bank, and a car that can take me almost anywhere I want to go. Anytime I feel like going. I really do have the world by the tail!"

After repeating these positive statements over, and over again for about ten minutes, I always seemed to perk right up and feel much better.

I believe the reason it works for me, is because all the positive statements, repeated with a positive tone of voice, actually penetrates deep into the subconscious mind.

73

Finally I felt good about myself, and the fact that I could somehow work out the difficulty that I was in. I must try to stay as happy as possible. I couldn't risk giving anyone I knew bad vibes. Otherwise, they might figure out that there was in fact, a serious, pressing problem. After all, right now I had to call my mom and let her know I was back home.

"Hi Ma!"

"Well-hello Frankie, where are you?"

"I just got back Ma, how are you? Is everything all right?"

"Everything is fine, Frankie. There's really nothing new here. Same old thing, I go to the clubs, every other day, you know? How about you, did you have a good time? How was the weather?"

"Oh yeah, Ma, it was great! I got a nice dark tan. The sun was really strong. My room was huge. It was a suite. You could fit six bedrooms in it. The place was gorgeous down there. You'd love the sun. It was hot, but you could burn to a crisp if you fell asleep for a few hours.

"I had a great time, Ma, It's a great place to just escape, very relaxed. Of course, I really didn't want to come back, but I had to. And the food - I must've gained ten pounds. How are you feeling Ma?"

"Oh, I'm just fine Frankie, I've got no complaints, and if I did, who'd want to hear them?"

"I heard it's supposed to snow tomorrow, is that right?"

"Yes, it's not going to be that much though. So, when are you going to come by?"

"Ma, I'll be by tomorrow, after work. I'm going to pick up a pizza and drop by, all right?"

"Oh, you don't have to, I can make something! Maybe pasta fasool, some homemade bread, no big deal."

"No, Ma, don't even think about it! Besides I want to tell you all about my trip. I have plenty of postcards and newspapers to show you. I'll see you about six-thirty okay?"

"Sure, all right, I'll see you then, Frankie."

"Bye Ma. Love ya."

"Okay, good-bye Frankie. Be good, I love you too, son!"

I felt good as I hung the phone up. I always feel happy after speaking to my mother. Sometimes, I feel guilty, because I know I don't call her enough.

I know I should call her more often, but everything always seems to get in the way. Mom always makes me see things as they really are. She helps me to keep things in perspective, no matter how old I get. She makes me laugh almost every time. She always had a great sense of humor.

All this reminiscing made the emotions come rushing back. The thought of losing my mother from my life for good. It almost started me crying. But I realized that no one can make me lose my memories of her, I'll have them forever.

I guess I realize this more now, than ever before, Especially since my plans to disappear will cut me off completely from my world. The only world I know, and everyone who's a part of my life now.

I vowed from this moment on, to wake up and spend more quality time with my family and friends, starting foremost with my mother. Being in my present predicament, makes me appreciate just how important family and friends are.

From now on, until I'm gone, I'll spend quality time with my loved ones. Because, I know, once I disappear, I'll be gone forever. I'll be cut-off... Unable to tell everyone how much I miss them.

So I must convince them all now. Show everyone just how much they mean to me. This way, when I'm gone from their lives for good, I'll at least remain forever in their hearts and minds. My mother always has, and still remains, my silent inspiration. I've always wanted her to be proud that she's my mother. Every time I was ready to give up, Mom would say, "My son doesn't quit, my son can climb any obstacle put in his way!" Hearing those words always drove me on.

I was all too familiar with this feeling of emptiness I now felt. I've lived through it before. A few years ago, emptiness was all I felt for a twelve month period. My father was abruptly and heart wrenchingly taken away from us some years ago.

It's been over five years ago that my father was killed. I remember it like it was yesterday. He got a flat tire on the Belt

Parkway, pulled over to change it, and as he did was hit by a van. The driver of the van was under the influence. He claimed he didn't remember hitting my father. Dad stayed alive in the hospital for twelve hours. Just as it appeared that he was improving, he quickly slipped into a coma. A short while later he died, with his whole family by his side.

I never thought my father could die so young, and I never thought he'd go so quick. With my father dead, I felt empty. I wished we had more time together. More happy memories. But with Dad gone, it made me stand up, take notice of my life. It probably made me stronger.

My father was gone for good and what brought this all back so vividly was the fact that everyone I know will instantly be gone from me - the moment I disappear.

Tomorrow doesn't always come for all of us. So I know the terrible feeling of emptiness. I know the sense of total despair.

This is what I'll feel when, finally, according to plan I disappear permanently from my suicide scam. And all my friends and family are gone for me for the rest of my natural life.

Chapter Eighteen

I eased the car carefully over the snow mounds, until it slid safely into a parking spot at Financial Life. I'd been gone for over two weeks and now I dreaded coming back.

The first thing I thought about as I looked at the office door, was the manager and warden, Tom Somi. For a split second, I pictured Tom waiting behind the door for me; with a whip in one hand, wearing a marine sergeant's uniform and barking out orders.

After opening the door and looking quickly inside, I entered the building confidently. Tom wasn't waiting for me. I tried to slip quickly and quietly by his open office door. It didn't work: my briefcase hit the wall making a scraping sound.

At that instant I heard, "Oh, Frank, you're back! After you settle in, I want to talk with you!"

"Oh, hi Tom," I said, sarcastically, "I'll be right in. I just have to check on something" Already I was sorry I came back.

My mail box in the agent's room was packed full. There had to be thirty or forty messages. I wished I was still poolside, with a cool drink.

I missed Alicia too. I felt sad not seeing her. There was a definite attraction there. I wondered what information she'd reported back to Tony. I also wondered, if in just some small way she might've missed me too.

Quickly flipping through my messages, I caught, Tony Vongemi's name three separate times. Two messeges from late Friday afternoon, and one from 9:01 am this morning. He knew I was on vacation and not returning until Monday. He's a wise guy I thought. Then it dawned on me, that he really is a wise-guy, a mob wise guy!

"Hi Tom!" I said, as I boldly entered the boss' office. "I saw your face on a wanted poster at the post office in the Bahamas."

"Very funny Frank! Are you practicing to be a clown, or is that the real you?"

"Did you miss me Tom? Who did you scream at for the last two weeks?"

"Yeah I missed you, Frank, my blood pressure went down for two whole weeks! Did you look at your messages? There's a couple of complaints!"

"No Tom, how could I? You wanted to see my pretty face," I said, showing my white teeth with a big wide smile.

"All I want Frank, is for you to follow up those complaints today! Now get out of here, you clown!"

Back to work again, I thought, as I closely reviewed my messages from the last two weeks. The top of my desk was cluttered with policies, forms and notes from all the agency meetings I'd missed.

"Boy, I'm lucky today!" I noticed I was the only agent in the office this morning. Historically, Mondays are always slow-going for agents. Sometimes the boss calls for a meeting, but most of the time it's slow. Most agents leave early on Friday and don't recuperate from the weekend until Tuesday.

Mrs. Tranphino called three times in two weeks, just so she could add her new grandchild as a beneficiary to her policy. She evidently wasn't told that I was on vacation. The third time she called, she started fighting with the secretary. Tom must've meant, Mrs. Tranphino, when he said I had a complaint.

There were a couple of referrals from good clients of mine. They were interested in health insurance. Of course Tony called those three times. Maybe just to bust my chops. Or maybe so I'd thank him for the wonderful accommodations.

I was in no mood for his Don - attitude today. I put his messages on the side and started my work.

As usual, Mrs. Tranphino was like a lamb when I spoke to her. The ones that mouth-off the most to the office staff are usually the most pleasant ones, when they finally speak to their agent.

Mrs. Tranphino wanted to know all about my trip to the Bahamas. I had no time for her, but casually told her the highlights of my vacation. Many clients like to know as much about their agents as they can.

After the small talk, I told her that I would mail her the beneficiary change form to add her new grandchild to her policy. I crossed her off my list.

By noon, I'd caught up, pretty much, on the urgent things. That's when Harry, the office gambling addict, walked by my desk.

"Frankie, you're back!"

"Yeah, I got in yesterday Harry. And I had a great time!" I said trying to head off a long boring conversation with an idiot.

"So what did you do?" he said as he drew up a chair.

He wasn't leaving. As usual he had nothing to do. Harry looked like crap, he must've lost all the weekend football games and the horses, and resorted to drinking the rest of the time.

"Oh you know, all the usual stuff. The weather was great, the girls were all gorgeous, and the casinos were ruthless. It's all the same junk when you go away,"

"Yeah, I know" he said, "I've been doing well myself, you know, Frank!"

"Yeah sure," I said, as I thought to myself, That's why you look like a homeless guy who just lost a fist fight" I smiled a big grin, at Harry, as I got up to go to the bathroom.

That'll shut him up. But Harry shouted after me as I walked away, "Maybe we'll do lunch Frank"

"Yeah, maybe" I said, as I disappeared. "When pigs fly south for the winter," I said, under my breath.

It was almost two o'clock when I finally, and reluctantly picked up the phone to call Tony. I figured that I'd better call him before he gets crazy and sends someone over for me for a command performance.

Tony answered the phone on the first ring. All he said was, "Yeah?" There was no mistaking that voice, that certain authoritative style, that same Don attitude.

"Tony, its Frank Granstino. How are you?"

"Frankie, you little weasel, where have you been? I've been looking for you!"

"Tony, I just got back yesterday. I was totally exhausted, and just got into the office a little while ago."

"How was the Bahamas, Frankie, good?"

"Excellent! Tony, everything was spectacular. The hotel was superb, the suite was just great! They treated me like a king, Tony!"

"They better have! I'll find out you know."

"Tony, I want to thank you for everything, It was fabulous."

"Good Frankie, you deserve it! We like you Frank."

"Tony you're like a hero down there, you must have a lot of clout?"

"Yeah, they like us very much there. We've given them a lot of business. That faggot treated you good?"

"What, who, Tony?"

"Jeremy Roberts, the gay hotel guy."

"Jeremy Roberts was great! He was falling all over himself. He sends his regards."

"Well Frankie, stop by later I've got to talk important business with you. I've got to go," he said as he hung up the phone.

Still holding the phone, I thought to myself, I don't want to see this thug, but what choice do I have?

Lately, I was trying to avoid Tony at all costs. Something's up. He doesn't want to break bread with me. He said, "talk business." That could mean another death claim. Or possibly a personal direct request from him to write a policy for someone else. Someone who may encounter an unfortunate accident in the not too distant future. A one way Vongemi car ride.

Slowly, but surely, I was catching on to this creep, Tony. He was a sly fox, though. I didn't want to go see Tony tonight, but I knew I'd be seeing him, either forcibly or calmly on my own. When Tony wants you he gets you.

Chapter Nineteen

It was 4:30 pm when I pulled up to the restaurant. The roads were glazed with a thin film of ice. The temperature was twenty four degrees, unusually cold for mid-December. Still dressed-up from work, I didn't bother changing, because I had no intention of hanging out. All I wanted was to get in and out right away. The place was starting to give me goosebumps.

The more I saw Tony Vongemi's face the more I realized that I was in deeper than I'd ever dreamed of. Little Frankie Granstino was helping organized crime in a multi-million dollar scam.

Nice accomplishment, Frankie, I thought. You've done real well for yourself, so far. You should've taken that job selling Cadillacs. That would've been easy. But no, I thought selling Insurance would be more prestigious, more honorable.

Once inside Tony's restaurant, I spotted Tony at the bar drinking. From a distance he looked a little sloshed. I wondered if that FBI probe had anything to do with him drinking.

Someone had ratted him out. Although the Vongemi's were known to have the best team of lawyers in the country, if he was found guilty, he probably would be dead from old age before he served any time.

Tony somehow saw me in the entrance way. He waved frantically as if he were in a large arena, motioning for me to join him. Tony immediately stood, hand outstretched for me. He grabbed my hand and squeezed it hard enough for my knuckle to crack. Tony always had to intimidate.

He pulled me in close and gave me a wet kiss on my cheek, as he said, "Frankie, you look great! How are you doing?"

"Great Tony, I'm nice and relaxed now." All I could think was, does he always have to kiss me?

There's nothing worse than a man with alcoholic breath kissing me, and talking right in my face. Not wanting to hurt his feelings at all, I gave him a big bear hug.

"So, Tony V, how've you been, my friend?" I asked with a big smile.

"Not too good, Frankie. Someone is trying to set me up!"

"Yeah, I heard, Tony," I said, not wanting to discuss any bodies, especially dead ones. You're looking good, though, Tony," I said, lying.

"What do you want to drink Frankie, my boy?"

"I think I'll have a white wine, thanks Tony."

After a few drinks Tony straightened up. He got real serious and said, "By the way, Rocco Conlini's dead. He drowned. I didn't want to tell you over the phone."

"Oh, Tony, that's terrible!" I said, even though I wasn't shocked.

I wouldn't be shocked even if he told me that five more people I insured were dead, all killed in a bus ride to Atlantic City and especially now, that they were trying to convict him on old mob hits. No, nothing would surprise me, not anymore. Slowly, I was starting to develop a thick skin.

Every so often I caught myself looking at all the entrances, thinking that any second someone would bust through with a machine gun blaring away.

I was so paranoid now at this point, that I expected to see something strange. I finished my second drink as fast as I could. I wanted out of there... fast.

All I could think of, as Tony was talking was this was the fourth death claim! Rocco was insured for one million dollars. That makes a total of three million dollars now that the Vongemi Family scammed out of the Financial Life Insurance.

Tony kept talking, but my mind was drifting. His voice was only background noise to me. First there was Joseph "Jo- Jo" Crucci, for five hundred thousand dollars. Then there was Liborio Tiullo who supposedly died of an accident. There was Anthony Proline, who died from an apparent heart attack.

Anthony's claim was for one million dollars. And now Rocco Conlini.

Rocco, they said, was fishing by himself of course. He drowned. Like all the others, he too was buried the next day in Italy.

Bringing my attention back to Tony, once again, I stood up to leave. "Tony I'll drop by with the death claim forms tomorrow. I've got to run."

All he did was get up, glare at me with bulging eyes, and scream, "Sit down! I want to talk to you!"

I smiled and said, "Oh, okay, I guess I can stay a few minutes more. Okay Tony, let's talk."

Tony wanted to talk much more than usual. After a few more scotches he started telling me things I didn't want to hear. By this time, Tony was babbling.

He told me personal family business about insider information. Where and when payoffs were made. Shake down money that was paid, and who was involved.

It was apparent that the Vongemi Family had many public officials inside their pocket. I didn't want all this private information and I couldn't believe all the names he was rattling off at me.

"We have Danny Caines, a lieutenant with the police department, on our payroll, and he has plenty of cops he pays off for us," Tony boasted. "You can't imagine how many politicians we have helping us, do you know..."

"Tony, please, don't tell me any names, I shouldn't hear all of this," I said, politely.

Tony kept drinking, and talking. I kept sipping and listening, not wanting to hear anymore, but much too scared to get up and leave.

Tony kept telling me all the Family private business, and I had no idea why. Why me? Why now? Was this my initiation? My welcome into the Family? Or was Tony just showing off, trying to impress me? Maybe it was the alcohol speaking. Or maybe he was just trying to scare me.

I felt like telling Tony to stop wasting his time if he was trying to scare me. I've already been scared silly for weeks.

Finally, out of desperation, I had to change the subject, "Tony, why don't you have a bite to eat," I said trying to get him to stop drinking.

I figured if he stopped drinking, he may just tell me to get lost. At this point I got up to put my coat on, like it was time to go home.

I felt at this point, Tony was too bombed to care. After all he'd just finished rattling off the names of businesses in Bensonhurst that were paying protection money.

Wanting to leave-while I still could walk, I said, "Tony, okay, I've got to go."

All of a sudden Tony's face got red, the veins in his neck pertruding, like they were ready to burst.

"Are you trying to hurt my feelings?" he shouted.

Shocked and scared, I sat back-down so fast I almost fell off the bar stool. "No! of course not. No Tony! I just thought you had things to do, I don't want to be a bother." I felt my hands shaking.

"Frankie, I want you here with me. You just don't understand me," he said, as he put his arms around me. "I like talking with you. You're a good listener."

He was definitely soused now, I thought. He smelled like rotten scotch as he squeezed me and smiled.

"You're going to stay and have dinner with me, Frankie, right?"

Reluctantly, I smiled and said, "I'd love to and I'd be honored. Tony, let's have something wild!" What else could I do?

This meant that I'd have to hang out for the night with this madman. At least Tony finally retreated from alcohol to coffee. He slowly started to calm down. Then, surprisingly Tony took a few phone calls while sitting in front of me.

All at once he started cursing and screaming at the top of his lungs. He sounded much like a dictator. Great, I had to eat dinner with the Godfather!

It was almost seven o'clock before things started to calm down. One thing I've got to say about Tony, is that we always ate well.

The food was always fancy, as if it was The Last Supper. I wondered if he ever did feed someone, and then have them killed? Tony always had the best of everything. Tonight was no exception.

We had huge twin lobster tails, and large thick juicy steaks. If I was going to go down tonight, at least I had a full stomach, I said to myself, as we drank expensive Poully Fouse wine. Tony always made sure the wine continued to flow. God forbid if anyone ever had an empty glass. Tony simmered down considerably and was suddenly very friendly once again.

We spoke about football, basketball, and whether Jimmy Hoffa was under the 50 yard line at Giant's Stadium. "What, are you kidding? Hoffa's got the best seat in the house, if he's buried there." Tony said, as we both laughed. It must have been the wine because I was feeling no pain at all.

"Are you happy Frankie? Do you want anything? Anything at all?"

"Tony, I'm fine, everything is great and business just couldn't be better thanks to you!"

"Good, Frankie, I want you to be happy. If you're happy, I'm happy, okay?"

"Yes sir, Tony, I understand. You're the man!"

Chapter Twenty

After dinner all that Tony did was raise his hand and the waitress came running over bringing him a full box of cigars and a bottle of cognac. Tony told me to smell one of the cigars.

They smelled great. Even though I usually don't smell cigars, I said, "Very nice Tony."

"Frankie, these are imported directly from Cuba. No one gets these. They're the best in the world! We have some special connections over there so we get the best they have. Castro himself smokes only these, Frankie, so enjoy. I want you to take a couple home, my friend."

"Thank you, very much Tony. I'll enjoy these for sure!" I said, while still wishing I was home and far away from this maniac.

But they were excellent smoking cigars. The aroma was fantastic, No doubt, it was the best cigar I ever smoked; I even took two for later.

Now, with a full stomach, and enough wine in me to help me totally relax, I wanted to get the heck out of this whacko's sights. Although I dared not show it. After all who wanted Tony to blow up again! In one minute he could kiss you, and the next minute he could kill you.

"Frankie you're going to join us in the back room for some fun," he said, with that glaring wide-eyed look.

"Tony, I'd love to, but I've got to be somewhere," I said as politely and as sympathetically as I could, hoping to finally convince him.

"Frankie, feel free to use my private office. Make some calls, and then you can join us!" He said, while grabbing my arm rather hard, but with a big smile on his face.

He expected only a yes from me.

"You got it, Tony," I said, knowing when to shut up and just play along. I know when I'm not going to win a fight, so why get crazy? Tony wasn't giving in, and I'm no fool. He looked like he was ready to snap.

Not knowing what kind of "fun" Tony was talking about, I went to his office to make some phone calls. Maybe Tony was planning on having some beautiful show girls. He also seemed like the type of a guy that'd get a great deal of satisfaction in beating a fat man up, just for laughs.

Tony's office had solid walnut planking on the walls, with a plush white carpet covering the floor. There was a large stone fireplace burning over to the left and to the right was his solid dark oak desk. Looking around the room I thought to myself, I could just imagine how many beating orders were given from this chair.

Tony no doubt was an important man, I only wish I knew months ago what I was getting myself into. I made a few symbolic phone calls just to make it look good. Especially if the place was bugged.

I called my mother, then I spoke with my sister Candice. Anything to waste a little time, I thought. I needed a little space, some time away from the pressures of watching every word I said to this wild man.

When I was done about fifteen minutes later, I casually walked out of Tony's office. Carlo, Tony's man, was waiting for me. He said, "Come with me chump, I'll take you into the back room!"

Hesitantly, I followed. I wanted to act tough, but who was I kidding? I was definitely out of my league. As we went through the doorway I was amazed, there was an entire hidden room behind a wall.

You'd never expect anything to be beyond the wall. The room must have been fifty - by - fifty, and completely soundproof. There were no windows, only many florescent lights. As I looked around the room - it hit me - this was an illegal casino. Great! I thought, "I don't want to see this, now I could get busted too. What am I doing here?" I said under my breath.

There were approximately forty slot machines, two craps tables, four blackjack tables, one roulette table and a few poker tables. I saw ten men dressed in black tuxedos. They must've been the croupiers.

As Tony saw me, he quickly stood up, started waving, and shouted, "Frankie, over here! Hey, Granstino!"

I went over to Tony, who was sitting at a poker table.

"What do you think Frankie?"

"I love it Tony; it's beautiful!" I said with a puzzled look on my face, like I just saw a ghost. "It looks just like Atlantic City, Tony."

"Oh it's better than Atlantic City. All the profits are ours. And there's no taxes! Screw Uncle Sam! Right Frankie?"

"That's it. You got it, Tony!"

Tony had a big shit-eating-grin on his face. I could tell this was his baby.

"Get Frankie a drink!" He shouted at Carlo, who was standing guard near Tony.

The six foot-four Carlo walked over, glared at me and without even a smile snapped, "What'll it be, hump-head?"

"Make it a white wine, smiley," I said, not caring anymore.

Carlo shot me a look that could kill. All I could do was smile a big wide smile showing all my teeth.

"Hurry up, Carlo!" Tony snapped.

Carlo disappeared quickly.

"Frankie, this place is a gold mine. You know everyone loves to gamble!"

"Tony, you hit it right on the head. Everyone loves the games," I agreed.

"Frankie, for four days a week; Mondays, Wednesdays, Fridays and Saturdays the gambling area is open. Now, only those people who we know are allowed in. We have everyone's pictures on file, and each person has to pass by two checkpoints. One of our checkpoints is visual. Our second checkpoint has a metal detector and we also have a weapons search point.

"We won't let a stranger enter at all. Any new players must all be checked out with us first, at least a day in advance. No new players are allowed to join, without being recommended by an existing member.

"Our boys would then check out any new player carefully. They'd run a check on the person, verify where they lived, where they worked and much more. There's too much at stake to be anything but thorough."

Tony continued telling me how, the next evening, when introduced in person, the new member would be escorted to the main office. They'd then be physically searched, and checked for proper ID.

Tony explained that as long as they knew where the guy lived, they were pretty secure in letting them in. After all, he said, "We could blow up his family, his house, even his entire neighborhood, if we wanted!"

"Sounds great, Tony," I said, with a smile.

"The security here is very tight, Frankie. And if anyone started any trouble they'd be thrown out and banned for at least six months. Then of course, we'd threaten the lives of his wife and children, just to assure his silence"

Tony smiled, "Frankie no one ever starts any trouble!"

Then Tony stood up, he moved his suit jacket aside, and revealed some type of gun.

"Frankie, it's a .45 Magnum, one of the most powerful handguns around... Clint Eastwood's gun! Remember, 'Go ahead, make my day!'"

"Yeah, that's right Tony," I said, wondering why I was hanging around with this crazy man with a .45 Magnum in his pants.

By eight o'clock the place was packed. It looked like Monte Carlo. The rule was that everyone must wear a jacket. If you didn't have one, the house would provide one for you.

The regulars knew the rule. Most of the members came over to Tony, immediately, out of respect to say hello. Many of them kissed Tony on both cheeks. I was learning an awful lot, maybe too much.

Respect is very important in Tony's operations. The mafia I learned, revolves around respect and rules. If you want to kill a mafia member the order to kill must be approved by a boss.

I looked around the room as people were being ushered in. Most of the men wore a shirt and tie, along with the mandatory suit jacket. It didn't matter how you dressed them, they still looked like thugs.

There were a lot of tough-looking characters there. Looking around the room casually, I visualized that someone took life-long convicts from a prison, dressed them up nice and pretty, and put them all in this room to gamble.

I didn't even want to look at them, that's how tough they all looked. Tony whispered in my ear; "We take in 50G's a night, Frankie. All cash."

"Fifty grand? From this place? That's great! Especially all cash, Tony!"

Then I thought, Shut up Frankie, you got a big mouth! You already know enough to get five people rubbed out.

"What do you want to play Frankie, just name it!"

"Well, Tony I don't like poker, with all the bluffing and pressure and the game of craps makes me too nervous. Maybe I'll play some roulette. I always liked roulette, Tony" I said, trying to sound excited.

"Okay, then, start with these Frankie," Tony said, as he handed me three one hundred dollar chips. "Just let me know if you need more. It's on the house."

I was awed, not so much that Tony handed me three hundred dollars of chips. But mostly because the chips were exactly like those used in the Atlantic City casinos.

"Thanks a lot, Tony!" I said as I hurried away, wanting to distance myself as much as possible; at least for awhile. Too much information... why was he telling me all this private information? I didn't like it.

I was starting to feel nauseous, just thinking about what I'd gotten myself into. For some reason I'd been getting myself deeper and deeper every day.

What was next? Maybe Tony was going to ask me to break someone's kneecaps. Or worse yet, was Tony going to order me to kill someone? I don't want to be in this Mafia game, but I can't get away from it, not until I disappear one way or the other. Maybe Tony was planning on recruiting me into the Family?

Chapter Twenty One

I walked around the illegal casino room, pitifully trying to look like I belonged; Trying somehow to look cool. But here I was; twenty seven, still with a baby face and weighing all of 175 pounds. How cool could I look amongst these hardened criminal type tough guys? I dared not look at any one of them.

After about three trips of aimlessly roaming around the room, looking at all the people and the action, and all the different types of games going on, I finally stopped at the one roulette table that had a few empty seats still available.

It appeared that roulette wasn't a tough guys game. The seat toward the middle of the table was empty. This of course was the best seat at the table. It allowed you to reach out and place bets on any number. Settling on this game, I reluctantly sat myself down. The place was jumping. Money was flowing like water, I tried not to stare.

There were crap tables, blackjack tables, roulette and poker tables all going at a feverish pace. The noise level was very high. There were many loud voices. Most were shouting their happiness at winning, or total disgust in losing.

There were even waitresses in low-cut blouses; rushing around serving complimentary drinks.

I handed the roulette dealer, a guy named Bo, my three hundred dollars in chips, and asked for one dollar chips in return.

"Any color in particular?" he said.

"No, just give me anything but pink please, Bo."

Bo was a big fella with wide shoulders, about thirty- five, who was starting to go bald.

"I'd never do that," Bo said, while smiling, as he reached for the blue one dollar chips for me. "You're a guy, guys never get pink!" He then pushed fifteen stacks of blue chips in front of me, and said, "each stack is worth twenty dollars, good luck tonight, pal."

"Thanks, my man," I said.

I quickly placed my bets on some of my favorite numbers between the 0 and 36.

All eyes were on the dealer as he spun the ball around the wheel. Round and round it went for what seemed like ten minutes. But in actuality it was only thirty seconds, as it noisily bounced in and out of slots until it settled on one number.

First the number 15 came up. Then 21. And then 29. None were mine, I lost three rounds in a row. I really didn't care though, as I was consumed by all the other activity around me. At least this was a very good diversion away from Tony, even for a short while.

What a bunch of characters, I thought as I looked all around the room. One was bigger and uglier than the next. Making sure not to stare too long at any of them, I thought, That's all I need to complete my day now - a beating!

Some of these guys surely were killers. But I did notice a lot of commotion at the table to my left. It was a poker game. It appeared to be for very big stakes. Tony was playing at the table, which seated about ten men.

As I looked over at the poker table, I saw piles of one hundred and five hundred dollar chips all over the table, with a big pile of chips in the middle. Then, suddenly, there was a great deal of yelling and cursing from the smoke-filled table.

A young guy, who looked to be about thirty years old, got up fast. He was yelling, and trying to leave. This guy looked a little sinister. He had long stringy blonde hair, an earring hanging from his right ear lobe, and a bad pock-marked face. His eyes were piercingly wild-looking, like that of a killer.

As he tried to quickly leave, everyone at the table jumped up screaming. All Tony did was get up, look over towards the doorway and give a high sign. The two big goons, Carlo and Benny jumped from the other side of the room to attention.

They both raced over quickly, and rather calmly got on either side of the guy. Then they lifted him clear off the floor, and proceeded to carry him to the back of the room.

Toward the rear of the casino there was another smaller room. Carlo and Benny carried the guy into the back room and closed the door. All the time I could hear the guy sobbing and begging for mercy. What was going on here? A sense of shock fell over the room. The entire casino went silent, someone turned up the backround Italian music that had been playing. All activity abruptly stopped.

Tony quietly got up. He walked calmly to the small room, opened the door, and slowly closed the door behind him. After about one minute, I heard frantic high-pitched screams, followed by two loud popping sounds-and then nothing. Just silence... total silence. No words, no more screams, nothing. Even the music was off.

It seemed like forever, but in thirty seconds, Tony slowly reappeared. The silence was ghostly, I could even hear the hum of the florescent lights above me, while all other natural sounds had been frozen still.

Everyone looked at one another, then at Tony. Tony had a sly smile on his face, as he walked calmly back to his poker table. He nonchalantly sat down, put his arms up in the air and said, "Let's play the game!" Then he continued smiling for all to see. Everyone looked at Tony again, then rather matter-of-factly everyone just started playing poker again.

I put two and two together and figured out that the guy was cheating in the poker game. You don't cheat with Tony Vongemi.

I didn't know anything about the guy, but it was plain to see that Tony had him killed, or better yet, Tony just killed this guy himself.

Great! I thought, just what I need now, to be connected to a murder. Me, of all people, I never even cheated on a test in my school days. Now I'm around criminals and killers.

My nerves were shot, I was scared and shaking like a leaf. My head throbbed, with a migraine. I wondered what I was doing here, and whether the police would show up any minute. Fear can do amazing things. I was so scared I felt like throwing up. Through it all I kept telling myself to act cool, to stay calm and hang tough, but in reality my hands wouldn't stop shaking.

All of a sudden, I had a tremendous urge to go to the bathroom. But I dared not move from my chair. I was still frozen with fright.

Play had quickly resumed on all the tables. It was a little less noisy than prior to the shooting. But you'd never know someone

95

had just been killed. How casual, yet how ruthless, I thought, as I looked around the room. Maybe this type of thing was routine.

Benny and Carlo never did come back out of that little room. I imagined that they were told by Tony to get rid of the body.

Maybe that's why Tony had a big smile on his face. He could kill someone and easily get away with it. After all, who in this room would call 911? If I was Tony, I probably would be smiling too! The power this man had was awesome.

Trying to think carefully, I placed more bets on the roulette table. I didn't want to looked spooked, although I was. I tried to act nonchalant, but I felt self conscious- like I wasn't fooling anyone.

My mind was so preoccupied that I now was betting subconsciously, not caring where or how many chips I was wagering. All I wanted to do was lose the chips as fast as I could, so I could go home. Maybe, if I made some stupid bets I could be out of here in ten minutes.

Unfortunately, to my surprise, I starting winning. So I just tried betting higher stacks of chips on each number. My betting increased to twenty chips, which was twenty dollars, each time on the numbers 0 and double 0. Now I was starting to lose again. Good, it's about time, I thought. It was the first time ever, in my life that I was glad to lose.

It took twenty minutes, but I skillfully and painfully lost all three hundred dollars worth of chips. Boy, was I thrilled. It took real self control to lose.

Now, all I had to do is wipe myself of all the sweat which had beaded up all over my face, and get the heck out of here. I told myself.

Chapter Twenty Two

It took a few minutes, but I got my nerve up and hesitantly walked up to Tony's poker table. The tension was thick. There wasn't a smile on any of the players' faces.

The chips were piled even higher than usual in the center of the table for an unusually large pot. I was too scared to say anything. After the poor guy that was cheating got killed, I decided to shut up until at least the hand was completely over.

These guys were serious gamblers, betting three hundred dollars each. Then they were raising each other at five hundred dollars each. The pot in the middle of the table- must've had five thousand dollars in it. Maybe that's why there wasn't a lot of smiling going on. Or maybe it was the fact that one of their players was just abruptly shot and killed for cheating.

Tony finally threw in his cards with disgust. "I'm out- with this crap hand!" he yelled.

I guess he wasn't doing very well, by the look on his face. Now it was a face-off between the two remaining players at the table. The tension was building and the pot was growing.

When they turned over their cards the first guy had three queens. The challenger had a pair of tens. I couldn't believe it, betting all that money on a pair of tens!

That's why I don't play the game. Too much tension for me. Too much bluffing.

The hand was finally over, the guy with the queens cleaned the table of all the chips, as everyone looked at him hatefully.

As a lull set in, some talking resumed again at the table. With my fist clenched, I reluctantly went over to Tony and said, "Tony I've got to go, I want to thank you very much for everything!"

"Hey, how did you do, Frankie? Did you win?"

"No, but I had a lot of fun, Tony, and too much to drink. I've got a splitting headache. So I've got to get going," I said, as I patted him on the back.

"Frankie, be good and stay well!"

"Thanks again Tony, you've got a great place!" I said, as I headed quickly for the door.

When I finally headed out of the parking lot, I let out a huge sigh of relief. All the way home I wondered, how I'd gotten myself in this lousy mess. How quick could I get myself out? The clock was ticking, slowly, but still time was running out. One day very soon I'd've outlived my usefulness to the Vongemi Family.

That's when Carlo and Benny would be looking for me. I was fully aware of what was happening. Now I was educated to the ways of the nasty organized crime business, the same Mafia many admire.

Tony was ruthless. There was no fear of God in his heart. He probably didn't believe in the hereafter at all. The average person has a fear of God, a fear of dying with a blemished soul. Not this man. That's what makes Tony and these organized crime types so dangerous.

It made me wonder, what was the life expectancy of a career Mafia man-anyway? Because, if the mob associates didn't kill you off first, the hard drinking and living would. It's not the kind of life I'd choose.

The next morning I started work bright and early. I had arrived purposely at the office by 8:30 sharp. Along the way I'd picked up a copy of the New York Times, a bagel and coffee.

Now with my breakfast and paper, I was all set to work. Working, somehow, took my mind off of Tony and the constant fear of Mob, at least for a little while.

Today I had to fill out another Preliminary Death Claim report. This report informs the home office that an insured has passed away, and that a death claim will be forthcoming.

As I stared at the blank report slowly my mind drifted to Rocco Conlini. Rocco was a friendly guy who was only thirty - three. He was married to a beautiful Italian girl, Rosie. Rosie was twenty - seven and slim, maybe five foot four and about 115 pounds. She had beautiful dark brown eyes, and long silky black hair.

I remember Rosie, mostly for her beautiful smile and sparkling eyes. Her eyes danced with excitement, they told me that she was full of life. Rosie and Rocco had a cute little boy who was about four years old. His name was Aldo.

Aldo was the type of child you just wanted to pick up and hug. The Conlinis were only in this country for three years. They'd moved here from Naples, Italy. They both loved America.

Rosie was still a little uneasy with our language, that's another reason why I found her so attractive. She had a certain amount of shyness and innocence, that made her more beautiful.

I didn't know if Rocco was killed, rubbed out, or in fact died on his own. Then again, maybe he's not even dead. I had no idea what had happened to Rocco, but I felt very bad for her and little Aldo.

Rocco was laid out for only one day here in Brooklyn. And like all the other Vongemi acquaintances that had died, he too was flown to Italy and quickly buried. Of course, I missed the wake in Brooklyn. Tony probably made sure everyone did.

There wasn't even an obituary in the newspaper. I would've paid to see the body. I was suspicious as to exactly whose bodies were really in these caskets. With the Vongemi family there always seems to be plenty of extra dead bodies just hanging around anyway.

Finally I managed to fill out the preliminary report, with the cause of death listed as: "Accidental Drowning" and I signed it. Once it was done, I put the report in the secretary's basket marked "New work for today." My estimation for the company to pay out on this claim was three weeks.

Of course, the company would surely have to pay double the face amount for an accidental death. Tony specifically asked for the accidental rider on this policy. So double the five hundred thousand dollar face value of the policy meant a one million dollar death claim.

The count had now reached three million dollars. That's what my association with Tony and the Family has cost the insurance company. Three million tax-free dollars collected.

Tony Vongemi had found a money-making machine, and his name was Frank Granstino. A sucker, who was too scared to stand up and fight back. Too scared to blow the whistle.

"Not for long, though," I said, as a devious smile crossed my lips.

By lunchtime, I had finished all my service work. I even completed all the call-backs, and all the past due reports for Tom. Angie informed me that she had "Big Tony" on the phone.

"He said you'll know who it is."

I took the call.

"Tony, how are you today?"

"I'm good Frankie. How's your headache from last night?"

"Much better now, Tony, thanks!"

"Good. Frankie, I want you to stop by Thursday night. I want you to join me for dinner, pal. Oh, and I'll also have that death certificate for you."

"Oh, all right Tony. I can see you at seven."

"That's good. Just make sure you're hungry and thirsty pal. I'll see you then Frankie. Take care. Bye."

Just when I was ready to leave for the day I received another phone call. Angie said, "it's an Alicia, and I don't think she's a client Frankie," as she smiled a big foolish looking grin.

"Thanks Angie!"

What could Alicia want? That game was over when my vacation ended. Even though I missed her, I was scared to talk to her. It could be hazardous to my health.

Could Tony have put her up to pumping me for whatever new information I'd feed her?

Knowing that she was already a spy, I reminded myself to be very careful. Watch what I say, and in what tone I say it in. Because Tony will of course find it all out.

"Well, hello Alicia! How are you, sexy?" I asked, sounding like I'd just hit the lottery for five thousand dollars.

"Hi Frankie, I'm doing great! I just wanted to talk with you. I've been thinking about you, and it's my lunch hour. So I figured I'd call from work. How does it feel to be working again Frank?"

"Oh, I'm alright Alicia, it only took one day for me to get back into the swing of things. Especially since I had twenty messeges waiting for me. My vacation already feels like it was months ago. This business really does bring you back to reality fast. But I like the intensity, I thrive on the pressure!"

"So Frankie, anything exciting happening since you got back?"

I wasn't going to bite on that one.

"No. Just your basic normal everyday stuff. How about you?"

"No, I just fell right back into work just like I'd never left. But it's been a little boring compared with the paradise we came from."

"Yeah, I agree Alicia, I miss that place!"

Now, wanting to shake Alicia up, I asked, "I tried to call you but I got the wrong number?"

"Oh, yes I wanted to talk to you about that, Frank. You see, I had my phone disconnected around a month ago and I didn't want you to get that stupid operator recording. You know the one, where the phone company makes it sound like the customer didn't pay their bill. And of course I knew I couldn't give you the work number here, because they don't allow any personal calls. I'm actually sneaking this one in on my lunch hour. I'm so sorry Frank. That's why I felt I had to call you."

She must really think that I'm an idiot. Well, I wasn't falling for the sweet voice and the beautiful girl. Not again. Even though she was gorgeous and it brought back sweet memories of us together. With the touching, the kissing and all the passionate love.

Although I missed that special time I was convinced it was all a setup. Still something inside me felt sorry for Alicia in some small way. Even if she was using me. I really didn't mind being used, manipulated, having someone watch my every move. After all, I was definitely attracted to her.

I might've even fallen deeper in love if we had a few more days together. She was someone I, probably, could've married; if only it was a legitimate love and not a prearranged affair.

"Oh that's alright Alicia, it's just so nice to hear your voice. I also miss your lips," I said wanting to lay it on heavy. Just to show that I wasn't on to her.

"I miss you very much too, Frank. We really have to get together again, as soon as we each can get away for a few days!

Listen, baby, I've got to run now before I get caught on the phone. I could lose my job. But I needed to speak with you."

"Alicia, it was great hearing from you. Please call me again whenever you can," I said, with a voice as sincere as someone still attracted to her.

We said our good-byes. Probably our last good-byes ever. I was tempted to run over to Tony's place just to see if he was listening in on the other line. I knew that no matter where she was, she now was giving Tony a complete and thorough report on me.

Tony no doubt would be asking her a million questions, like, "Did Frankie sound scared of anything?" "Was he upset, or disappointed?" "Was he mad at anyone?" "What was his mood?"

The only thing Tony would get out of Alicia though, was that I missed her terribly. That I tried to call her and that I probably was madly in love with her.

Ultimately, Tony would be convinced that his little scam on me worked. That I never once suspected the setup on my vacation. Or that I was being monitored by Alicia, who was reporting every move and attitude back to Tony.

He must've been having a hearty laugh right now, thinking just how stupid his pawn, Frankie was. How naive the twenty - seven year old kid was. Since I told Alicia nothing out of the ordinary, this can only mean that I don't suspect Tony of anything. He must be thinking, "Frankie, the sucker!"

As I thought about it, I realized, I'd rather be thought of as a sucker, an idiot, than smart and looking like a piece of Swiss cheese full of bullet holes.

I had ingeniously bought myself some more time, which I desperately needed to complete my plan. Time was all I had, and adding a few days could mean my life. Time also could help strengthen my plan. A special, well thought out plan, that had no holes in it at all. And every time I saw Tony's wild looking stares, it reminded me of all that could be lost if the plan failed.

As I caught myself drifting into fantasyville, I took a deep breath and snapped out of it. My dreaming will hurt me one day, Maybe I'll be crossing the street and wandering off mentally, but

I know I can't change now. This inquisitive mind got me this far,
I might as well hold onto it.

Chapter Twenty Three

"Advantage Accounting, how may I help you?" the sweet-sounding female voice asked.

"Paul Luggi, please," I said.

"Who may I say is calling?"

"Frank Granstino of Financial Life," I said.

"One moment, please."

"Frank buddy, what's up? How are you today?"

"I'm doing good, I'm pretty much caught up now with the backlog of calls. What's up with you, buddy? Do you guys have any good tickets for tonight?"

"Surprisingly we do. It's been a little slow lately so there's a few extra tickets."

"What do you have? I'm looking for the Knicks against the Nets."

"Frank, believe it or not, we've got a set of Knicks tickets."

"Great, Paul, let's go tonight. You don't have anything else to do, do you?"

"No, I was just going to hang out tonight and take it easy. I'd love to go see the Knicks, I've been working much too hard anyway, I need to chill out!"

"The game starts at 7:30 Frankie, so just meet me outside of the Garden at 7:00, ok buddy?"

"Great! I'll see you later, guy, see you at 7:30."

Paul and I both loved basketball. With it's speed, intensity and momentum you can't take your eyes off the court. We both loved the Knicks.

We met outside the Garden. Paul was dressed up, as was I. We both were coming from work.

I think there was a sell out crowd on hand, over 16,000 seats.

The Knicks got a tremendous standing ovation when they were introduced. They'd just come off a six game west coast road series, where they won four games.

The Knicks had an easy time, beating the Nets on this night. The final score was 110 to 93, another masterful Knicks victory.

We had a great time, Paul and I. It made me wonder why we didn't do this more often. But life is funny in a way. Time moves much too fast. So hectic with work, family and friends. we never seem to have enough time to spend with all of the people we're close to. With the pressure of sales, I've never felt at ease, even when I did try to enjoy myself.

Paul and I hung out after the game. We went to some sports bar in the vicinity of the Garden. We each had a few more beers and I had a few more than Paul.

Since Paul drove to the city each day, we'd drive back to Brooklyn together. Paul was fine driving. He only had two beers after the game and we waited around for a while before we hit the road.

Paul and I spoke about sports some more. We also spoke about work and pretty women - all the usual stuff. Paul asked me about my old girlfriend, Lisa DeVoe.

"No, I haven't seen her at all. In fact I'm completely over her and don't even think about her anymore!"

Those were my words, but something inside of me said I still did miss her - very much.

"Yeah, I hear you. My love life is like the John Starks three point basketball shot, It never happens anymore!" Paul said jokingly, maybe just to make me feel better.

Only to myself, would I finally admit it. I did miss Lisa. Not as someone I wanted to marry. But I missed her company. I missed the dating, the romance, And I missed the lovemaking.

Being with Alicia reminded me of the special times I had and only can have with the company of a woman. I knew that I needed a woman, someone I could love and share all my innermost thoughts with, it would just have to wait.

I wanted to call Lisa, but I dared not. Not because I was scared because we broke up, but my total respect for her stopped me from ever calling her.

The tears filled my eyes every time I thought about all the pain that would be felt by the people I love when I'm gone. They all would know only one thing: Frank Granstino committed suicide. For some unknown reason, Frank killed himself. Took the easy way out. All of my family, my friends and associates will feel tremendous sorrow and pain as they desperately try to figure out what went wrong.

No, I didn't want to get closer to anyone new. No new friends, no new lovers. No one else needs to be hurt. I also didn't feel like being too friendly to anyone I already know.

But I knew in my heart, that once I disappeared, I could never come back. No phone calls. No letters. No disguised visits. Nothing. A complete cut off. Anything else would only put everyone in danger.

There was only one way to do it. I had to make it a clean and permanent break. All because of that creep Tony Vongemi. Lisa would definitely feel something, I was sure of it. But she'd feel a lot less than if I were to bring our feelings for each other back to life.

We called it a night when I told Paul that I had a terrible headache. I blamed it on the noise of the Garden, although I really wanted to go home and go to sleep. It was the only time that I truly felt at peace.

Chapter Twenty Four

Once I was back at my apartment, I got ready for bed. It was a weekday and it was almost 2:00 am. I was dying for some restful sleep. Sleep to me was a pleasant escape from reality, my way of forgetting. A way of giving my mind a rest from racing, from worry to worry.

Tomorrow's another day and all my problems will be there waiting for me. I knew I had to meet Tony again. I only prayed that he wouldn't be drinking. I can deal with Tony when he's sober. "God help me, I can't take him any longer," I said aloud.

I didn't want to be there, and I definitely didn't want to witness another rub-out. My fear of ultimately getting killed by the Vongemi Family was starting to fade.

Worrying so much over the last couple of months somehow takes the edge off dying. I was exhausted from worrying about it. I was only thinking about the pain it would cause my family and friends, that bothered me now.

Wednesday at the office was fairly uneventful. There were no calls to answer, thankfully. Just the basic daytime prospecting pressures.

Candice called just to say hello. "How you doing champ?"

"Great! The sales just keep rolling in, Cand, I can do no wrong! They all love me here!"

"Well, Frankie, You just keep your head on straight, and your eyes wide open. Remember one thing: life runs in cycles, just like the seasons. There's good and sometimes great, but you must also accept the bad too. Keep this phrase for when things get tough, 'And this too shall pass'. If you can remember that, then you'll weather any storm."

"That's great Cand, I'll remember that one. Thanks."

"Ok, Frankie, let me run. I'll catch you later. Bye."

"Take care. Bye-sis."

Looking at my desk I reviewed some pending work. Once we sign up a client up for life insurance there's a lag-time. Of course, there also was the usual administrative detail work. There always is in life sales.

I quickly made calls, following up on a couple of reports. When my work was done, I hung out with a couple of other agents in the office. Never one to socialize much in the office, I always try to keep my conversations brief with the other agents.

Tom was out of town at a managers' meeting. The office atmosphere is totally different when Tom is out. The place is so much calmer. There's no tension and no pressure. Every so often it was nice to see Tom leave the office for a few days.

Harry Lest and Audrey Lewis were both in the office and seemed to have nothing to do. Harry as usual was studying the horses in the racing form, trying to hit a winner.

Audrey was hoping Harry would find a hidden diamond amongst all the listed horses. Everybody is always looking for a sure thing. Harry, though, couldn't hit his head, much less a good paying horse.

"Harry, Audrey, how are you? Have you hit anything Harry?"

"Oh, I've been holding my own lately. But I feel very good about a horse running today, Frank."

"Oh, I see. What's it going off at Harry?"

Audrey pulled her chair up closer to Harry.

"At Belmont, in the third race there's a horse called, Mamma Run He's a good horse and he's running in a race where all the horses are non-winners in their last three races," Harry said, with a twinkle in his eye, and a smile on his face.

I could tell Harry was getting off on this stuff.

"What are the early odds on him?"

"Oh, he's running at 20 to 1, but he's a much better horse than the numbers show, Frank," he said, while shaking his head in disbelief. I'll let you guys in on this horse, if you want to part with some cash for a while"

"Oh, that's nice, Harry," I said, "but I'll pass. I'm still broke from the casinos in the Bahamas,"

"Don't worry about it, there'll be plenty of others. They run every day," Harry said, with a big smile.

"I've got a few bucks, Harry. How much do you need?" Audrey asked all excited.

"Oh, let me see now. I think we could do it for thirty dollars. We could bet the horse to win, and of course in the triple. Yes, we can do thirty dollars each and we'll split fifty-fifty."

"Okay Harry, thanks for letting me in on it, we should win, I hope?"

"Audrey, my dear, it's money in the bank... right in the bank!"

It's sad how some people live their whole life and never learn lessons from their mistakes. Harry, has never even had a bank account! He drove a bomb of a car that burned oil through the exhaust pipe. His own family disowned him because of his non-stop gambling habit. His house was foreclosed on by the bank, because he couldn't make his mortgage payments.

Now, he was sucking Audrey into the fantasy he created: the illusion of winning, the rush of adrenaline a gambler gets by just being in the game, much like a drug, excitement of gambling gets in their blood.

After a while it doesn't matter whether they win or lose, but merely that the potential to win is right around the corner.

Audrey was all excited, her face lit up, her eyes sparkled. She was getting the gambling rush. Harry's face was all aglow, also. He was busy staring at Audrey's exposed legs and thighs, in her short mini skirt. He too was getting that rush of adrenaline, but a totally different kind.

Audrey knew she had a live one; like a fish nibbling on the bait, Harry was practically drooling. Audrey kept making small talk about the office, all the while watching Harry's uncontrolled stares.

I noticed Audrey's antics. Ever so slowly, she moved, exposing just a little more leg at a slightly different angle. There was no saving Harry now, I thought, as I got up to leave. "I'll see you two later, I've got to finish up some urgent paperwork," I said, with a quick smile.

"Oh, Okay Frank, I'll let you know what the horse pays," Harry said sarcastically.

"Great! Good luck you guys, I hope you win big!"

"Bye Frankie," Audrey said, with a big sexy smile.

111

She really was a flirt! I said to myself, as I disappeared back to my own private corner.

I tinkered around at my desk for a little while longer. With my calculator in hand, I added up all the commissions I had coming in on all the new sales.

The money was flowing in so fast I couldn't keep up with it. Mostly due to all the cases written through Tony. And now as the leading agent of the office, I had won the admiration and respect of everyone. Even Tom, the big man himself, who couldn't stand me at one time, was now actually asking how I felt, and if I had any ideas for the office.

Chapter Twenty Five

By two o'clock my work was finished at the office. Feeling like having a drink, I dropped in on one of my favorite hangouts. The Goal Post Inn on 86th St. in Bensonhurst. It was a pretty active and hip sports bar. No matter what time you got there, they always had some type of game on TV. Today, it was soccer from Italy.

As usual, I ordered a Heineken draft. Today I was, especially, in the mood for a meatball parmesan hero. I was more hungry today than usual.

The food was good at this bar, or, maybe it was their beer that was so good that the food didn't matter.

Mike Prenelli, the owner, was tending bar, as usual. Mike knew his sports and his beer. This guy could hold a conversation on any sport or team around.

My meatball sandwich came, so I moved myself to one of the empty tables available and got myself another fresh brew.

While I ate I realized that I had to see that maniac Vongemi tonight. There was no way that I was going to stay with that clown tonight, I thought.

I still couldn't forget that man's face before he was rubbed out in the back room the other night. That sight was branded deep into my brain. The fear on his face was bone chilling. The casual way he was eliminated by Tony's men and the insignificance of a human life felt by Tony Vongemi really shook me up.

I carefully reviewed in my mind my escape plan, so far. The details of just how and when I would disappear. No doubt, I'd have to lead up to the so-called suicide. My lifestyle and character would have to slide rapidly into decline. I continued to plan, while slowly sipping my beer.

I'd have to appear despondent to the people I cared about. Everyone I know would have to believe that I was upset and not myself for some time before I jumped.

As for where I'd jump from, a bridge was definitely out of the question. First of all, there would be no hard impact. The water below would do little or nothing to disfigure the body. No, the body would have to be unrecognizable, or at least as close to unrecognizable as possible. The only way to do this correctly, in my mind, would be a leap off a tall building. A choice building of substantial height would be the World Trade Center. That would do very nicely, I thought. Once the body smashed into the concrete far below, there'd be little left to recognize or identify.

Now, since I wouldn't be actually jumping myself, I'd have to find someone similar to me in size and age. That shouldn't be too hard. At least not too hard to find someone that could resemble me. Though it would definitely be harder to find someone willing to take my place jumping off the building.

As far as someone looking like me, that would be fairly easy. I'm about five foot ten, my hair is dark brown, my build is slim, or average, at best.

I have no special identifying marks on my face or body. My eyes were a standard brown color; nothing special. At least none of the girls ever made a fuss about them. Even my shoe size was a standard.

My hair was too long, but slightly longer than the way the guys were wearing their hair today. Most of the younger guys have buzz cuts or short hair. I hated to admit it but I was just an average Joe. Nothing was very outstanding about me, except for my big mouth. I always did have a big mouth.

There's no way that I'll be able to convince anyone to die for me, I thought, with a smile. I'll just have to find someone. Someone down and out. Someone ready to die. Someone like a homeless alcoholic, that'd work. That'd definitely solve that problem, I thought as I ordered another beer.

The plan, just like a jigsaw puzzle; was starting to take form, and rather nicely. My mind has been working overtime on this plan.

After calling the office for my messages, I was told I had none because, as Mary put it, "This place is like a ghost town"

After talking to Mary for a few minutes longer I headed home. My plan was to show up at Tony's place at around 8:00, I could get out of dinner without hurting his feelings and still be able to walk.

The last thing I wanted to do was hurt Tony's feelings and possibly speed up my execution. Tony was under a tremendous amount of pressure lately, anyway. So I didn't want to push my luck. After all, I have not been feeling very lucky at anything for months.

Tony still needed me. I don't know why, but for some unknown reason he still needed me. I had some unforeseen value to him. Otherwise, I knew for sure that I would be fish food somewhere.

I was probably the only person that could link the Vongemi Family to the multi-million dollar insurance fraud. Amazingly, little Frankie Granstino could have one of the most powerful mob families busted.

That's precisely why I was in a such a jam, I realized this months ago. For the first time in my life, I knew too much.

I headed home to take an afternoon nap. After all that thinking and projecting I was exhausted, not to mention the meatball hero and four beers I consumed.

My stomach felt like it was ready to explode. Three hours is all I needed to recharge my batteries, then, I told myself, I'd take a quick shower, shave again and head out.

Chapter Twenty Six

There was one stop I had to make before going to Tony's. A quick call to the Engel's home so I could pick up an overdue premium. Their life insurance policy was always in danger of lapsing because of late premiums, or bounced checks.

The Engels consistently fell behind in their payments, so of course, it was Frank to the rescue; calling, reminding and collecting. After all, if Sal Engel should die and his life insurance wasn't in force, I'd feel terrible and somewhat responsible. So I believe, as their agent, I must do everything I possibly can to keep my clients current with their premiums.

It was 7:50 when I pulled into the parking lot of the Little Part of Italy. I dreaded seeing Tony again.

I prayed that he wasn't drinking this time. All I had to do was drop off a life insurance claim form for the death of Rocco Conlini. How many more young people were going to turn up dead? How many more of Tony's so called personal friends and associates was I going to have to fill out claim forms for?

Reluctantly, I entered the restaurant carrying my briefcase. Not that I needed the briefcase to carry the one form, but I wanted it to look official. Also, it would help me get out of the restaurant that much quicker. Especially when I told Tony, "I've got to make one more sales call Tony, sorry, but I have to leave!"

Once inside, I quickly glanced over at the bar. I hoped that Tony wasn't sloshed again. I didn't need or want to see him out of control. Tony wasn't there. He wasn't at any of the tables either.

Angelina, one of the main waitresses, came over to help me. "Angie, where's Tony?" I asked.

"Is he expecting you?"

"Sure, just tell him Frankie's here."

"One moment, Frankie, I'll be right back," she said with a smile.

Angelina, was a short slim Italian girl with a cute accent. She had short straight black hair, and sparkling blue eyes. She was of average height and weight.

It took her five minutes to return. I'd taken a seat at the bar area and just observed. Sally was the bartender for the day.

"How about a drink on the house while you're waiting?" she offered.

"Thanks Sally, but I'll pass. But I may need something strong later!"

"I hear you!" she said, smiling. "I'll be right here for you, if you need me," she said.

Sally was a real looker. A hot-looking blonde with her hair set in a kind of wild-looking but sexy way. She must of had some kind of perm done to give her that sexy look.

With that hair and her green eyes, along with her beautiful white smile, she was just outstanding. The guys just couldn't help themselves. They just had to try their luck with her. I sat back and patiently watched. The bar was packed full of guys, all with silly grins on their faces. They were each taking turns, trying to sweet talk Sally into a date.

Enjoying the free entertainment, I sat there looking toward Sally. Studying her, She was enjoying all the attention she was getting.

I also got a kick out of the cash register, which was all computerized. No keys, only a touch screen. When a customer ordered a drink, all Sally did was touch the appropriate drink on the computer screen. After which the price for the drink would automatically appear. Sally then would touch how much the customer gave her, and the correct amount of change would show up on the screen.

While I sat there taking it all in, Sally shot me a big grin. The kind that makes your heart skip a beat. All I could do was smile a big stupid self-conscious grin right back. But I fully understood what these guys were thinking and why they couldn't help themselves as they stood and kept drinking.

Just then, Angelina reappeared and motioned me to follow her. She said, "Tony's waiting for you in the back room."

"Thanks Angie," I said, as I took one last look at Sally.

I wondered if Tony was fooling around with Sally. After all, who could blame him for wanting her? But could she actually want him? Even I wanted Sally, or maybe I just wanted anybody nice at the moment. Maybe it was a relationship I needed. I did miss that steady relationship with a woman. But I dared not look twice at a woman now, knowing that I'd soon be disappearing. No, I couldn't dump that on anyone new.

As we walked through to the back room Tony was seated at a table on the left side of the room. My friends Carlo and Benny were standing on either side of the doorway. When I looked at them they didn't even blink. They stared me down, not cracking a smile, just staring. Maybe they were trying to intimidate me. These two guys could look at you one minute, and then turn around and kill you in the next.

"Hi Tony," I said, "how are you today?"

Tony quickly looked up, he stood up and slowly came over to me.

"How you doing? Everything good Frankie?" He smiled as he reached out to hug me.

"I'm great, Tony! The same old, same old."

"Nice to see you," he said, as he kissed me on the cheek.

Again the kissing.

I didn't want any kisses, thank you. At this rate, I'd never know which kiss was my "kiss of death".

I shook hands with Tony and said, "I've got that claim form for you."

Tony shook my hand, he squeezed it so hard I thought my fingers would fall off. Tony had the habit of squeezing your hand as if he were trying to squeeze the blood right up to your head.

I figure that Tony just wanted to remind everyone that he was the main man and that he wasn't one to be taken lightly or ever taken advantage of. He didn't have to remind me. I knew not to screw him. I smiled at Tony and said, "Nice to see you again, Tony!" while trying to get some feeling back in my hand.

"Tony, I've got the form you requested right here," I said, as I opened my briefcase to get it.

"I'll pick it up from you in a couple of days. I've got to be going, though Tony, I have to make another stop."

"You've got to have a drink with me Frankie," he said. "I can't Tony, I have an appointment and I don't want to smell of alcohol."

"Okay, then have a soda!" he said. "Carlo, get Frankie a soda... Now!"

Carlo quickly ran out of the room like someone was chasing him. In just one minute Carlo returned with my soda. Carlo gave it to me along with a look like: I hope you choke on it. All I could picture as I looked at Carlo, was him with his hands around my neck and a sick look on his face.

Sucking the Coke down so fast that I almost choked, I excused myself as I stood to leave. Apologizing that I had an appointment. I promised Tony, "I'll be back another night just to hang out, Tony. A night when I don't have an appointment, we'll have a ball, I promise!"

Chapter Twenty Seven

It was Friday morning at 10:30am when I got the message from the new secretary, Josephine. Josephine was a hot looking Spanish woman; of maybe twenty-five. Just what an office full of men could use.

The message was taken at 8:30 AM, as soon as the girls opened the front doors. It read: "8:30 PM sharp. Meet me in the restaurant; Be there! Tony Vongemi."

Great! The last place I wanted to be was with Tony at his place. Not again. I cringed at the thought. Settling in at my desk with a fresh cup of coffee and with a calm, cool attitude, I dialed the restaurant.

"Yeah, what is it?" was the harsh voice on the other end.

"Oh, hello; it's Frankie, Tony Vongemi please."

"Yeah, hold on!" he snapped.

I didn't recognize the voice, and really didn't care to know who this particular goon was. Maybe it was a goon in training?

After about five minutes of waiting on hold, I heard,

"Yeah, Tony here!"

"Hello, Tony, its Frankie. Listen, I can't make it tonight I've got a sales appointment. I'm sorry, Tony."

"You've got an appointment alright. Your appointment is with me! Right here at 8:30 and don't disappoint me!"

He slammed the phone down with a slam so loud it startled me.

Was he pissed off about something? Maybe he got a letter about the insurance claim; maybe they caught him in his multi-million dollar scam? My feelings were mixed. Either way I was a dead man so what was the difference? Kill me now or in a month.

Was this the end? Was this how my life would end? In a Mafia-owned restaurant, laying at the bottom of the ocean wearing a concrete suit? I thought of running, possibly hiding, or maybe talking to the law, maybe even the FBI.

Then it finally dawned on me as I leaned back in my chair, contemplating my future. If the mob and Tony wanted me dead they probably wouldn't invite me to a public restaurant. They'd just have me eliminated, quickly, quietly, and before I knew what hit me.

No, I thought, Tony must just want to talk to me. Maybe I'm just overreacting. Calm down, Frankie! I told myself. In disgust I cancelled my appointment for the night, I had no choice.

Tony changed my plans. How ironic, I thought, I had an appointment with a prospect, trying to protect their life with insurance. But the funny thing was, my life was the one that needed protecting. My life, I felt, was the one that was truly in danger.

I was consumed by the constant thought of dying, although I was only twenty-seven and in perfect health.

It made me wonder, what had I accomplished in my twenty seven years? What did I have to show? Had I done anything outstanding? Would I be remembered for anything?

It's amazing but most people don't know their true friends until they've died. The more I thought the more depressed it made me. So I stopped thinking and snapped back to reality.

The sales office was empty for a Friday morning because of the two inches of fresh snow that had fallen overnight. Life insurance agents look for any excuse they can to avoid going to the office.

Usually I'm no different, but, I had to be there. With all the worrying I have been doing lately it helped me keep my mind occupied. It helped me channel my energies. The worst thing I could do at this point was to stay home and sulk. Why should I feel sorry for myself at this point? After all, I did have a plan. Even though it wasn't finalized, I still had formulated a strategy. All I had to do was fine tune it. This alone should make me feel better. At least I had a direction I was heading in.

I did worry, though, that something might happen before I could implement my elaborate plan. I felt like a tire with a nail in it. You could drive on that tire for days or possibly weeks. But sometimes the tire would go flat by the time you went around the block. You could never tell. This was my most pressing concern. How much time did I have? Weeks. Months. Or just maybe right around the corner someone would be waiting for me.

With time on my hands, the quiet empty office, and the faint humming of the overhead lights as my background, I did some soul searching. There's so much I wanted to do. So many places I still wanted to visit.

All at once Alicia popped into my mind. I could see her with such clarity, it was like she was right next to me. In my mind I could still smell her perfume and the soft fragrance of her hair.

I knew full well that Alicia was a set-up. That the time we had together was planned right down to the last emotional kiss. But I didn't care and probably would do it all over again.

It felt good to be with Alicia and I knew I would be able to meet someone again, someday, when this whole Vongemi-thing was behind me.

Finalizing, refining and strategically planning my game plan, that's where I was now. A plan to beat the mob to the punch. Why not kill myself off! At least dead in the mind of Tony and the mob. If they were truly convinced that Frankie was dead, then they'd finally be satisfied.

I kept going through the same scenes in my mind. How could I appear dead to the mob and the entire world, yet still be alive and happy somewhere? How could I convince the all powerful mob, that I was finally dead, out of the way permanently, and no longer a threat to them, individually, or their operation as a whole?

Where would I wind up to spend the rest of my life, safely and away from the mob? Would I still be able to live a normal life? How far away should I go? Would the Bahamas be far enough? Or should I go to a smaller island somewhere in the Caribbean? Maybe an undiscovered island somewhere in the South Seas?

All these questions and so many more were bouncing around in my head. Every time I thought I had a solid answer, I started doubting myself. I thought, no, it's still not good enough! Or no, they'll never fall for that one!

Then I realized, all they really wanted was for me to go away and stay away. And not talk to anyone at all about their fraudulent scams. By the time it's all over, maybe the total figure would be five to seven million dollars that the Vongemi's beat the insurance company for.

That's a nice piece of change to the mob and I couldn't care less, anymore. But the mob would never believe me. Not now. I did know one thing though: with me out of the way they'd never have to worry about my talking to the Feds.

As it was, the Vongemi Family was getting into some more trouble. With all the dead bodies that were being dug up recently, all they needed now, was for me to shoot my mouth off about a multi-million dollar fraud scam.

The only problem with me talking to the FBI is, the FBI and the judicial system in this country moves so slow. By the time it was all over I'd surely be dead before any conviction was rendered. Or, perhaps one-by-one my family would be executed, in order for me to stay silent.

I'm sure the FBI would assure me complete safety. They could give me security protection around the clock. They could even give me a new identity and relocate me.

It all might look good on paper, and maybe I'd be safe somewhere for many years. But I knew full well who I was dealing with. I knew their style, their reputation. The mob was ruthless and would stop at nothing to silence a witness. Especially one with such damning evidence.

The mob's funds would be unlimited-to invest in saving their crime boss or mafia operations. No, I was one step ahead of them. I wouldn't rat them out. I knew better than to go head-to-head with the mob. But if all went perfect, I'd still be alive somewhere. My family would all be safe and unharmed, although very sad about me.

My suicide would greatly affect them all. But it was my only way out alive, I knew this now. The only way to protect my family and completely satisfy the Vongemis would be the death of Frank Granstino.

Chapter Twenty Eight

It was 8:15 Friday night when I got to the restaurant. I knew that I'd rather be in a street brawl than there.

Suddenly, I got a flash of inspiration. What if there was some way to hurt Tony Vongemi and his entire mob operation! Since I'd be dead anyway why not let the Vongemis suffer a little too. Especially for all the torment and heartache- still to come. As I walked to the front door of the restaurant I had a smile on my face. I'll pick this thought up later, I thought before I entered the restaurant.

As I walked into the restaurant I was surprised. Tony was there waiting for me. He was actually hanging around near the entrance. This time there were no hugs, no kisses. Tony merely shook my hand, patted me on the back and said, "Let's go to the back room, Frankie, I've got to talk with you."

Tony appeared very concerned about something, almost distant. Not his usual happy-go-lucky I'm-in-total-control attitude. It struck me as odd, that this man of so much power was acting a little nervous. Something was up.

We sat at a nice table in the back room. No one was there except for the usual apes. Carlo and Benny each stood post at either side of the doorway. But this time they seemed more intense. They both were looking around cautiously, their eyes constantly moving around the room. It was as if something was about to happen any second and they wanted to be prepared.

This wasn't good, to say the least. Once again I felt myself shaking. This time I was so scared I felt ice-cold, like my blood suddenly stopped pumping. There was also a sharp pain in the pit of my stomach, like a knife was lodged in there. The burning sensation I felt was like sulfuric acid was pouring into my stomach. Was this it? Was this where my life would end? Was Tony five steps ahead of me? Did he figure out that I had a plan brewing?

Thoughts of my childhood quickly came to mind.

"Frankie, the reason I asked you here is because we lost another friend last night. A close personal friend!"

Oh good! I thought to myself, another one. Feeling a great sense of relief, I finally felt the blood returning to my legs that had been cold and numb.

"Tony, I'm so sorry" I said, trying to muster as much compassion and sympathy as I could, while feeling so relieved that some other sucker got it instead of me!

"Yes, it was Pio Abbatomi. Last night he was driving his station wagon. The brakes gave out and he struck a telephone pole at about midnight. What happened then was the car caught on fire and the whole car was engulfed in flames when the cops showed up. Pio burned to a crisp. It's a crying shame, Frankie."

"Tony that's terrible, what a way to go," I said as I thought to myself. Sure, who are you kidding!

"I'm so sorry Tony," I said, while trying not to crack a smile.

"Benny, hurry up and get us a bottle of champagne!" he yelled.

Benny ran off and was back in about a minute, without saying a word. The champagne was Dom Perignon.

We spoke of poor Pio, the accident and Pio's family. I sold Pio the life insurance, so I remembered his wife Anna, who couldn't speak any English. His children; Pio, Aldo and Santo all spoke English and Italian.

"Such a nice family, Tony," I said as I reminisced. "They were all so happy. They were as perfect a family as anyone could ever hope for."

I wondered if in fact Pio was really killed. Or was it someone else's body planted in the car? Was it planned that the car would go on fire? Was the body able to be identified?

All I knew was I had another death claim on my hands. No matter how you looked at it, my clients were dying one by one, and they were all Tony's leads.

How many more deaths would there be before I'd be called into the company home office for an investigation? What would I say? How do you explain away five deaths as coincidence?

It was only a matter of time before the bells would go off. It felt like any second the whole thing would explode in my face. Either I would be killed by Tony and his gang, or I'd be in real trouble from the insurance company for all the suspicious death claims.

It was a no win situation. I felt like I was in a pressure cooker. I knew I had to do something pretty quick. I was biding my time, but my time was rapidly running out.

Tony said, "Pio was a close and dear friend of mine Frankie. We go way back his family and mine."

"Yes I know, Pio said only nice things about you, Tony," I said.

"It's a shame, Frankie, you know. I just saw Pio the day before yesterday. Everything was fine, he looked good, he was happy."

"Tony, life is short, we never know when it's going to end, that's why we've got to live life to its fullest," I said trying to sound philosophical.

"So true, my friend, so true! By the way, Frankie, I have the death certificate and claim form on the Rocco Colini policy, if you want to take them back with you."

"Sure, Tony," I said, as I folded the forms and put them in the inside pocket of my suit jacket.

As I looked closely at Tony Vongemi's face, all I could think about was all the deaths. All of Tony's so called recommendations. Joseph, 'Jo-Jo' Crucci and Liborio Tiullo for five hundred thousand dollars each. Then there was Anthony Probine and Rocco Conlini for one million apiece. Now, the most recent death was Pio Abbatomi for one million dollars.

Tony and the family was up four million dollars. The way I looked at it, either he had all these people killed, or he switched bodies with others he had killed, or something. Maybe all these people were hiding somewhere in Italy and he had other dead people he used as impostors. But no matter how he did it, all I saw was four million dollars in Tony's pocket and I was the only one who could blow the whistle on him.

Carlo came over to our table, bent down and whispered something to Tony. Tony told Carlo to bring another bottle of champagne. Tony then shouted to Carlo, "Bring us fried calamari and some mozzarella sticks!"

My stomach was still in a knot. I felt nauseous, so I said nothing.

Tony then stood up as a gentleman was escorted into the back room. The man kissed Tony on the cheek and then they each hugged. Tony said, "Frankie, this is Louie G., Louie, this is Frankie, my dear friend, Louie have a seat; Something to drink."

Louie sat down and thanked Tony, Tony then poured him a glass of champagne.

"So Louie G, what's new in the jewelry exchange?"

"Well-not too much Tony, it's been quite slow ever since the Christmas rush ended. We've all been losing our shirts," he said as he shook his head, like he was in some kind of pain. He quickly drank another glass of champagne.

Tony made some small-talk with Louie G. while I ate and drank. I loved fried calamari, and Tony's place made it perfect. Not overcooked, not dark. It was light and just right. Tony was a stickler for details. He wanted only the best food in his restaurant. Louie G. on the other hand wasn't eating anything. He was drinking pretty heavy and perspiring a lot. Louie looked rather nervous. His eyes were darting back and forth all over the place. He was starting to get me really nervous. When I'm nervous, I eat a lot.

There was definitely something bothering Louie, his eyes kept moving back and forth, first to Carlo, then Benny. I looked at Louie sweating profusely, then I shot a quick glance at Carlo and Benny, who looked even bigger now.

We had some more champagne and some more appetizers. The waitress, Rose, brought us some chicken wings. I kept eating, Louie kept drinking, and Tony kept staring at Louie. Louie said he wasn't hungry, but he was thirsty.

I felt Louie was entertaining in some strange way, especially since he couldn't stay still. It was like he had ants in his pants. He looked like a character from a cartoon, skinny, unshaven, always fidgiting like a little weasel.

Chapter Twenty Nine

Louie tried to leave twice but Tony wouldn't let him go. The third time Louie tried to leave, Tony shouted at the top of his lungs, "Shut up and sit down!" It was getting late. I wanted to leave in the worst way and I really had to take a leak. But I was willing to pee in my pants rather than ask Tony anything at this point.

We made some small talk about hockey and basketball, and some movies, but it was just to pass the time. Louie didn't look very well at this point.

As late as it was, I didn't bother to tell Tony that I really should be going. I didn't dare. I was feeling a nice buzz from all the champagne. Even though I wanted to get out- so bad, I wasn't that stupid.

After Tony screamed at Louie, I figured I'd stay; drink until I fell asleep, and hopefully wake-up sometime in the morning still at the table - God willing. In any event I wouldn't feel any pain, I thought, as I poured some more of the fine champagne.

Tony raised his hand to Carlo. Carlo, with his eyes always fixed on Tony, ran right over to him as he said, "Yes boss?" Louie almost leapt out of his seat. His face was now red from fear. Tony told Carlo to bring something. Carlo quickly returned with a fresh box of Cuban cigars and a clipper.

Tony pointed out to Louie how rare the cigars were in America. He told Louie, "you know Louie these are the same cigars that Castro smokes."

All Louie did was shake his head, "yes", as he stared down at the table. Out of the corner of my eye I watched Louie, he had a queer look on his face.

Tony was nice enough to clip the cigars for us, with this large gold cigar clipper. It looked to be 14 karat gold. Tony then lit us all up. We got another fresh chilled bottle of champagne and we leaned back.

I started to relax. I guess the champagne was taking over. Maybe soon, I'd get up the nerve to ask Tony if I could leave. Or at least pass out at the table. Either one was alright with me.

Louie was now so tense I thought he'd bite right through the cigar.

I really enjoyed Tony's Cuban cigars. They were quality. They smoked cool yet gave off a very nice aroma.

Louie G. just kept his mouth clamped down tight on the cigar and kept squirming in his seat, ready to jump out of his pants. The sweat was running down his face even though the temperature felt very comfortable.

After about five minutes, Tony stared long and hard at Louie. He looked Louie square in the eyes and asked; "So Louie, you like to screw me, huh?"

"No, Tony, I wouldn't!"

"Shut up!" Tony shouted. "So you think that you're a big shot, Louie?"

"No, Tony, don't talk like this. Especially in front of the boy."

"Shut up your face!" Tony shouted, his face now red with rage. Tony's veins were now bulging in his neck. Now I was squirming too.

"You want to screw Tony Vongemi! You, Louie G.? You want to mess with me? You're nothing but a sissy. A fairy-jeweler. You're a faggot. A nothing! A cockroach, Louie! You were nothing. Not a thing without the Family. We made you Louie, don't you remember? Remember the old days?"

Louie said nothing. Not wanting to be noticed, I made believe I wasn't there.

"You played with the books, Louie, didn't you?"

"No! absolutely not, Tony, no way! Tony I wouldn't! Tony, please listen!"

I didn't know where to look, it was so uncomfortable. I tried to slide down in my chair but it didn't help. Still squirming, I was too nervous to breathe. Tony looked straight in Louie G's eyes, for what seemed like five minutes.

"Tony please listen to me!" Louie cried. Tony just stared, not blinking once. Periodically, I'd peek at them for only a second at a time.

Louie now had tears running down his face. Then he burned his hand on his cigar while trying to put it out. Tony finally looked over at Carlo and Benny. With a flick of his hand he motioned towards them. They both quickly ran over and grabbed Louie, one on each side.

I turned away, not wanting to be there. With my mouth closed, not breathing, for fear that I'd make some noise and be noticed. I was frozen still in place.

Louie was now screaming and crying intermittently. The tears were running down his face. I was still observing, but only out of the corner of my eye. My eyes weren't even blinking, to my knowledge. The rest of my body was still paralyzed with fear, as if I were in a coma.

Carlo and Benny each had a smile on their face. This was what their whole existence was about, and they loved it. They were in their glory; true professional killers on call.

Tony had a fierce war-like look on his face, like he was going to do hand to hand combat, one-on-one, with the enemy. I'd turned and faced my left side. Everyone acted as if I wasn't there.

Louie was being held in place to the right of me. The whining and crying went on for a full five minutes. It seemed like hours, I only wished I had much more to drink. My stomach was now completely knotted up and I felt a terrible cramp.

With Louie now motionless and being held down by Carlo and Benny, Tony moved closer. Tony, now cool, calmly took hold of the gold cigar clipper. He grabbed Louie's right hand and he took hold of his index finger. Louie was now begging, "No! not my finger. No, Tony, please I swear, anything!"

Tony took the finger, inserted it in the cigar clipper and swiftly clipped it off. The clipping sounded like a large carrot chopped in half by a cleaver.

There was a blood-curdling cry from Louie. Blood splattered all over the table; on Tony, Carlo and Benny. Louie wasn't breathing for what seemed like forever. But in reality must have been sixty seconds. Much like the baby that loses his breath in a crazy fit of crying.

I couldn't look, but from the periodic glances out of the corner of my eye, I took it all in. My stomach lunged. I fought it back, but twice I almost threw up. Out of shock I still couldn't

131

move. I don't think I was breathing for at least a minute. Was I next?

Still not breathing for fear of being noticed, I started to breathe only slightly through my nose. I couldn't believe what I had just witnessed! All I could think of was, "Thank you, God, it wasn't me!" I had the rest of my drink. Trying to act cool, not wanting to make a scene I sat there, like a little boy; like absolutely nothing had happened.

"Louie, no hard feelings, pal! We'll just forget about what you stole!" Tony said.

Tony waved his hand. Carlo and Benny quickly took Louie away and at the same time wrapped a bar towel around the balance of the stub of the finger on Louie's hand.

All Tony did was look straight in my eyes and stare. Not a word was spoken. There was no need for words. I got the message, loud and clear. The message was simple, "Don't ever screw Tony Vongemi! Don't even think about it."

It hit me right at that moment, that this was the only reason I was ordered to show up at the restaurant. Tony wanted me to see what happens to anyone who crosses him or the Family.

No words were spoken. Tony got up. Then I got up. Tony hugged me. As he did he stared once again into my eyes. That kind of stare that makes you shake. The kind that you can't stare back at too long. I couldn't, and I didn't dare.

I felt that I didn't have too much time left. As I left the restaurant I walked as if I were an 85 year old man. Like all the energy of my body was completely drained out. I walked with little steps, almost as if I was a convicted criminal condemned to the electric chair.

I knew in my heart that soon Benny and Carlo would be coming for me. My time was almost up. Tony wasn't ready to dispose of me at the moment, but his eyes said it all; I'll be a dead man soon. This I believed as sure as the sun rises every day. Maybe I had a month, maybe six. But not much longer than that.

He just wanted me to keep my mouth shut. He didn't want me to squeal about his operation or about the multi-million dollar scam. That's why the fear tactics were used, and they were convincing.

As I headed for the car I was still shaking like a leaf. I shook like a young child who'd lost his mother. I was scared out of my wits. In my case it just made me more determined to carry out my plan of action. Systematically, carefully, but most importantly, flawlessly.

I drove home like I was an old man, driving 10 miles an hour. When I got there all I wanted to do was walk. I must've walked for hours. Losing track of all time, just walking and walking and thinking.

My mind was reeling off thoughts in rapid succession as I continued. My thinking was of Tony, what he did, and Louie the Jeweler, now missing a finger on his right hand. The finger, that was cut off, probably was casually thrown away in the garbage.

This was the mob. This was reality. There's no turning back now, Frankie, you must move forward! I thought, as I walked on.

The walking was like a therapy of some sort. I was now more determined than ever to see my plan through to a successful end.

I couldn't rest now; Not until I was somewhere on a tropical island. There was so much to do and so little time left to do it in.

Chapter Thirty

By the time I reached my apartment I was all psyched up. Now, I was walking at a much faster pace, since I started feeling the bone-chilling air.

For the first time that night, my nerves settled down. For some reason I wasn't as fearful of Tony as I was before. Maybe my brain was being freeze-dried, or maybe I was just plain tired. But after so many times of feeling deathly scared, it starts to wear thin. The fear subsides. After all death can only happen once to a person anyway, I thought.

The wheels were turning, my mind wouldn't stop working in overdrive. Just like a computer my mind was calculating all the scenarios. Taking into consideration all the possibilities. Weighing all options.

My concocted plan must be perfect, Tony was too smart for anything less. After all, it was a life or death, My life that was at stake here. But also, all of my family could become targets, if the plan backfired. Or if the mob got an inkling that a plan was in the works.

With time running out I knew I'd have to step up my strategic planning. As I settled into my kitchen chair I felt the urge to have something relaxing. I had a year's worth of excitement just tonight.

Warm milk, that sounded good. That would help me sleep good tonight. I made some warm milk and went to my favorite chair in the living room.

My Lazy Boy recliner was the most relaxing chair in my apartment. I've done some of my best thinking in that old chair. It was given to me by my father, so it had sentimental value and a special place in my heart. I could swear there were a handful of times that my father would send me an answer to my problem or question.

While thinking deeply about the details of my plan, I could sense strong feelings, telling me that I was doing the right thing. Somehow, I felt it was my father, reassuring me. I continued working on the details of my plan. I had be precise in my actions and clear in my thinking. I must stay controlled at all times, no matter how hard it may be. I couldn't shake the thought of losing all my family and friends forever.

I'd been crying myself to sleep almost every night- lately. My body and mind were both exhausted, as my eyes started to close.

Just then I thought of Louie the jeweler. I could see his hand as clear as day, missing the all important index finger. I wondered if Carlo and Benny finished the job, Did they take him out and kill him?

Poor Louie. If he cheated Tony, he'd never do it again. I'm sure all of Tony's other associates found out about this stunt.

My eyes closed one last time. Totally exhausted now I gave in. Once again in my father's old recliner, feeling his strength and his presence, I comfortably fell off too sleep.

Chapter Thirty One

It was 10:15 am Saturday morning before I opened my eyes. I had slept all night in the recliner. The night before had been draining to say the least. After all, how many nights do you get totally scared out of your wits. Along with the likes of Carlo and Benny, Vongemi's gorillas gaping at you, just waiting for the order to kill.

The late night marathon walk also helped me sleep like a baby. I've noticed for weeks now I've been sleeping much more.

A pattern was forming, I could sense it and I was concerned. What was happening to me? Was I sick? Was it the stress? Because I had enough stress for ten people. I didn't know, but It was getting worse. I was sure that I was becoming slightly depressed. Who wouldn't be with all the worrying I've been doing.

Every night I found myself repeatedly looking out of all my windows. Constantly, I checked to see if anyone was watching my house, waiting outside for me, watching all of my movements.

Was I paranoid? I guess so. But I knew I was very concerned - and scared. My depression was real. Still, there was something inside me, that convinced me that I could handle it. My plan was taking form, I was moving closer to putting an end to the madness.

Mr. Coffee, my obedient and faithful automatic coffee machine, had my fresh coffee waiting for me. It automatically brewed each morning at 8:00 am.

For breakfast I made a frozen bagel in the oven; just ten minutes in the oven and almost as good as fresh-baked. Not bad in a pinch.

Sitting in the kitchen, with my coffee and bagel, I called in to see if I had any messeges. Even on a Saturday, with the office closed, we can work.

At the office we have something called, Voice Activated Messenger Service. A new system, installed a year ago, allows us to get or leave messeges 24 hours a day, all by voice command. It's an intricate computer, that recognizes the spoken word, and allows interaction with the caller.

On the weekend or any time when you call, the system answers with a friendly female voice. It proceeds to explain that the office is closed. But "Harriet", as the computer calls herself, "is still working, and can help you."

"Hello, it's Frank Granstino; calling for my messages," I said to Harriet.

"Hello Frank Granstino, please tell me your personal pin number," Harriet said.

"Three zero one," I said-telling the computer my mother's birthday, which I used for all my pin numbers.

"You have one new message, your new message was left for you at 9:05 am Saturday morning. The length of the message is two minutes and seventeen seconds. Would you like to hear your message now or later?"

"Now," I said, Approximately five seconds later my message played.

"Hi, Frank, its Alicia. I hope all is well. It's early Saturday morning, I was just thinking of you. I've been busy lately. I'm taking some college courses and working part time as a waitress. I still don't have a phone hooked up, so I'll have to call you again at work. I just wanted to know what was new and exciting with you Frank. You know I do miss you. If you need me I could always travel to be with you.

"Well Frank, I've got to run right now but I'll call you again on Monday. I can still vividly remember our time together. It was special Frank. It always will be. I hope it will always be special for you. Maybe we can do it again... Think about it. I can take the time, if you can afford the time, the air fare, and play money. Well, bye for now, sweetie!"

"You have listened to all your messages, should I save or delete them?"

"Delete," I said.

"Thank you, good-bye Frank Granstino," Harriet said, as the computer phone disconnected.

Chapter Thirty Two

As the phone call ended I had a smile on my face. Who was Alicia kidding! I thought, while looking at the ceiling and wondering. The memories came rushing back, as I thought of her

Was Alicia trying to con me again? I knew she only wanted to hear the dirt. She wanted to pick my brain, snoop, as only she could. I knew Tony told her to call and report back to him.

Of course Tony wanted to check up on my attitude, see what I was thinking, especially after last night. He probably was hoping that I'd spill my guts, and tell all to beautiful Alicia. He wanted to know if anything was bothering me. Tony hoped that I'd somehow tell her what I'd witnessed last night. Maybe Tony was secretly hoping that I'd be shooting off my mouth about him. Then he'd have a perfect excuse to silence me now, instead of down the road.

In my head, I had it all planned out. I knew what I'd say, what tone of voice I would use. And exactly what attitude I would project to Alicia when she called me at work. There was no way I'd be anything but a positive, happy-go-lucky guy. I'd project an attitude of a person with everything going for them. I'd exude confidence, total satisfaction with every aspect of my perfect thrilled-to-be-alive, life.

Totally prepared now, I played it over in my mind at least five times, Mentally I was prepared for the show. My acting would be flawless. I knew how I'd act towards Alicia too.

There'd be no way that Alicia would be able to tell Tony anything, except, that I was one of the nicest, most level headed and upbeat guys around. That there was nothing bothering me at all.

I reminisced once again, thinking about Paul. We've been friends since junior high school. Paul was tall for his age, even at age 13, he towered over everyone. He loved playing baseball, and played it well. Everyday, after school, we'd play.

Those were the good old days. So many times I wished I could go back to that simple laid back life again. The good old days, where all you had to do was show up at school each day.

Just sit still, wait for the bell to ring, then go home so I could start our daily ballgame.

The girls always liked Paul. He was average looking but had great blonde hair. He kept it on the long side, so with his blonde hair, his above average height, all the girls just went wild.

We've been best friends ever since then. We even would go out on double dates together when we were young. Or if one of us had no girlfriend at a given time, we'd tag along on a date. We were such good friends that we never felt out of place, even being without a date of our own.

Since it was the weekend, I called Paul and asked him if he wanted to come over to my place and watch some old movies. He said that he had to go over and visit his sister, so he couldn't make it. But Paul suggested that we get together tomorrow, Sunday, and watch the Bulls and the Orlando Magic basketball game on cable.

"Sure Paul, let's get together. Come over to my place, we'll watch the game. Pick up a couple of heros at Blimpies hero shop. Make sure you buy the Blimpie Best, extra bite sandwich."

"Alright Frank, I'll be there in time for the pre-game show."

"Great, Paul, I can't wait!" I said, as we said our good-byes.

As I poured myself another cup of hot coffee, I thought about the morning newspaper. The paper boy should've delivered it by now.

I went outside my front door and sure enough the Daily News was sitting there waiting for me. As I looked up and down my street, I noticed the same black car I'd been seeing before. The car quickly took off from up the street, and turned at the corner. I caught them again. It didn't even bother me that someone was watching me. I was doing nothing to rat the mob out. Let them look, I'll be gone from this mess soon, anyway.

I went back inside and sat back in my recliner, took a big sip of coffee and casually looked at the front page of the paper. I almost choked. I stared in disbelief at the front page-for what seemed like three solid minutes. Then I slowly repeated the headline out loud: MOB RAT RUBBED OUT- FOUND WITHOUT LIPS. The headline was type-set in big three inch bold letters across the front page.

140

What I'd first suspected was true, "Willie the Ears" Shoteri, the Mafia informant, who ran to the FBI to testify against the Vongemi Family, was killed yesterday.

Willie "The Ears", had ratted out to the FBI where they could find the bodies of people who were supposedly killed, Mob-style, by individuals from the Vongemi Family.

Shoteri gave the FBI dates, names of the dead, how they were killed, and who specifically killed each one of them. He had turned FBI informant in exchange for a new life, and a new identity. Willie was to start his court testimony in about one week. He was telling everything until they killed him.

In smaller print, under the headline it read, "Mob Informant found impaled on goalpost, without his lips." Under the sub-headline was a picture, not a close up though, of a body. It was lying on top of the crossbar of the football goal post with the upright post impaled through the torso. He looked like a shish-kebob.

I couldn't make out any of the features. The picture was purposely shot from around 30 feet so as not to be too gory. This guy's lifeless body was slumped backwards resting across the crossbar of the goalpost.

If you wanted to send a message, loud and clear, there was no better way to do it. It appeared that the goalpost was sticking straight through his chest.

The News said it was the goalpost in Giants Stadium at the Meadowlands in New Jersey. The newspaper went on to state: "whoever killed Willie 'The Ears' Shoteri, also cut his lips off his face."

The first people on the scene were the police, who described it as "the goriest slaying we've ever seen!" The lips were sliced off the face probably with a utility type of knife, according to the authorities. "A knife with those straight-edge blades in them. The kind you use to cut open cardboard boxes," stated one of the officers on the scene. They added: "whoever did this wanted to send out a message. A loud and clear message. One that announced they meant business."

There were three pages of coverage on the killing. Showing pictures of some other well-known, major mob hits. The stories covered the background of Willie "The Ears", and his long life of crime with the mob. It also featured stories about all the main players of the mob. Including Bobby "The Bull Dog" Vongemi. As well as Tony Vongemi, and the rest of the Vongemi Family.

The News didn't point their finger at any one Family of the mob. They wouldn't single out anyone in particular. Although, they did mention that the Vongemi Family did have the most to gain with the "silencing" of Willie Shoteri; especially Bobby "The Bull Dog" Vongemi.

I knew of course that the Vongemi Family was responsible. Ever since the FBI dug up the first body and identified it as Sammy "The Ponies" Skatti, the mobster who used to fix the races for the Mafia until he was caught squeezing out too much money for himself.

"This could've been me," I said, still somewhat in shock. If I hadn't caught on to Alicia's game, and let love blind me, I'd've spilled my guts to her and be dead already.

Chapter Thirty Three

Yes, I truly considered myself to be lucky. Lucky to still be alive. Also, I was relieved that Willie "The Ears" wasn't one of Tony's referrals I'd written life insurance on.

How could I explain that one to the insurance company. If we turned in a death claim like that? It would set off an internal company investigation. One that would surely include me, and be an all-out in-depth investigation, which would include all of my clients. No doubt it would blow the lid off the whole deal. Tony would then have to kill me immediately, for fear that I'd rat him out.

He probably would also rub out a few more people who knew anything about the scam including insurance officials. "It's a tough business, this Mafia business. Someone out there can always rat you out!" I said, as I stared at the picture on the front page.

No matter how big you get someone is always preparing to topple you. You can't trust anyone when you're in the Mafia. Not your brother, friend or mother.

As I continued reading the story, page two of the News explained more details about the hit. It appeared, according to the News, that Willie's lips were "sliced off his face along with his mustache."

It was then thought that the killers took a plain piece of white cardboard and glued the lips on the cardboard. The lips were put on the cardboard as if there were a picture of a man's face on it, and the lips just had to be added. Because as the News put it, "The lips were positioned like a child would add Color Forms onto the picture of a face".

I read the story over again. I'd never heard of a mob hit that was this brutal before. It definitely was a message: "Loose lips may just be cut off."

My salvation was I knew the message. I fully understood the message months ago. No one had to hit Frankie Granstino on the head. These people meant business. You just don't play with the Mafia's money or their business. No, I knew that these people were nasty, and I wasn't purposely-going to get them annoyed at me.

I won't bring this incident up to anyone. If Paul speaks of the mob hit, I'll change the subject. When, and if I speak to Alicia I definitely won't speak about it. And I'll skim right over it if she does.

I'd have to program my mind every morning from now on. No slip-ups. My thinking, my attitude must be precise and upbeat. I dared not slip and show any concern, or connection of any kind to the Vongemi Family, Tony or the restaurant. I couldn't allow anyone I came in contact with to know that anything was bothering me. Even though I definitely feel nervous and spooked. Constantly though, I kept wondering if I could escape before Tony puts that all too certain hit on me.

Finally I decided, I must pull this great escape of mine off within the next couple of months.

Hopefully I'll be one step ahead of Tony and the Family. If he gets the slightest indication that I'm planning to escape I'll be signing my death warrant. Tony would never allow me to sing to the authorities.

Tony blatantly killed Willie "The Ears". He didn't even try to make him disappear quitely. The Family made a public show of it. They might as well have set off fireworks, and had cheerleaders dancing and chanting. Maybe they should've televised it.

The Vongemi clan won't go to jail, and I know they'll spend any amount to avoid a conviction. If they can't buy a way out they'll simply kill anybody who could be a threat to them. The Mafia cannot be beat. They can be slowed down. They can be intimidated. The mob can even be summoned into court to stand trial, but in its futile attempt to rid society of organized crime, law enforcement won't be able to stop the mob.

Whatever doubts I had about running away from the mob were now silenced. The thought of turning to the FBI were now a distant memory. I knew I couldn't turn informant against Vongemi and live to talk about it. I feared what might happen to my family more than myself.

The newspaper described what happened with Willie "The Ears." They said Willie was in the Witness Protection Program. But, because he was getting very close to testifying against Vongemi, Willie was moved around a lot.

The paper stated that Willie was being transported to and from the district attorney's office and various other locations.

It was only speculation that someone had followed Willie from the district attorney's office and uncovered his hiding place. Then somewhere between 1:00am and 4:00am Saturday, someone abducted Willie. The law enforcement guards who were protecting Willie were shot with tranquilizer guns. The kind used in the wilderness to knock out animals. The FBI agents were now in never-never land

The FBI wouldn't say how or at what time it took place, but they did admit that three of its agents were put to sleep for up to six hours. No one was hurt except for Willie. The FBI admitted no wrong doing in the death of Willie but stated, "That an investigation of tremendous proportion was underway."

It was simple. The mob knew where the FBI was hiding Willie, or they bribed an insider to tell them. There was always someone who'd spill their guts for a lump sum of tax free money.

Now that the FBI lost not only their witness, but their case against the Vongemis and organized crime, no one will ever prove who actually killed Willie Shoteri.

Tony, and his older brother, Bobby "The Bull Dog" Vongemi were home free. At least now Tony might calm down. I hoped I wouldn't have to meet with him again. But I knew better. Pio Abbatomi was dead. That would mean another death claim. Still another report to be filled out by me. Another story of how death occurred. Then, I'd have to visit Tony once again. I knew Tony would want to see my face, my attitude as I picked up the latest death certificate. He'd be watching closely for any changes in my personality.

Chapter Thirty Four

My thoughts remained on Tony. I thought about the man and how he sucked me right into the trap. Money is definitely a motivator and sometimes an evil culprit. I realized now how skillfully Tony dangled the golden carrot in front of me. Knowing he could provide the easier sales quickly, he hooked the unsuspecting hungry, ambitious and young agent.

Tony had me coming back for more, like a drug addict addicted to cocaine, who has an uncle that'll give him as much as he wants for free.

In life when something is "too good to be true," it usually turns out not to work out. In my case, the dream come true, turned out to be my worst nightmare! The only way I could end this nightmare - was to end my life. End it myself, before it was ended for me.

Because of the commissions, I'd managed to save one hundred and twenty thousand dollars. Which now was in a safety deposit box at the bank. After realizing that something was fishy and knowing that Tony was big-time organized crime, I dared not show money anywhere. When I finally made my move, I'd have enough money saved to start a new life. A life with a new identity, new hope, and somewhere far away.

Tony evidently was a genius. A ruthless criminal with a brilliant mind. Someone who orchestrated a multi-million dollar scam. He probably had worked it out using the district sales levels.

He also knew when an agent starts making one hundred and fifty thousand dollars a year, when he's used to earning only twenty five thousand, that agent will be thrilled and keep his mouth shut. I did keep my mouth shut, but only out of fear for my life. Other than the agency, no one knew I was pulling in big dollars.

I didn't show off, and I purposely didn't tell anyone. I didn't want a soul to know my business. Especially, I didn't want anyone to know that I got suckered into helping the Mafia and a cold-blooded killer.

I was exhausted from thinking and reading the paper. I needed a break, an escape from this world of madness. As usual, whenever I felt depressed lately I went to sleep for a few hours.

It was the only peace I could find in my life. At least during a silent sleep anyway. This time was different though.

Before I fell asleep I gave my mind specific instructions. I commanded, "While I sleep I want you to figure out how I can get even with Tony Vongemi. How I can make him pay for taking my whole world away from me?"

Feeling somewhat relieved I woke up 35 minutes later with an overpowering idea. What I planned to do was to change the names of the beneficiaries on all the insurance policies that Tony referred to me. I would change them all to non-profit organizations such as the Red Cross, Cancer Society, local churches and other religious organizations.

The first time Tony tried to collect, he'd be shocked to find that the beneficiary will be a non-profit group. Maybe the next death claim Tony would try to collect on would be for two million dollars. If I only could see the look on his face, see him squirm. Two million dollars, vanishing right before his eyes.

I don't need any of Tony's stinking money. Besides, I want him to believe that I'm dead and dead men don't need money. Just changing all of the beneficiaries will fix his wagon. The fit of rage he'll throw after one or two million dollars is paid out to a church will be enough for me.

To date the Financial Life Insurance Co. had five death claims as the result of Tony Vongemi.

Tony Vongemi had suckered the Financial Life Insurance Co. out of some four million dollars in death claims. My record was piling up. Five death claims and four million dollars against me.

Still, I thought carefully about the five deaths, I wondered if these five men really were dead, or was that too an elaborate scam. Maybe the dead bodies weren't even the actual bodies of these guys. Maybe they were other dead people being passed off as these five identities.

The Vongemi Family would have no problem coming up with dead bodies to switch identities with. From their reputation, the Vongemi's could probably supply a body a week. Freshly killed, but slightly bullet-ridden bodies. All you could use.

Chapter Thirty Five

The problem I faced was this, I had already written at least 200 polices so far, on Tony's so-called referrals. The damage was done. If I didn't write another case from Tony, he had all that he needed. All sitting ducks, all nicely insured.

Tony could clean up with just claims on twenty more lives, which if added up could reach an additional twelve million dollars, in tax-free insurance claims.

The main problem was if I stopped accepting his future leads and if I didn't write another policy on any of his paisans, Tony would definitely know I was on to him.

No, I had to continue doing business as usual and not let on that anything was wrong. I could play a very convincing jerk, I thought to myself. Much better than I could try to breathe while being choked to death. All I knew was I was being used like a well-worn door mat. Tony was walking all over me, and all I could do was smile.

Pio Abbatomi was the latest death claim when his car, a Ford Taurus station wagon, hit a telephone pole at about sixty miles an hour. The impact was so powerful that his car exploded into flames. The fire was so intense that all the fire department could do was let it burn. Pio Abbatomi was burned beyond recognition. They scrapped him out of the car. The newspaper stated that Pio was dead instantly from the severe impact.

It was six o'clock when I reached my mother's house in Staten Island. The family moved years ago to Staten Island, where it was quiet. A few years ago, I moved back to Brooklyn.

My mother kept the house, even after my father's death, over five years ago. Every few weeks I try to visit her, if I can. But time moves so quickly,

Since I had called ahead, and told her I was coming, I reminded her not to cook. It was the weekend and my philosophy is: no one should have to cook on the weekend.

In Brooklyn there's a famous pizza parlor on Third Avenue called, A Pizza Magic. They make the best pizza in the whole state of New York. People even come from out of state.

I brought her a large Sicilian fresh mozzarella pie. It's her favorite because of the crispy crust. And I got her a dozen mussels in red sauce. She's always loved them.

When I reached her house I parked right in front of the red all-brick ranch home. My sister Candice and her daughter Michele were there as usual. They lived around the corner so they were frequently at Mom's house. Michele was now nine years old. it had been almost five years since her father Ray ran off.

I admire Candice for raising Michele by herself, and not taking in just any man, like many other single mothers do. My sister has always been a great source of inspiration to me. She reads a lot, and always looks for the good in everybody. I know she picked up a lot of these traits from my mother. She always makes me feel better whenever I feel down.

I love my little niece, Michele. Every time I see her, I pay extra special attention to her. I feel terrible that she doesn't have a father figure in her life.

As I entered my mother's house, Michele came running over to hug me almost knocking the pizza out of my hands. "Whoa, take it easy, little girl," I said, as I quickly found a place to set down the pizza and mussels. Michele always loved to see me.

"Uncle Frank, I missed you!" she said, which almost brought tears to my eyes.

"I know, I missed you too, Michele, I said, softly.

My mother and sister were in the kitchen.

"Hello, how's everyone?" I asked, as I kissed them both. "What's new and exciting?"

"Oh, the same old stuff, Frankie, you know," Candice said.

Then my mother asked; "Are you feeling alright, Frankie?"

"I'm fine; never been better, I'm just a little tired, Ma, that's all!"

My mother could always tell whether I was pale, real tired, sick or happy. She knew whether I was in a good mood, or even if one of my hairs was out of place. She must do a five second scan of my whole body every time she sees me. And in just those five seconds she'd come up with a list of what was wrong. She's amazing. And she had no problem telling me just how bad I

152

looked on a given day, either. "You know Frankie, you're only going to be 28 years old. You better start getting some more rest. You're starting to look 38 years old!"

"Thanks, Mom, anything else?"

"No, I'm was just trying to help you."

"I know, Mom, I'm only kidding!"

"You know, Frankie you could also use a haircut," Candice chimed in, with a big grin on her face. "Right mom?"

"Yes, Frankie, Candice is right!"

Looking at my sister's hair I said, "Hey, listen curly, I heard that Einstein used to cut his own hair, so I figure I'll wait a little longer and start to cut my own hair."

"Oh, you'll really look good then," she added, laughing hysterically.

"That's all you'll need to do, cut your own hair!" Candice said.

"Ok, you two, let's eat, the entertainment is over," my mother said, with mock sarcasism.

Chapter Thirty Six

As the night progressed we watched I Love Lucy reruns on TV and chatted some more. I caught myself staring more and more at my mother, my sister and my niece. Casual glances, just enough so I wouldn't be noticed. I knew that my time here was now quickly running out. That I'd have to leave for good shortly, never to return again.

Still staring, I noticed little things, like the way my mother smiles when she's happy. That my mother reminds me of a young girl of sixteen-whenever she laughs. I can see the young happy-go-lucky child still in her, the sparkle in her eyes. I loved my mother, and I knew that if she knew what I was planning, that she would be one hundred percent behind me.

As I looked at my mother's wonderful smile I felt happier and more determined than ever. She always did give me strength to do the seemingly impossible.

Then I looked at Candice. All I could think of was where did this curly red headed sister of mine come from. Nobody else in our family ever had red hair, or curly hair for that matter.

Even the neighbors thought someone left her on our doorstep. I figured that someone in our family tree, maybe 200 years ago had red hair. It must be in the genes.

We always got along, Candice and me. When we were growing up we'd always play together. Mostly, she'd play with all my toys. Candice was somewhat of a tomboy, as we were growing up. Now, she was a lovely woman of thirty, with a beautiful little girl who was growing up fast, right before our eyes.

I'll miss my little Michele. All those little hugs and kisses she so willing would give. There's nothing so precious as young, loving, and innocent children. So sweet, so pure. Before the cold world we live in brainwashes them-into thinking like we all do with jealousies and pettiness.

Children like Michele are so innocent. No prejudice, no motives, just pure loving affection and trust for everyone they come in contact with.

155

It was getting late, about 11:15 pm, when Candice got up to leave. It was way past Michele's bedtime. She must've been exhausted, although she looked much more energetic than the rest of us.

I also said my good nights as I kissed everyone again. My mother said, "Make sure you get some more rest, Frankie. Don't burn the candle at both ends. Watch your partying. I hope you're taking vitamins, I heard that vitamin 'E' is supposed to work wonders."

She should only know, I thought. I said, "Mom, I'm not burning any candles, I don't even like the smell of candles!"

"You know exactly what I mean, I see dark circles under your eyes, again. You know those dark circles mean too little rest, Frankie!"

"No they don't Mom, it means too many drugs!" I said, with a big grin.

"Get out of here, before I give you a shot in the head," she screamed, as she waved her fist in the air.

I always seem to bring out the best in everyone, I said to myself happily as I drove down the secluded side street in Staten Island.

All the way home I thought about my family and friends and wondered why we didn't see each other more. The demands of the job, the hectic rush of daily living and all its chores leaves most of us too exhausted to socialize during the week.

I was aware that when my plan started to unfold, I would have to cut my family and friends off from my world. As hard as it might be I'd be alone. No one to ask anything of or get assistance from.

And most of all no one to help me complete my plan of suicide and escape from Vongemi Land. It's so lonely when you have a serious life threatening problem you can't discuss with anyone. Other than Paul, my only true friend, I wouldn't be socializing with other people. I didn't want the extra pain, for them or me. When I'm gone I want there to be as little grief and despair as possible. My family's suffering would be more than enough. How do you explain to a loving, adoring niece that her

156

uncle took a leap off a tall building. What do you say, when she asks, "But why Mamma? Why?"

At this point I was almost at home, I had just crossed the Verrazano bridge into Brooklyn. It was then that I realized, "We must do what we must do!" I knew my plan would go forward. I must do what I must do, I thought. I felt much better. Now, I also knew that my suicide plan would definitely work.

I felt a tremendous surge of confidence. And I knew in my heart that this was the only real way out. My suicide plan would put to rest, once and for all, Frank Granstino.

Chapter Thirty Seven

Sunday morning was cold. Extremely cold. The temperature was 15 degrees with a wind chill of 10 degrees below-zero. The weather report on the radio stated that this was the coldest January on record.

Pipes were freezing and bursting all over the city. The frigid temperatures left many people without heat. It felt like months instead of weeks that it was Christmas. My Christmas was the worst holiday I ever had. There was no spirit, no cheerfulness for the season.

The entire city was on "special cold alert," which meant at the first sign of no heat, the fire department would be sent immediately to the person's home. They would then transport the person or family to special temporary shelters.

It was 10:00 am on Sunday, Paul called. "Frank, let's go get some pancakes!"

"What are you - crazy, Paul? It's 10 degrees below-zero. It's too cold!"

"Stop being a sissy, the sun is shining bright, and the temperature is going up. I want to get out of the house, I feel like crap! Frankie, I'll pick you up in 10 minutes; be there or be square."

"Alright, then we'll hang out for the Knick game, it comes on at 1:30 pm today," I said.

Today I gave into Paul. Mostly because I felt I owed him as much time as he wanted with me and because I knew before long I'd be gone.

It was exactly ten minutes later when Paul beeped the car horn. He must be hungry! I thought, as I put my heavy coat and hat on. I was one of the fortunate ones this season. Many people were sick with the flu, or pneumonia.

I guess I didn't have the time to get sick, I was too worried about the Vongemis and staying alive. I also took real good care of myself, eating well, and taking a lot of vitamins.

Over the last few months I put on 15 pounds. My weight was now up to 185 pounds. Recently, I caught myself-eating much more than normal. My nerves were on edge. It's no wonder, with crazy Tony killing people.

As I got to Paul's new Honda Accord, I said, "Howdy partner, where do you want to go for breakfast?"

"I feel like pancakes. Let's go to the Pancake House, ok?"

"Sure Paul, that's fine!" I said.

As I sat down next to Paul I noticed a bandage on his forehead. "What in blazes happened to you?"

"Please, I'm still sick over it, that's why I need a treat at the Pancake House. I got in an accident last night. Well, let me clarify. Some clown hit me, and ran while I was waiting at a light. It was almost as if he wanted to hit me. There were no skid marks, no screeching of his brakes, and I could swear that he had a smirk on his face after he hit me."

"Oh yeah, I see he hit you on the driver side front quarter panel. Are you alright Paul?"

"I'm fine. Just a splitting headache. He hit me at about nine o'clock last night. The ambulance wanted to take me to the hospital, mostly for observation, I guess, but I refused. So they fixed me up in the car, no stitches were needed, so I guess I'm lucky."

"Well I'll be dipped. What kind of a car was it?"

From what I can tell, it was a late model Cadillac. There were two guys in it. They didn't even have license plates when I looked."

"Well, as long as you're not hurt."

"The only thing that hurts is the damage to the car, but I'll be covered, I have a two hundred and fifty dollar deductible. So that's all it'll cost. I could've tried to follow these guys, but they looked pretty big. I didn't want to get beat-up."

"You did the right thing Paul! Why push your luck? People are crazy today. They probably had bats in the car. You don't fool around today!"

"Yeah, I guess. I still can't believe how they plowed right into me!" Paul said as we drove to the restaurant.

I had a sick feeling that Vongemi sent his goons to show me that he knew my friends and my family. Tony probably was just sending a message to me through Paul. This possibility troubled me.

Chapter Thirty Eight

"Uncle Jimmy's Pancake House" was located at Third Avenue and 86th street in Brooklyn. This place had the best pancakes around.

"So what did you do last night Frank?"

"Oh the same old thing, you know. I visited my mom, Candice and my niece, Michele."

"Oh that's good," Paul said, "How's your mom holding up?"

"Oh great," I said, "My mom's one tough lady. She always seems to do good. She eats well, takes care of herself. You know, vitamins and other things.

"Yeah, your mom always did take good care of herself.

"It's her attitude, I think. She has a positive attitude about life. I think she'll make it to a hundred easily with her attitude."

"Frank, I know, your mom was always a happy person. At least until you got in trouble. You always were doing something wild and crazy, Frankie."

"Oh - give me a break Paul, I was a good boy."

"Oh yeah? How about the time you climbed the telephone pole, and then you were too scared to come down. The fire department had to rescue you?"

"I don't remember that."

"Oh sure you do, Frank."

Paul was laughing hysterically all the way to the Pancake House. I thought he might pee his pants he was laughing so hard.

"Frankie, I think your mother deserves to be made a saint, just for raising you."

We each had the Pancake Special of the day. Uncle Jimmy's had more ways to make pancakes than I ever saw before. He even had ham pancakes.

Paul and I had the strawberry pancakes. Strawberries were inside the pancakes and on top. It tasted like strawberry shortcake.

We spoke about work, his family and about the Knicks. While we were eating, Paul asked, "Hey Frankie did you read about that mobster, Willie that got killed?"

"Oh yeah that was wild, wasn't it?"

"Did you see the picture, the one with the goal post sticking out of the guy's chest?"

"Of course I did. It was all over the papers,"

"Did you speak to any of the Vongemi's about the mob hit on that Willie character?"

"No, Paul I haven't seen any of those Vongemi guys in a long time. As soon as I found out about them, I kept my distance."

"That's good Frank, Do you think Vongemi had him knocked off? he asked, with a sly smile on his face.

"I don't know, it's very possible, they're capable of it aren't they?"

"You bet they are. They have some reputation!"

We each polished off six big pancakes. We were stuffed when we headed back to my apartment. On the way home we stopped off and picked up two big heros at the Blimpie hero shop.

Since we both liked the Bulls we couldn't bet against each other. We both wanted to see Michael Jordan flying through the air and slam dunking the ball. He was still a great player, probably the greatest basketball player there ever was.

The game progressed as expected, Michael Jordan was flying high through the air. He was slam dunking the ball, stealing the other team's passes. He was fabulous.

Our hero sandwiches were great, and we washed it down with a few light beers. We couldn't watch one of the best games of the year without some beers and munchies.

While they ran and played; we watched and drank. That's the life. By the fourth quarter the Bulls took complete control of the game.

By the time it was over, the Chicago Bulls had won easily. The score was 106 to 93. It was a great, fast moving game. One you just couldn't look away from. The excitement level was tremendous. If you wanted to forget about your problems, then this type of exciting basketball game was the answer. It was intense. It worked for me. For three solid hours I thought of nothing except beer, eating and basketball.

After the game, Paul and I watched a couple of movies on HBO. Before we knew it, time flew by, it was 9:30 at night and tomorrow was a work day for both of us.

"Boy we had a great day Frankie, didn't we?"

"We sure did!," I agreed, "That was some game,"

We both headed for the door. For the first time in a long time, I was happy, but at the same time I felt pangs of sadness. I'll miss him when I have to disappear. In fact I'll miss everyone. But Paul was my buddy. Like a brother to me.

It was 10:00 Sunday night when I got an overpowering urge to do something I've neglected for years. There was something inside telling me to go to church. I didn't know where or why but I had this intense urge to go to church.

It had been six years since I last went to church. At that time it was for a happy occasion. It was my sister Candice's wedding. The church, Regina Pacis, was truly a spectacular church.

It's huge. When you enter the front, through the thick heavy mahogany doors, you instantly sense that you're in a very special place. There's an incredible feeling that comes over me every time I enter this church.

For the first time in months I wasn't scared of anyone or anything. God, and my belief in heaven had a calming effect as if someone lifted a tremendous weight from my shoulders.

Not until I walked through the doors of the church, did I feel the intense sense of spiritual relief I'd been longing for. As I sat down in the pew, by the aisle, I looked toward the altar, and said several prayers.

I stayed in the church for a few more minutes, praying, planning and formulating the strategy for the plan to break away for good.

My plan was to disappear in about one month. This gave me enough time to work out all the finer details. There would be one shot at it. If it worked I'd get to live. If it failed, I'd be dead. When put in perspective, my choice was crystal clear. Failing was just not an option!

Chapter Thirty Nine

The next week passed quickly and, surprisingly, was very quiet. There were no new death claims to report from Tony and no special requests for me to show up at the restaurant for any meetings. I did my job all week, seeing four appointments for service and new sales. It was business as usual.

On Tuesday morning, I got a call from Alicia. Of course I was expecting her to call me. Tony was trying to set me up by using Alicia to pump anything she could out of me. This time once again I was totally prepared.

When Alicia asked me how everything was, I told her, "Fabulous!" I told her that I even went to the movies over the weekend. That I saw, Gone With The Wind, with a girl I'd met in a bar. We decided to go out on one date, nothing serious. I explained to Alicia that the girl wasn't attractive to me but she was good company.

Of course I made the whole thing up, and I down played my feelings for the girl as, just friends. But I sounded as upbeat as I could. She had to sense a feeling of complete happiness on my part, convincing Tony that I'm nothing but a sex-hungry young man.

Alicia then asked, "Frankie, did you hear about that murder in your area of "Willie the Ears?"

"I didn't even get to read the newspapers. It's been non- stop lately. But these things happen Alicia, what are you going to do? I don't even follow world events, lately, I just can't keep up with it. The business keeps me running, you know?"

"You must be going crazy, if you're that busy."

"Are you kidding? I love the action, I thrive on it!"

By the time it was all over, I told her I missed her and we should get together in about a month. I even offered to wire her money if she needed it. She turned my offer down.

Alicia now claimed she was selling Avon cosmetics door to door and doing very well and she'd have her phone turned on again, as soon as she paid the back bills.

The week was uneventful for the most part. Tom Somi, the office-enforcer never even yelled at me once. He only called me a putz, once. Tom should only have heard what I called him - under my breath.

The week went fast. It seemed like time was moving faster now that I had a plan to run. Was it because I felt that my time in this town was running out?

It was now 8:00 am Saturday morning. I'd come to the office purposely at this time because I knew no one would be here.

One advantage of being single is, you can basically do whatever you want to, anytime you want. It's nice not having to answer to anyone, not like some crazy married couples I know. But I have to admit, sometimes it's lonely.

Every so often I'd come in just to be by myself. A productive time when I can get some serious work done. Today I was adding up all the Vongemi referred sales, and what potential claims were still outstanding. As I added, I got more disturbed. The numbers were mind boggling. Four million dollars in proceeds were paid out, and there could be much more.

Rocco Conlini's claim for one million dollars was just paid out late last week. My claim instructions to the company was to mail the check directly to Tony. Then I told Tony that it was a new company policy to pay claims of one million or more directly to the beneficiary's representative. And that they send the check by certified mail. But in reality I just didn't want to see Tony's mug so soon. My patience with Tony was gone but I couldn't let him sense it.

According to my calculations, there were more than fifty larger policies that Tony could potentially put a claim in for. There were many more policies than that-written, but the largest ones amounted to fifty. The total amount of Insurance on just the largest fifty policies added up to 20 million dollars. So it was conceivable that Vongemi could collect an additional 20 million dollars in phony future death claims.

Looking back, I can't believe Tony had suckered me into this scam, into the mob. And as a result I felt indirectly responsible for four million dollars worth of phony death claims so far.

Even though it was innocently done on my part, I was still partly responsible in this scam and now faced an additional 20 million of potential future claims. That's lovely, just lovely! I thought.

I took a large yellow pad out of my desk drawer and stared at it blankly. Now, how can I become real dead? I thought, while looking and studying the office ceiling.

Reaching inside my right desk drawer, I grabbed the Cuban cigar that was hidden there for weeks. Boy, these really were quality cigars, I thought, as I bit the end off one. Leaning back in my swivel chair, I lit it up.

Chapter Forty

I put my concentration fully on the task at hand, as I wrote on my pad, "Frank Granstino's, Suicide Plan." Under the heading I wrote the following: Place: World Trade Center because it's one of the highest points in New York - a hundred and ten stories.

It was of utmost importance that it take place at a high point because I need what ever I throw off the roof to be totally unrecognizable. Also, the World Trade Center was like a ghost town on weekends and no one was working and few lived in the immediate vicinity.

Next, we needed a body. I wanted to be safe and sound-somewhere far away, especially when the authorities found the body that was supposed to be me.

The entire operation revolved around the dead body. It had to pass for me. So I wrote down, the body is to be that of a newly deceased homeless man. The body must also match my build, complexion and age as closely as possible.

Since my statistics were common it worked in my favor. For the first time ever I was glad that I was five-eleven and a hundred seventy five pounds, and a shoe size of 10 1/2.

I'm just a regular guy, It should be easy to find a body match to mine. As long as I stay away from black or old homeless men.

By the time the body hits the ground, there should be nothing left to it. Once the body started to fall from the roof, it will drop at 32.2 feet per second. The gravitational pull of 32 feet per second on a 175 pound lifeless body will pretty much disfigure even the hunchback of Notre Dame, I thought, as I pictured the fall.

The World Trade Center's roof was more than one quarter of a mile off the ground. "Great! That's just what I need," I said emphatically, "No one will ever know that I'm still alive!"

I started to think of potential problems that might arise. I'd have to be ready at a moment's notice to pull this scam off. After all, a matching dead body doesn't magically appear every hour. It may take two weeks, maybe even longer to find one. My estimation was that the west side of the city would be the best place to stake out for my body double, because many homeless stay there, not far from the water.

Next, I'd have to clean-up the body before I could pass it off as my own. I'd have to cut and clean all of his nails, make sure his teeth were in good shape.

I started to gross myself out, just thinking of touching the body of a dead man. I hate dead things, I can't even touch a dead bird. But I had no choice. I needed to do these things. No one said it would be easy. My options were few.

This plan had to be tight, I needed to be absolutely precise in all my movements for me to be able to pull this thing off. My mind must not get off track. I needed to think carefully. My emotions must be controlled, no matter what.

I can do it, I can pull this off, I told myself. My fear of dying, of being killed by the mob, was starting to subside. If Vongemi should beat me to the punch, I was secure in my belief in God. In my heart I didn't want to die, I was going to do everything in my power to beat the Vongemis.

I just needed a few more weeks to escape with my life. I wrote a big "3" at the top of my page. Just three weeks, and counting down, I thought.

West 33rd Street, that's where I'll find a body. I wrote it down. From reports I had read in the past, the homeless bodies were found in this vicinity.

Many of the homeless died from drug overdoses, and Aids. The sub zero-record setting, low temperatures were also a factor.

My planning continued, with my thinking intensified while I kept writing. I realized I'd have to start drinking in Manhattan's West Side bars. At least for the next few weeks.

After the authorities found my body, I'd want them to find a trail. And the trail they'd find should be specific. The trail should lead to despair, desperation and of course depression. There must be no doubt in anyone's mind that Frank ended his life out of total depression and desperation. As sad as it sounded to me there was no getting around it. I had to destroy the nice positive character of Frank Granstino. As much as it hurt, Frank Granstino had to become a drunk and a drug user. It was the only way. This way, when the police did their investigation they'd report that poor Frank was drinking and an addict and had been depressed for weeks before his death.

The suicide must be believable. The Vongemi Family would surely get a copy of the police report. They had connections with everyone, especially inside the police department. The Family had to be convinced that I did in fact commit suicide, and I was dead.

By 12:00 I had four pages full of notes. My planning was going well, I had my outline of what had to be done. There'd have to be some fine tuning, but overall I was pleased with the first draft.

My planning session lasted four hours. I was now mentally exhausted. I packed up my briefcase and started for the door.

All of a sudden I realized that the pad with all my notes couldn't stay in my briefcase. I had to hide them somewhere. But where? Was there a safe place? Some where no one would think of looking?

My apartment and my briefcase were out of the question. These were the places that would be searched first. The car was no good, and I dared not keep them on me. If Tony's men ever found the plans, I'd be dead very shortly thereafter.

Just then it dawned on me: I could simply hide the plans right here and nobody would be the wiser. Inside my desk drawer I took a plain envelope. I then folded my notes, put them in the envelope and sealed it.

Then I flipped over my desk chair and taped the envelope to the underside of the seat. Now, no one would ever think of looking there.

By the time I was done, I was happy, finally my thoughts were put into a strategic plan. With a smile on my face and a sense of accomplishment, I headed home.

Just before I reached my home I saw a large black car. It was a late model. As I proceeded with caution, I saw that it was parked right in front of my house. My first thought was: How odd, why is a limo here? Nobody was getting married. The only people in the house were the owners, Jodi and Alan Goudi and myself.

My apartment, located upstairs was a spacious three room apartment. Still looking around, I thought, The Goudis were retired, had no children, so what's the deal?

Reluctantly I parked my car and cautiously walked toward my house. As I got closer to the front of my house I saw the doors of the black limousine open up.

Before I knew what was happening two guys rushed at me from the car. There was nowhere to run. In a split second I was surrounded and held in place. It took only another second for me to realize that it was Tony's men Carlo and Benny.

Carlo said, "Tony wants to see you, now!" while squeezing my arm tightly. "Come with us," he said, while pulling me forcibly toward the car. My arm hurt and I was scared. Is this it? Is this where it all ends? I was completely caught off guard. Why would Tony be looking for me today? Why now?

"Carlo, I can't go with you, I've got to go upstairs!"

"No, you don't. Frankie you are coming with us, right now!"

"But, Carlo, I've got to go to the bathroom!"

"Do it in your pants!" he growled as they both dragged me into the limousine, with its engine still running. As soon as the doors of the car closed, the car screeched off leaving skid marks on the street.

"What's up, Carlo?" I said, while shaking like a leaf.

"Tony wants to talk to you. What are you deaf?"

"Carlo, at least tell me where we're going,"

"Why are you so nervous? Were going to the restaurant to see Tony. Now shut up. You're giving me a headache!"

Trying to be nonchalant I said, "Carlo you abruptly grabbed me off the street, what do you expect!"

Finally feeling just a little relieved that I wasn't going to be wasted, at least for the moment, I started to wonder what the heck is so important that Tony has to practically kidnap me. It took ten minutes for us to reach the restaurant. Finally I'd find out what Tony had on his mind.

Chapter Forty One

As we entered the restaurant I quickly looked around. Not a soul was in the place. It was about 1:00. I looked over at the bar, Tony wasn't there. No one was. Carlo and Benny pushed me towards Tony's private office.

Carlo knocked on the solid walnut door once and entered. Tony looked like the President, while sitting majestically at his desk. On seeing me, Tony rose from his black leather chair. With a smile on his face, he said, "Frankie, my friend nice to see you. Come in. Come right in."

With the back of his hand Tony waved once at Benny and Carlo and they quickly left, slamming the door behind them.

"Frankie, how are you feeling?"

"I'm alright, Tony, I just don't like being forced into a car and dragged over here!" I said feeling frustrated and annoyed.

"Please excuse Carlo and Benny Frankie. Sometimes they don't understand. You know Frankie they're not too smart," he said, while hitting his head with his palm.

"Please accept my apologies Frankie, OK?"

"Sure, Tony, no big deal! You wanted to see me?" I said, feeling apprehensive.

"Yes, Frankie, I trust you and I like you. But some things you have to discuss eyeball-to-eyeball. You understand don't you?"

"Of course!" I said, trying to sound like I fully understood.

"Frankie sit down. Make yourself comfortable-my friend," he said, as he waved towards the chair next to me.

"You want a cigar, Frankie? Maybe a drink?"

"No, thanks, Tony," I said as politely as I could, "I'm fine"

I remembered all too well the last time I had cigars at Tony's restaurant. I remembered Louie, I remembered when Tony cut the jeweler's finger clean-off, splattering blood all around the table. And I remember the crying, begging and screaming from Louie.

No, I think I'll pass on Tony's cigars. At least for now. I was still on pins and needles as to what was so important, why Tony had me abruptly picked up.

Was I in trouble now? Did Tony figure my plan out? How could he? No one knew but me. I'd kept it all a secret. I hadn't shared any of Tony's scheming, his killing, maiming, or other inside mob secrets with anyone. Even my best friend Paul.

"Frankie, I had you brought here so I could tell you in person, what I have to tell you," Tony said with a grim face.

Here it is, I thought. This is the moment! Were Carlo and Benny waiting just outside the door for Tony to give the order to take me away and kill me?

"Frankie, this is the deal, Keith Brava is dead. He had a policy with you for one million dollars, didn't he?" Acting cool, I said, "Yes, one million."

"Good. Very good, Frankie," he said, smiling at me now.

"What happened?" I asked with a puzzled look.

"Well Frankie, I'm going to tell you a little secret. You see Keith Brava had a big mouth. He started shooting his mouth off to everybody about our business. You know, Family business."

"Tony you don't have to tell me anything, I don't need to know anything," I said while looking him in the eyes. Feeling relieved that I wasn't going to die just yet. At this point I couldn't care if he killed a nun. I did a quick check with my hand to see if I'd soiled my pants. I'm all right, I thought.

"Frankie I want you to know and see some of our world. Maybe you should see what happens to someone with a big mouth, a squealer. Frankie, anyone who jeopardizes our business, anyone that disrupts the flow of the Family will be eliminated. Anyone. Do you understand me?" Tony's eyes had that wide-eyed-fierce look. The look I've seen him get before.

"Tony, please, I don't think I should be hearing all this! I'm just the insurance man. I only want to sell insurance, and stay out of trouble!" I said, with my voice quivering as I spoke, showing Tony my exposed fear.

"I want you to hear! I want you to see what happens when men turn on their friends!"

"But Tony, this is your personal business..."

176

"Frankie, you are a paisan. You wouldn't hurt us. You know better, don't you?"

"Of course," I said while getting up to shake his hand. As I did I felt my sweaty palm. But I didn't care.

Tony squeezed my hand very tightly this time, and wouldn't let go. With a sick little smile on his face he said, "Cause I'll break your neck too, Frankie my boy! You just stay a good boy, OK, Frankie?" he said while pinching my cheek.

"Tony, you don't have to worry about me!"

"Well, Keith Brava started talking too much. We found out that he was all set to talk to the Feds about our operations. We couldn't let him do that Frankie. You understand don't you?"

"Tony, I don't know, I guess I..."

"Frankie, I know what you would've done if you were me. You would've taken care of it, eliminated the problem, shut him right up. Do you want to know how we shut him up?"

"No Tony, I don't think so, I said, as I shook my head no.

"Well I'm going to tell you anyway, because I like you. We snapped his neck Frankie. Yes, we broke his neck and then we threw him off the roof of his house. We made it look like he was cleaning the leaves out of the gutters on his roof. That's how he broke his neck. The authorities bought it as an unfortunate accident. An accidental death. Frankie, doesn't that pay us double or triple? Or should I say the beneficiary?"

"Tony I wish you wouldn't tell me any of these things. But since you have, I must tell you that the policy will only pay out one million dollars. We didn't put a rider on that policy. Only with the rider attached would the policy pay double for an accidental death. But Tony please don't tell me any more details. I'd feel much better not knowing too much. Especially since I'm the writing agent. It makes me feel like I'm a part of a cover up. Do you see where I'm coming from Tony?"

"I understand fully. So you say we're only going to get one million dollars? You mean we're going to lose a million bucks? Whose fault is it Frankie? Tell me, who messed up?"

"Tony, please, listen to me. No one screwed up and no one is trying to screw you out of a million dollars. First of all, Keith purchased a term life policy. Term insurance as you know, is the cheapest form of life insurance available. So we don't normally put the accidental rider on Term insurance. You see the accidental rider cost almost as much as the base policy, which pays for any kind of death. So when someone wants the accidental rider we inform them that it's much wiser just to increase the base policy. Tony, do you see? Do you understand?"

"You're not trying to double-talk me are you?"

"Please, don't hurt my feelings. I've never misled you before, have I?"

"I'm sorry, Frankie, it's just that the Family was counting on two million dollars. You understand. That's a lot of money."

"I understand fully. But I also understand that you and the Family have enjoyed a total of five million dollars in death claim benefits, including this one. And I've helped you all the way Tony. Five million dollars tax free, that's nothing to sneeze at, is it?"

"Frankie, you're a good boy! And you've been helping us. Just don't get stupid, and don't get too smart for yourself, you hear me?"

"Yes, I understand completely. You don't have to worry about me." I said.

"Lets go get us a rub-down and a sauna, Frankie, I've got some nice connections in the city. Beautiful girls. Frankie, they'll do anything you want them to. Trust me. They even dress up as little girls for me. Come on, let's go!"

"No, I'm just not in the mood, not right now. I've got a splitting headache!"

"Frankie, you want for me to make Carlo get you something?"

"No, please don't make Carlo get me anything. Thanks anyway. I just need to rest. Tony, you keep telling me that I'm a good boy and I am. But you're throwing far too much at me too fast. I want to stay a good boy. I don't want to know all the inside, private stuff. Right now what I really need, is to go home and lie down. I feel exhausted. We can go out another time, okay?"

Tony rose, not saying a word. He walked to the office door, opened it and yelled out for Carlo. Within five seconds Carlo came running into the office.

"Carlo, I want for you to take Frankie home. Make sure he gets some peace and quiet. You're responsible, I want Frankie to get some sleep. Do you understand me Carlo?"

"Yes, Tony I'll get the car ready and bring it to the front door."

With that, Carlo was off and running.

"I'm sorry I told you too much Frankie. I just wanted you to see that we reward loyalty and we destroy all who are disloyal!"

"Tony, I've always wanted to know, how do they break someone's neck?"

"Are you sure you really want to know?"

"Yes, I'm just curious"

"Remember what they say - curiosity killed the cat!" he said. "What you do to break someone's neck is first sneak up behind them. You put your left hand firmly on their left shoulder, then quickly pull them close to your body. You then put your right leg in front of their right leg, keeping their body firmly pressed against your body. Then with your right hand you grab their head at the left side of their forehead, and with one quick motion you yank their head all the way to the right side. Just one big snap. It's a quick and painless death. They're dead before they know what happened. Why do you want to know Frankie? You need some help with some low- life? Just let me know."

"No, Tony, I don't know, I was just curious that's all."

"You just go home now and rest. Feel better!" he said, as he rose to shake my hand. "Oh, and by the way, I expect to see you with the paperwork tomorrow. You know it's for one million dollars. That's a lot of bucks. I don't want any screw up!"

"Tony, the guy just died. At least give me a chance to do the paperwork."

"Frankie, we killed Keith two days ago. That should be plenty of time. How long do you want to hold our money?"

"Ok, Tony, I'll get the paperwork going in the morning. Then I'll drop by to see you. Maybe you'll have a death certificate for me?"

"Oh, I'll have one. Don't you worry about that!"
"All right, let me go home now, I'll see you tomorrow."

Chapter Forty Two

As promised, Carlo and Benny were waiting in the car with the engine running right outside the front door. Not a word was spoken. No looks, no faces. Just dead silence until I reached my home.

Once I reached my apartment, I quickly opened my door and went inside. Only when I closed the door behind me did I finally feel safe. My hands, as I looked at them, were shaking.

My worst fears were true, Tony was a killer. A cold blooded killer. Vongemi would stop at nothing to protect himself and the Mafia Family. I was just a pawn, a piece he moved on his board of business. He used me and continues to use me. Now, I honestly believed that Tony was very capable of snapping my neck, all by himself.

There was that certain look in his eyes. The look of a killer. "The eyes are the window of the soul," and Tony Vongemi's eyes were cold. When he was showing me the technique of breaking someone's neck, his eyes were gleaming.

I still can't believe how I got myself into this mess, and just how easily I could've avoided it all right from the beginning. But I didn't, and now I must deal with it.

One thing was certain, Tony had just given me the extra motivation, the much needed conviction, that I was doing the right thing in all my planning. I felt stronger, although scared, I knew that I'd succeed.

Walking over to the doorway I double checked all my locks. I thought they were locked, but I just had to make sure. There's no question about it, I was spooked! Today could very easily have been the last day of my life. Mentally, I don't know how many more life threatening scares I could take.

I poured myself a glass of white wine. The wine tasted good, as it went down real easy. With the knowledge that all three of my door locks were secured, I poured myself another glass. There was a certain comforting feeling that had come over me, as I sipped the wine.

For the moment I felt safe, maybe it was the wine. Either way, I didn't really care I just wanted to forget. After my second glass, I was relaxed. I needed to forget, even if only for a little while. A nice deep sleep, a rest of my brain, maybe an hour or two, that's all I wanted. It was only 3:00 pm, with daylight shining through the windows, but I needed some rest.

Abruptly I was shocked out of my sleep, with a rapping sound, coming from my front door. As I leaped out of my bed, I caught a glance at the alarm clock. It was 5:30 pm. It took me exactly two seconds to reach my front door.

"Yeah, who is it?"

"Open the door, Frankie, it's Carlo, Tony sent me!"

"What do you want, Carlo?" I said, now fully awake as if someone had just slapped me.

"Frank, just open the stupid door, I've got something for you!"

Carlo sounded annoyed now. I wondered what was going on. Did Tony send him back so soon? Was he here to waste me?

The rapping got harder as Carlo screamed, "Open it or I'll knock it off the hinges!"

I realized, either I faced the music, or wore a door on my face.

"Ok Carlo, I'll open the door. Just wait a second!"

As I opened the door two inches, I peeked through it and said, "Carlo, I was sound asleep!"

"I'm heartbroken!" he said, sarcastically, as he kicked the door wide-open.

"So what's up?" I said, trying to sound calm and cool. But I must've been red in the face from fear. I sure felt flushed.

"Calm down, Frank, Tony told me to drop by with some Chinese food," he said as he handed me a shopping bag full of food. "Enjoy your food Frank," he said, while smiling at me- with a sick little grin. Then he quickly turned and left.

I stood there, door open, gasping with my mouth open, as I watched Carlo. He walked down the front steps and got into a black Lincoln Town car and drove away. Looking down at the shopping bag, then back out at Carlo driving away, all I could do was shake my head.

182

Tony was really getting on my nerves now! But I had to bide my time.

I sat at my kitchen table, looking at the bag of food. "No, they wouldn't poison me, would they?" I said outloud. Looking closer at the bag I inspected the top of it. The bag had the restaurant's name imprinted on it. The food was from the Three Fortunes Restaurant, on 86th St. I'd eaten there several times. They had a reputation of being one of the most exclusive Chinese restaurants in Brooklyn. The food was known to be fabulous there.

The top of the bag was stapled, the menu was also stapled on the top of the bag. Feeling pretty secure about the food being authentic, and not tampered with, I tore the bag open and looked inside.

The choice of food was mouth watering. There was spare ribs, egg foo young, moo shu pork, an egg roll and sweet and sour soup. There was enough food here to feed four people. But, since I liked leftover Chinese food, and usually ate it cold the next day, I didn't mind.

Suddenly, feeling quite hungry, I didn't wait. Instead, I dug right into the moo shu pork. If they wanted to poison me, I'd find out quick enough. I was feeling pretty confident as I started to eat.

Since Tony would rather snap my neck than poison me to death, I was certain, now, that the food was untainted. And if I was wrong, then at least I'd have a nice full stomach.

Chinese food isn't so bad if it has to be a last meal. I had a few more glasses of wine with my meal. I enjoyed the variety of Chinese food I'd been given. Trying to forget about my plans, and my problems for awhile I watched some basketball on TV.

By the time I awoke and looked at the clock radio it was 6:00 am. Since this was my third time up already, I didn't even try closing my eyes. I had already woken up at 4:00 and 5:00 am. There was just too much on my mind. My mind kept racing, I couldn't sleep so why try? With my eyes wide open I did remain in bed resting. There was too much to do: the planning, the refining, the thinking; who could sleep?

By six thirty I was out of bed and taking a nice hot shower. Mondays are slow in the insurance business, I didn't have to report in by any specific time. Today though, I wanted to beat everyone in and out of the office.

I really didn't want to be there, but with all the pressing things to do, I showed up at 7:30. This was way before anyone with any sense would show up at the office.

I wanted to file the death claim preliminary report on Keith Brava, but I also wanted to be out of the building way before everyone else started to show up. The Brava claim report took only ten minutes.

"One million dollars face amount. Cause of death: fell off the roof of his house. What a laugh!" I said out loud.

I filed the report in the out-going basket, for the secretaries to send away when they came in. Then I left a message for the office manager, Josephine.

I told her that I was coming down with the flu, which had been making the rounds as of late. I think they called it the Japanese flu. It was a potent strain that was knocking all its victims out for about a week at a time.

With the excuse of the Japanese flu, I could now achieve some of my urgent goals for the week. The priority for the day was purchasing a police scanner radio, so I could monitor all police activity in the city.

What I was particularly interested in was activity on the West Side. I had to zero in on the homeless area, near the West Side highway, where many homeless people stay sheltered and unsheltered against the winter. It was one of the harshest winters in years. Many homeless people died.

Chapter Forty Three

Within two weeks I felt that I could expect to locate an acceptable body. Monitoring the scanner and keeping records would give me the exact location for future homeless exposure deaths.

My only problem would be to get there close to the time of death for a good match to my size and shape. I didn't see this as a problem though, as there were always quite a few homeless drug and alcohol deaths in my general age range.

Vongemi had me spooked ever since his goons forced me into the car. Now I was paranoid. Was there someone waiting for me in a secluded area, waiting to pounce on me as I came out of the house?

Every few minutes I found myself looking out the window, looking for anything even remotely suspicious. My comfort level was now zero. From here to the end, when my plan has been completely carried out, I wouldn't feel safe.

This morning I lost count of how many times I looked out of the window already. I wondered how much a man could endure? Would I crack up? I thought about my present mental condition, and was a little concerned.

One last look outside the window. This time I took a mental note of the car alignment on the street. The colors, the cars and the placement of them.

Next, I headed out to my car. It was parked on the street directly in front of the office. I wanted to see if anyone was looking for me. So I got in my car, and drove up the block, keeping an eye on my rearview mirror.

I looked for anyone that appeared to be following me. The deli was two blocks over, so I stopped and ordered a roll and coffee. Again, looking around.

Then I saw it: a black car, moving very slowly around the corner. There was something about the full sized car. Like I had seen it before. Was it tailing me? I wasn't sure. But it did get my attention. As I drove back to my office, I continued to watch everything carefully.

This whole expedition was a test. Once I was back in the office, I immediately ran to the street side window. I took in the street, looking around, trying to see if there was anything suspicious. There was nothing. All clear. No other tails. No suspicious looking cars.

Once I was back in my car, I drove around for a while, watching my mirrors closely. Nothing. With no one watching me I felt at ease again. This time I headed back to my apartment. No more fooling around, I thought. Once again there was no one following. Since it was early I still had some time left before the electronics store would open. I headed back to the apartment.

As I headed up the stairs to my front door I smelled something strange. I couldn't put my finger on it, but something smelled. Then, as I opened my front door, the smell hit me right in the face. It was gas! It filled the whole apartment.

I ran over to the stove. The knob on the oven was turned to 300 degrees. I quickly shut the oven and ran to the window which was stuck closed. With a tremendous thrust, the window finally shot up. Quickly, I ran out into the stairway, and outside to catch my breath.

I was stunned. Someone had tried to kill me. If it had been the nighttime, I surely would've set off an explosion, as soon as I would've switched on the apartment light. My only lucky break was I was only gone for a short time, I didn't have to switch the lights on and I wasn't smoking.

It was twenty minutes before I went back inside the apartment. But first, I carefully inspected my door locks and door jamb. There were no marks, no forced entry. My oven hadn't been used for at least six months. I don't do any fancy cooking, So I knew someone was trying to kill or scare the crap out of me. And it was working. My hands were shaking and my legs were weak, as I slowly sat down in the kitchen.

After about ten minutes, I quickly got up and began searching the entire apartment, including draws, and closets. Not looking for anything in particular, just inspecting everything. I had to know if there were any other surprises waiting for me.

It was then that I found something I didn't immediately recognize. Then it hit me. Right near the living room phone, attached to under the end table, was an electronic listening device. After examining it closely and not saying a word, I quickly stepped on it. After hearing it crunch, I threw it out the living room window.

How long had the Mafia been listening in on my every conversation? I felt good only about one thing: the fact that I had not shared any of my fears of the mob with anyone at all.

My fear of dying was at an all time high now. There was no doubt now in my mind I was a dead man. Just the place and time were still to be determined.

The morning newspaper was outside, so I quickly grabbed it, took off in my car, parked on a side street, and watched the apartment from a distance.

Intermittently, I glanced at the paper. As I turned to the front page, all of a sudden, it hit me, like a slap in the face on a cold day. The headline almost screamed at me. It read: "Bobby the 'Bull Dog' Throws the Bull at Feds."

Of course, I knew immediately the story was about Tony's brother. The story stated that Vongemi, a capo in the Vongemi Family of organized crime was brought in for questioning by the FBI. I was stunned.

Bobby "The Bull Dog" was specifically questioned regarding the death of Willie "The Ears" Shoteri. The newspaper claimed that Bobby was eating with approximately 20 people at a restaurant in Little Italy, when the FBI made their arrest.

The FBI questioned Bobby for four hours, but they had to release him. According to the Vongemi Family lawyer, named Joseph Brinni: "They have nothing on him, the FBI is just wishing on a star. They're just so excited about trying to indict Mr. Robert Vongemi that they all wet their pants. And that's all they are going to get. My client is an upstanding business man in the community."

The News went on to explain that Bobby was released after four hours. The FBI, when asked about the interrogation down- played the whole incident, stating that, "we only had a few questions for Mr. Robert Vongemi."

Howard Smith, the bureau's lead investigator said, "We've been looking into Bobby Vongemi's actions for some time now.

We also have confidential sources, that have linked Bobby Vongemi to the abduction and ultimate demise of Willie Shoteri."

I kept watching the front of the house. Nothing. No one even walking around. The message was already received loud and clear, I understood fully.

My attention returned to the paper. The picture in the News, of Bobby The "Bull Dog" showed him with a grin from ear to ear. When asked by the reporter about the FBI inquisition, Bobby replied, "The FBI? They've got nothing on me, they wasted my time, but that's alright, the coffee wasn't too bad."

What seemed amazing to me was, as much as Bobby Vongemi looked like a hardened criminal, his lawyer looked even more crooked. Joseph Brinni, the Vongemi lawyer looked like the biggest weasel to come along in years.

Money does buy the best defense, and the Vongemi Family had an unlimited source of income. Their lawyers could run circles around the government and state prosecutors.

My mind was made up, the Vongemi Family would be here for good. Unscathed and more prosperous each and every year. Anyone who attempted to dethrone any member of the Vongemi Family would be silenced, and in any manner needed to save the Family name. They just proved to me that they could kill off anyone they want, any time they want to. The gas filled apartment could have easily blew me away, if I only came back later and no one would've been the wiser.

The only threat that the Vongemi's could succumb to, would be the maddening violence of their own kind. Only their own kind could dethrone them.

My mind raced, it envisioned the classic Mafia rubouts. I remembered seeing the picture vividly of the mobster shot dead in the restaurant, blood all over the place with the cigar still hanging out of his mouth.

Many people though, have a secret admiration for the Mob: the way the Mafia bosses dress, their arrogance and their power. It's sad in a way, just how many people are sucked into that life. Even unknowingly, like me.

My watch showed 9:30 as I threw the newspaper down in disgust. I was disgusted, not just about the Vongemi Family, but in the lack of justice in our country. The fact that too many people constantly beat the justice system. As much as I wanted to, I couldn't change it. Frank Granstino is only one little man.

What was wrong with the justice system, was much too big for even the whole city. What was really needed was government intervention. We needed a complete overhaul of the whole legal system. A change in the rules, the definitions, the players.

Maybe some of my disgust came from my disappointment, I hoped against all odds, that somehow the entire Vongemi Family would be put behind bars for good. That I'd get a reprieve of some kind, from this Mafia chain that had been tightening around my neck. A chain I couldn't break free from, unless and until I disappeared - permanently.

There were many things to do, and the first thing was purchasing the police scanner. I needed to run over to the local Radio Shack store. It was already 9:30, the store was twenty minutes away. I loved this store.

I refrained myself from purchasing any gadgets I would have to drag with me when I ran, and purchased only what I came for: the police and fire scanner.

Of course, I'd need to interpret whatever would be broadcast over the scanner. So I found a dictionary of terms and codes, this way I could decipher what was happening as it unfolded.

I couldn't wait to hook it all up, but I left it in the trunk for later, I had more important things to do first.

Chapter Forty Four

My next stop was the local liquor store. What I wanted to do from this point on, was to show everyone that I came in contact with that I was not my usual self, not the regular, totally in control and all professional Frank Granstino. The old Frank Granstino would never go out in public drunk. He'd never be disrespectful, not unless something was deeply troubling him.

Well, I was going to show the world, that Frank Granstino was in fact, deeply troubled. From this day forward everyone I came in contact with would see a totally new, and repulsive Frank Granstino. I would appear to be drinking excessively from this point on.

If I committed suicide, if the world knew that I ended it all, then there had to be a motive, a problem, something unusual. Totally normal, happy-go-lucky people, with everything going right, just don't end their life.

Once I was at the liquor store, I decided to purchase a case of cheap whiskey, something which I felt would smell foul. The way I figured it, I'd need to show many bottles, all strewn throughout my apartment. Then I'd show a few mostly empty bottles in the car.

For my plan to work, I needed to establish the fact that I'd finally gone over the edge. That I couldn't take life anymore, and had become an alcoholic as an escape from reality.

I purchased a case of one-litre bottles of Smithline blended Scotch whiskey. It was the cheapest brand that I could find. "This stuff will be perfect," I told myself, as I carried the case of bottles out to the car. Once I reached the car, I opened up the case.

The first bottle I opened gave off an aroma that was so strong it made the hairs in my nose hurt. The smell made me feel like throwing up. I never could get used to Scotch. The only alcohol I enjoyed, was red or white wine and beer.

As I closed my eyes tightly, I tensed my whole body and took a big mouthful of Scotch. Swishing it around and gargling with it for what seemed like an eternity, I spit most of it out the car window. I let some of the whiskey drip down my face. Then I stepped outside the car, and with the bottle in hand, I poured some of it on my clothes.

Since I knew what I'd be doing today, I had dressed in my older work clothes, which fit in well with an alcoholic mood. I soaked my shirt and my pants. Then I poured some of it on the passenger side seat area.

It's funny in a way, but amazingly I was starting to get used to the pungent smell. My new car stunk. It hurt me at first to ruin the car, until I realized that this car would die when I died, I couldn't take it with me, and I couldn't give it away.

Feeling that I was finally complete in my preparation, I headed home. My next action would be the apartment. I needed to fix the apartment up, with a couple of empty bottles, and wet the apartment a little with some scotch. The person that smells, generally can't smell themselves.

Carefully, I hid the police scanner radio, so no one would find it. Next, I hid all the full bottles of Scotch around the apartment and tore up the cardboard in little pieces. So I could throw it into the garbage bags in the alleyway.

I knew full well that I couldn't keep the case of Scotch in the trunk of the car, just in case someone were to look there. I had to take these measures. Better to be safe than sorry. Also, the house was too clean, I had to mess it up a little, make it look like the apartment of someone who didn't care. Someone who didn't have the strength to fix it up.

To look the part of an alcoholic, one must work hard. To keep in line with the plans of the day, I had to definitely smell, look, and act the part. That's why I was glad that I hadn't shaved since yesterday. With a full days growth of beard I was able to look exactly the way I wanted to. With alcohol breath and Scotch soaked clothes, I'd smell as ripe as any vagrant.

My plan was unfolding nicely as expected. My next move could be my last. If I really wanted my suicide plan to work I had to fool them all. The most important person, of course, that had to be fooled, was Tony Vongemi. If he caught on to my scheme, if he figured me out too soon, then I was truly a dead man!

With the house and car all set with all the pieces in place, I proceeded. The next step was to drop in unannounced, on Tony, while reeking of Scotch, and acting more obnoxious than I'd ever been. If I acted superbly, I'd get away with murder. If I goofed, then I'd probably be whacked.

The half filled bottle of Scotch was in my hand as I pulled into the Little Part of Italy parking lot. I needed one last gargle, which I purposely let dribble, once again down my chin and neck, which in turn ran on to my undershirt. I smelled worse than a stagnant sewer. I really stunk, as I deliberately parked the car on an angle-across three parking spaces.

I opened the front door to the restaurant with a tremendous burst, which in turn slammed it hard against the inside wall - as I yelled: "Tony, oh Tony, where the hell are you!"

People at the bar, waitresses setting tables, all looked and stared at me. Then I saw someone jump from the bar stool and run towards me. Staying in form, I didn't flinch. It was Benny, Tony's goon.

When he reached me, he said, "Frankie, what's your problem?"

With a big stupid-looking grin, I slanted my head, squinted my eyes and said loudly, "Hi-ya Benny-Boy, where's big Tony?"

Benny grabbed me hard by the shoulder and forcibly led me over to the nearest table.

He pushed me down into the chair, and said angrily, "Sit down, and shut up. I'll go get Tony. You just stay there. Don't move. Do you hear me?"

Benny must've been gone for five minutes. No doubt he was explaining to Tony, that Frankie was totally wasted, and making a fool of himself. Still in character, I was amusing myself by playing with the silverware. Waving them through the air, as if they were jet fighter planes on a mission. Of course, anybody that was still in the room was staring.

I didn't care, I was way past caring. It was now a mission. Much like the old TV show, Mission Impossible. And my acting was superb. I was fully focused and in control. There was no turning back now, I had to complete my mission.

Out of the corner of my eye, I caught Carlo, with Benny leading the way, and Tony one step behind. No doubt, they were being cautious. All it takes is one nut-job with a gun to rubout a mob boss. They weren't taking any chances. As soon as I saw Tony, I got up fast and said, "Tony, my pal, how are you?" I then slapped him hard on the back.

With that Carlo and Benny both grabbed me and forced me back in my chair. Tony's face was now red, I wasn't sure if it was anger or shock. I'm positive that no one with any sense would approach him, a mob boss, in this manner.

He cracked a phony smile and said, "Frankie, are you feeling all right?" Then before I could answer, he screamed angrily, "Carlo, get Frankie some strong black coffee, right now! Frankie, you just sit right there, we'll get some coffee for you. You've been drinking Frankie?" He said slowly, as if he were talking to a little boy.

"No Tony, honest," I said, right in his face, so he could get some of that stagnant Scotch aroma. He quickly pulled away.

"Something must be bothering you, for you to get like this and come into my restaurant. Do you want to talk about it Frankie?"

"No. Well I don't think so. It's a girl Tony, a stinking, lousy girl," I said, now with tears in my eyes.

"Oh, I see," he said, while shaking his head, "You don't have to say anymore, we've all been there. Women are all the same, Frankie. Our mistake is showing them that we care. We should just use them, like they use us for everything. They all stink. Once you realize that, you'll never get hurt again. The trick my boy, is never, ever give your heart up to them. That's when they hurt you. Can you understand this, Frankie," he said, like a father talking to his son.

"Yes, oh yes," I said, as I put my head on the table as if I'd given up on life.

Just then, Carlo came running with a small pot of espresso, of course, he didn't have the sambuca I love so much whenever I have espresso. Mission accomplished! I thought to myself.

With my head back down on the table, I heard Tony tell Benny, "Make sure he drinks all that coffee. Even if you have to

194

force it down his throat! Then bring him straight home. Get him out of here before I lose all my customers. You drive his car and make sure he's fully awake when you give him this death certificate. He better not screw this million dollars claim up, or we'll end his stinking misery right now! Do you understand what I want, Benny?"

"Yes boss! I got you. You can count on me. You want for me to give him a shot in the head?"

"No, Benny, not yet. Not just yet."

There's an advantage in playing someone totally wasted, you can hear exactly what's being said about you behind your back. And in what tone it's being said. I heard it all and I didn't like the tone. My suspicions all along were correct. As soon as I'd outlived my usefulness to the Vongemi Family, I'd be wasted. Dumped like this morning's stale coffee. I wasn't smart enough to stay out of the mess I'd gotten myself into. But at least I was now smart enough to know when to disappear on my own. Before the concrete shoes were fitted on me.

I could hear Tony walk away, right after he said, "Hurry up and get him out of here, he's stinking the whole place out! By the way, take a quick peek around his apartment, let me know what he's been up to!"

Just then, Benny picked my head off the table by the hair on the back of my head.

"Hey you mug!" I said, as if I'd just been woken up.

"Shut up your face and drink this down, or I'll pour it down your stinking throat for you!" Benny said, with a sadistic smile on his face.

Meanwhile Carlo smiled, watching, enjoying the whole scene. It took me fifteen minutes to finish the espresso coffee. Which I kind of enjoyed, as if it was a celebration drink, for a superb acting job.

All of a sudden, I felt Carlo feeling me for my car keys. I dared not move or let on that it bothered me.

"You really stink!" he said in disgust. "And over a woman?"

With my keys in hand they dragged me to my car, which also stunk by this time. Benny drove my car, with me in the back

195

seat and all the windows wide-open. Carlo followed close behind, in a black Lincoln Town Car.

Chapter Forty Five

When we arrived at my apartment, Benny and Carlo roughly pulled me up the stairs to my apartment. They sat me in a chair at the kitchen table, while they started to look in all my cabinets. He finally found what he was looking for: it was the coffee maker. Benny made me a pot of coffee, so strong, I might just as well have poured the coffee grounds down my throat. But again, I didn't show that I noticed.

Benny said to Carlo, "This place stinks too, let's get the hell out of here as soon as possible, Carlo!"

Carlo was quickly running around the apartment. I could hear him opening all the dresser drawers and all the closet doors. He looked under the bed and even in my checking account register. He probably was looking for anything that showed an affiliation to the FBI or the local authorities. He found nothing. "Let's get out of here," he said.

Benny shook me until I looked at him, then he slapped me hard with his right hand across my face. Again, I didn't flinch, I stayed in character, with my teeth clenched tight I straightened up and looked at him.

"Frankie, look at me, can you hear me?"

"Sure, Benny, what's up? Do you want a drink?"

"No you idiot, listen to me! Tony wants me to give this to you. It's a death certificate. Do you understand?"

"Yes, this is the death certificate I need for Keith Brava. The one million dollar death claim, I know exactly what to do," I said, as if I'd sobered up enough to understand.

Happy that his job was done, Benny motioned for Carlo, as if he'd said, "Let's go!"

"By the way, you won't be needing this," he said, as he took a half-full bottle of Smithline Scotch. He then threw my key chain on the kitchen table, turned to leave and said, "Bye sucker!"

All I did was put my head back on the table, while still clenching my teeth, in case he tried to hit me again. With Keith

Brava's death certificate in my right hand, I kept my head on the table for five minutes.

Thrilled with my little charade for the day, I smiled and said, "All right!" Although I was becoming accustomed to the stench, I really didn't like it. Disgusted, sweaty, and smelling quite ripe, I took all my clothes off. I put them in a large plastic bag and tied a knot in the top of the bag. At least this would stop the smell, and at the same time, preserve the Scotch smell for later use. I might as well use the same stinking clothes, over again.

I could accept the smell of the stagnant Scotch on the clothes, and even on my body. But I knew that I'd never get used to, or enjoy the taste of the Scotch, even if I tried a better brand. To me, It felt like trying to drink down a bottle of Windex glass cleaner; The mind said go, but the body said no.

Finally, I felt relieved. I'd gotten away with an important part of my major plan, and didn't get caught by Tony Vongemi. Tony easily could have had me killed today. I probably deserved it, and if not for the death claim papers I might've been shot through the head. That's a quick and painless way to go, I thought, as I prepared for a steaming hot shower, which I fully understood I needed. I was never so happy to take a shower in my entire life. I felt clean, I even added a splash of cologne for a refreshing new smell.

Now it was finally time, I was so excited about trying out my new police scanner radio, I'd thought about it the whole day. So I just opened it up and delved right in. Instructions? Not for me. I probed, and I played, pressing every button available. After ten minutes of getting absolutely nowhere, I gave in. Only because I was frustrated, did I pick up the owners manual.

The rest of the evening was spent becoming familiar with the 10 Code manual. The manual I'd purchased explained in intricate detail all the police language, used in their everyday communication. Terms such as: "10-4", which means yes, or affirmative in police talk. After playing for five hours, I finally had enough. I needed my rest tonight. After a cup of hot tea, I laid down. In less than five minutes I was unconscious, sleeping like a baby.

The easiest way to become the new low life of the office, is to show up stinking drunk. And that's exactly what I did. Except I showed up right at 9:00 in the morning, as soon as the office opened for the day.

Mary Silone was the office manager. She was the biggest gossip around. If you wanted something spread around the entire office, all you had to do was let Mary know about it. She'd inform the whole world, and probably change the story while she was passing it around.

There are some people who gamble, some people who sew, some who watch the television religiously, and some who gossip as a hobby. That was Mary Silone. I don't know if she gossiped out of boredom, or because she was insecure, but she never stopped talking about people. Mary's whole existence, it seemed, was just to gossip.

Mary was about fifty, with curly short black hair, which made her appear even larger than her 270 lbs. At about five foot three she was like a house.

I purposely put my Scotch-smelling clothes back on. Taking a big mouthful of Scotch, I gargled with it and spit it out into the kitchen sink. I wanted to show up early enough to catch her, but too early for the rest of the office personnel.

I circled the office from 8:50 am. As I suspected, Mary was as usual, seven minutes early. Mary always wanted to start talking as early as possible. She would talk to anyone who'd listen, and talk about anyone who wasn't in the immediate area.

As soon as I got out of my car, I messed my hair up with my hand. I really stunk, Mary would get a nose full of Scotch today, and I was so glad. When I entered through the front door of the office, I started to wobble as planned. Mary was standing at the counter near the doorway.

"Hi ya sexy!" I said, sounding smashed.

"Oh, hi Frankie, I thought you were sick with the flu?"

"I am, I just wanted my messages."

As she came back with my messages, and got close to me, I said, "Thanks Mary!" as close to her face as I could get.

When she got a whiff of the putrid smell, I saw her back off quickly. With a look of disgust on her face, she said, "Well, I'll be! You take care of yourself, Frankie!"

"Oh don't worry about me," I said, "I've been taking strong medicine!" As I made my way out the doorway, I purposely hit my shoulder hard, on the right side of the door jamb. I wanted to leave Mary with that one final impression of the condition I was in. I could tell that my intoxication act was working, Mary's contorted face told the whole story.

As planned, I was in and out of the office before 9:00. Mary was the only one who saw and smelled me. "She'll have a party now," I said, as I pulled away in my car, with a sly little smile on my face.

My next move was to get in some more hot water, as soon as I reached my apartment. I wanted to rile someone up, get them so disturbed that they'd put in a formal complaint against me. I could always bring the worst out of a person. People have almost pulled their hair out trying to deal with me over the years. Some hate me, some love me, but there aren't too many in the middle.

As I flipped through my messages, I picked out Mrs. Flossi. Now, Mrs. Flossi is always mad at someone, or something. Every month, without fail she calls with a problem over something stupid; something trivial. And since she's on my old debit route, I have to service her, and listen to her nonsense. "Well not today," I said, as I sat down at the kitchen table, while reaching for the phone.

"Hi, Mrs. Flossi, it's Frank Granstino, what's your problem now!" I said, trying to be as obnoxious as I possibly could.

"What? What do you mean," she asked sounding stunned. Then after a pause she said, "What's the matter with you?"

"What's the matter with you?" I said, "You're the crazy woman, always with problems. Why don't you go get yourself a job, and stay out of my hair! Why don't you try and bother someone else for a change!"

"Don't you want to help me?" she asked, giving one last desperate attempt to let me off the hook.

"No. You bother people! You're annoying! Take your business somewhere else! Call Prudential. Bother them!"

"I'm going to call your manager!" she screamed. "That's it for you buster!"

"Aw, go chase yourself. Go feed your face again, you fat pig!" I screamed, as I hung up the phone so hard it almost came off the wall.

"Mission accomplished!" I said. I expected to see results before the day was over. There was no doubt in my mind, that Mrs. Flossi was on the phone this second with the manager. She must be bending Tom's ear. I could just see Somi, with his face flushed red with rage. As she told him all the nasty things I said about her, she must be frothing mad.

By now, it was only 9:30am, I had managed to get myself in big trouble in less than a half hour. I was starting to enjoy this self destruction thing. My goal was to change my image. My boyish, clean-cut image. I wanted to be known as Frank Granstino a deeply troubled man. Everyone I came in contact with must realize that something is terribly wrong. That I must be devastated over something, for me to act as self destructive and irrational as I have.

I've got to get out of the apartment, I thought. There's nothing good that can be accomplished, at this point from home. Time is passing, much like a basketball game, when your favorite team is behind, and there are only ten minutes left in the game. Too much to do, and too little time left to accomplish it all.

The way I was feeling, I didn't want to hear the phone ringing. I knew that any minute now Tom Somi would be calling. He'd want to see what was wrong with me, and if I'd lost my marbles completely. By now, he would've heard from a very distraught Mrs. Flossi, telling him all about my horrible disposition, and my terrible repulsive behavior.

Mary Silone, no doubt told the entire office all about Frank Granstino the drunk. How I was stinking drunk, loud, and out of control at nine in the morning. Tom, wasn't a big Frank Granstino fan as it was. So he had to be relishing the thought of screaming at me. But more than just screaming, he'd want to know why I was suddenly acting so irrational and what had suddenly and mysteriously turned my personality around.

Chapter Forty Six

I was hoping somehow, against all odds that the temperature outside had warmed up. Earlier in the morning the car made all kinds of whistles and whining sounds, as it labored to start. At 8:00 in the morning, the radio station reported that the temperature outside was 5 degrees, with a wind chill factor of minus 30 degrees.

There were cars stranded all over the streets. The people walking, and waiting for buses looked like mummies. They had wrapped every part of their bodies with scarfs, hats, mittens, and anything else they could find.

The car once again sounded like a sick, out of tune orchestra, with the weirdest whining sounds you could imagine. The laboring sound of the engine cranking made me feel happy to hear the engine finally turn over, especially with those crazy sounds. I dared not stay out too late in the sub zero temperatures.

With the same stinking clothes on that I'd worn before, I was all set to party. With the car still warming up, I was fooling around with my police scanner. Earlier, I was able to tune in on the 110th precinct in Manhattan. This precinct was in the vicinity of the west thirties.

Tuning into the 110th precinct would allow me access to all emergency activity in the west thirties area of Manhattan. I would need to take the pulse of the city every day. With my scanner tuned to their frequencies, I can monitor police movement in the area, especially at the crucial times during the execution of my plan.

As I started my drive to the city, it dawned on me that the traffic was extremely light. For weeks now, many people have either left their cars at home, to take public transportation, or because their cars wouldn't start. The weather reporters scared people, on their TV and radio reports. They warned, "If you don't - absolutely have to go somewhere, then you should stay indoors. The wind chill factor accompanied with the sub-zero temperature is taking lives."

Traffic was very light both in the Brooklyn Battery Tunnel and on the West Side highway. With my scanner on the seat next to me I was able to monitor all pertinent police transmissions, but only the transmissions I chose to listen to. I eliminated all the other precincts, except for the 110th. After all, this wasn't pleasure, it was serious business. I was fighting for my life.

The stench of my Scotch-aged clothes was perfect, I thought. I had a new image to uphold, one of a troubled alcoholic. I figured out that it was all an attitude. That if I envisioned myself as an actual troubled alcoholic, I could easily pass as one.

It would take me approximately two minutes to get into the alcoholic role. I felt that when I was in character as an alcoholic, I was marvelous, very believable and I enjoyed acting the role. Somehow I felt that I was in control of an audience, I was the center of attention.

At 11:00 in the morning, I had reached the west side of Manhattan. I drove around for about 20 minutes. The foot of West 33rd Street right near the water was the target area of my mission. According to the latest reports, there were more homeless men congregated in that immediate area, than in any other part of Manhattan.

There were even reports of former college professors, and Wall Street executives who were now homeless. These homeless men had just given up on life. Life as we all know it to be. They checked out from reality. Maybe it was a woman, maybe the pressures of everyday living, but something pushed them over the edge to the point of no return.

Continuing on my excursion, I drove around the immediate area. I parked the car, so I could walk around the vicinity. As I looked around, there were cardboard boxes set up to act as shelters. There were wooden boards used as roofs to keep the snow out of their sleeping area. Anything they could use to protect themselves from the frigid cold.

I observed carefully, taking in all the sights, the degradation, the various souls of the once brave men.

There were many black men as well as white men. Men of all ages. Many more younger men then I expected. There were far too many men. Men who gave up life as we know it. I thought, as I looked at the lost souls, bundled and numb from the cold.

I observed all the empty liquor bottles lying carelessly around. Mostly they were of brands I had never heard of. Probably they were the least expensive of the brands around. Anything to get the job done, to deaden the senses. Maybe they just wanted their inner-most pain to go away. Even if it was for a short time, I thought, as I looked at the half-dead bodies spread throughout the area.

Most of the homeless want peace from the real world, the world that was too hard to deal with, at least until the liquor wears off.

My research was correct, I had hit the jackpot with my location. The West Side at 33rd St. was the area I would target. Now all I had to do was wait for a body. A suitable, matching body for my operation.

The clone I was waiting for would have to be a male, white, approximately thirty. Someone with a full head of brown hair, and with no distinguishing marks.

It was colder than I expected as I made my way back to the car, which I had to park way up the block on West 32nd Street. With all my expensive and heavy clothes, the cold air still chilled my bones.

With the car running, I waited patiently for the heater to warm the car up. I turned on the police scanner, my little spy friend. With the squelch control on high, I didn't have to hear any static. The radio was set so that I'd only hear a broadcast transmission on the frequency I programed.

Action was nonexistent at the west side police precinct. All was quiet for now on West 33rd Street. At least nothing I was interested in. I did hear of a pocketbook theft, some guy on a bicycle snatching an old lady's pocketbook. I hung around the area a little longer. I wanted to get a feel for the neighborhood.

At three o'clock it was time to leave. Now it was time to cruise the downtown Manhattan area. Specifically the World Trade Center area. Since the World Trade Center would be an instrumental part of my suicide operation, I needed to do my homework. The view is still breathtaking, I thought, as I looked straight upward from the base of the Trade Center to the very top.

I was convinced that my estimate was correct. Anything that was thrown off the roof of this tremendous building wouldn't be recognizable after hitting the ground.

No one would ever know that the body isn't mine. As long as I did all the instrumental, pertinent, and flawless planning, and execution of the operation correctly.

Chapter Forty Seven

The bar was located near the World Trade Center. First I changed my good wool overcoat, I put on a heavy wool lumberman's jacket, it was red checkerboard and very old. I think it was my father's coat from more than thirty years ago. All I know is that I looked and felt like a bum in it. Exactly what I wanted to portray to the public - at least right now.

To add the finishing touch, I had to gargle once again with the Scotch and of course my act wouldn't be complete without letting the whiskey dribble down my chin.

My goal was to become known at the biggest and most popular bar in the area. After my suicide scam, I was positive that the police would try to piece together the last few weeks of my life, including all my movements. They'd surely interview all the bartenders in all the bars, all around the area of the death scene. My goal was to project a certain personality, one that would fit in well with a suicidal person.

The name of the bar was, The Broadway Pub and Grill, it was located at 111 Broadway, just blocks away from the Trade Center complex. The bar occupied an older building, which looked like it was built around the turn of the century. It was a building made of old red brick. The detail was unique, with bold concrete moldings and carvings; a nice looking, old fashioned watering hole.

To think that a hundred years ago businessmen came and sat just like me at the bar! The inside was as old as the outside of the building. There was dark mahogany wood on the walls, old fashioned tables, and what appeared to be the original bar, with the original brass rail along with the old mirror behind the bar. Above the mirror, close to the ceiling, were all old fashioned collectibles, such as beer steins, statues, and wood carvings.

Covering all the walls were pictures of famous people, taken many years ago. I sat at the historic bar, on an antique-type bar stool. It was made out of oak and darkened by the many years of age, and it had a high back to it. As soon as I settled in my seat, a big guy came over and said, "What'll it be?"

As the bartender looked at me, I looked at his name tag and said, "Give me a Johnnie Walker Black on the rocks with a beer chaser, Charlie."

"You got it pal!" he said, as he took off. Charlie looked like a big Swede or Irishman. Maybe about forty eight years of age and six feet tall. He had to weigh about two hundred sixty pounds. A big man, who most wouldn't tangle with. From the looks of Charlie he'd been bartending for some time.

There was a certain flair, a flow with all his movements behind the bar. There wasn't a wasted step or gesture. When he returned with the drinks, I made it a point not to be too nice. Trying to stay in character isn't easy, but I was aware that I had to project the personality of a troubled man. A man who overindulges in alcohol. Someone with deep, dark troubles on his mind, a very depressed person.

I had no intention of drinking the Scotch. I'd drink down the beer though. I liked beer. There weren't too many people at the bar at that time. With the first glass of Scotch, I took the whole shot in my mouth. I waited for Charlie to go to the other end of the bar, then I turned to my left, leaned down and spit the full mouthful of Scotch onto the floor. I quickly drank down the beer. Scotch always tastes nasty to me, I never could, nor wanted, to acquire a taste for the potent formula.

After ordering another one, I basically did the same thing. Except this time, I took the full shot in my mouth as if I drank it. I waited thirty seconds, then got up and went to the bathroom. Once I was safely in one of the stalls, I looked around, then spit it all out in the toilet. Shaking my head from side to side I rinsed my mouth out with hot water; the taste of the Scotch was still stinging my tongue.

When I went back to the bar stool I acted drowsy. I told Charlie, "Hit me again,"

"You got it pal," he said, as he gave me a crooked look, like he was trying to read my mood and my condition. I made no small talk at all. Small talk can only blow my character, I thought. The real key to staying in character, is to give only one word answers to any questions or comments made.

Charlie asked, "So, how you doing today, bud?"

As I slowly looked up at him, I said in a monotone voice, "Good!" I quickly looked back down at the bar top, and then at my drink. Then I turned my whole body around - ignoring Charlie and stared out the window of the front of the bar.

Charlie got the message and quickly turned his attention to another customer, saying, "So what do you think of this crazy weather?"

Taking one big mouthful of Scotch once again, I turned, bent down and spit it out again. Carefully, I looked around and thought, successful again!

I went back to sipping my beer, trying to get that nasty Scotch taste out of my mouth. As much as I tried not to, I was getting a little buzz in my head. Even though I wasn't actually drinking it, some of the Scotch was entering my bloodstream.

All I had to do now was just exaggerate a little. Charlie cautiously brought me another drink, as he eyed me up and down.

I waited again until the coast was clear and Charlie turned his back to me. Now, once again I took the Scotch in my mouth all at once. Then I got up slowly and casually went to the bathroom. This time I spit it out, rinsed my mouth, wet my face, messed up my hair a little and went back to the bar.

Now, it was time for real action. Acting very sluggish in attitude and movement, I wobbled as I went to sit at the bar. I promptly laid my head down on the bar and knocked the glass of beer over, spilling it all over the bar, right where I laid my head. All in a day's work, I said to myself, as I waited for the action to begin.

I could hear quick movement, I knew Charlie was coming over to me. "Hey pal, you all right?"

No answer.

"Hey bub, wake up! Come on, time for some coffee. Come on now, let's get up!"

I raised my head slightly and said, "Oh hi, hit me," then I put my head down.

Charlie came around from behind the bar lifted me off the bar stool, at which time I purposely knocked it over, which resulted in a big THUD. Charlie started walking me around slowly, three times around the room and back to the bar stool, which he set back upright again.

As he fed me some black coffee, he asked, "You're not a heavy drinker, are you?"

Sounding half asleep, I said, "No not really!"

"What's wrong pal, what's bothering you?"

"Nothing!" I said, as I closed my eyes looking like an owl.

"Is it a girl, pal?"

I opened my eyes wide, looked at the ceiling and just shook my head. "Yes, it's Lisa!"

"It'll be alright, just have some more coffee," he said, as he patted me on the back. "Are you driving?

"No, I said, I'm busing."

"OK, but you wait a little while before you go!"

I drank the coffee down and straightened up in my seat, acting much more awake then before. Twenty minutes later I said my goodbyes. I purposely left a nice size tip so Charlie would remember me. He had to remember me. This was important, I thought.

Chapter Forty Eight

For the next week I did basically the same routine, on three separate days, all in Charlie's bar. Drinking far too much, and needing help sobering up.

With my frequent visits I was becoming a regular. Each time I opened up a little more to Charlie. Telling him about my insurance career and how hurt I was over the breakup with my girlfriend. I told Charlie how alone I felt, and how all the girls that I do meet can never come up to what Lisa and I used to have together.

As planned, I continued to show my out of control drinking. Occasionally I'd cry, just enough to make an impact. Surprisingly, I was a much better actor than I ever suspected. I needed Charlie and the other regulars, to help piece together for the police the last few weeks of Frank Granstino. How sad he was. How lonely and totally despondent he had become. They had to believe I'd become suicidal. After his death, it would be apparent just how troubled a young man he really was.

The scanner kept me well informed. It even told me of two separate homeless deaths. Both were related to the extreme cold weather, which was gripping the area.

The two dead homeless men were of no use to me. One was Caucasian, and in his late seventies. The other was black, bald, and in his forties. Both made the police scanner, as they were picked up by the emergency medical technicians, and transported to the hospital, and then the morgue.

My time hadn't come, yet. During the week I'd made my plans to fly away. As soon as I was ready I now had my escape route. My escape would be aboard a TWA 757 jumbo jet out of Newark International Airport. I'd be headed for the remote island resort of Barava, near the Cayman Islands.

I forget how long the reservation clerk at TWA said it would take to get to Barava. It really wasn't important. The only thing that was important was, would the distance be far enough that no one would think of looking for me there?

Barava was also a hot place, with plenty of sun, beaches, and women. All the things I could start to think about, once again, as long as my plan was successfully completed. Also during the week, I had successfully taken the identity of a dead man.

The way I planned it, after my escape from New York to the Cayman Islands I'd need to assume a new identity. The old me could no longer exist. Everything associated with my life and family in New York, had to be put to rest. I had to assume a completely new foreign identity. One that was not going to be traceable in any way, to the life and times of Frank Granstino.

The name I chose was Mario Taini. Mario Taini was a man who was insured through Financial Life. Mr. Taini passed away sometime last year at the age 77. He had never married, and never had any children. Mr. Taini was insured by another agent in the company, but we all have access to the records. So late one night, I reviewed the Deceased Client Records and discovered his file. It seemed perfect. After all, he didn't need the identity any longer! I thought.

Since Mario Taini had no living relatives, no one would ever match up his name or realize what had been done. The name was also unique, which I liked. This way, there'd be no association with anyone with the same or similar name. It was a perfect match for what I needed it for. Since I had all of his records, which included his social security number, I felt secure in taking his identity.

A few months ago, in Detective Magazine, I'd found someone in the Manhattan area who made up different forms of identification. All types of identification, including college diplomas, doctorates and master degrees. What they were especially adept at, was their specialty for making up driver licenses and social security cards, exactly what I needed. The place was called Documents To Go.

When I finally found Documents To Go they'd changed their phone number three times and moved to another location. It seems that they were always just one step ahead of the authorities. They even claimed to be able to forge police department identifications also.

It took four days for my new drivers license and social security cards. Both were perfectly executed in the name Mario Taini. The drivers license had my picture laminated onto it, just like New York State does it.

All you need in this world is money, and your health, all the rest you can buy. I had money, plenty of money, but now I was trying to work on guaranteeing that my health would continue to stay perfect. The only way I could stay healthy, I was convinced, was to disappear quickly, while I still could.

So with my new identification in hand, I was well on my way to carrying out my disappearing act. My open airline ticket to Barava, along with the documentation of my new identity were all in order. All I needed now was a body. A nice dead body.

With my frequent traveling to the city lately, no one had been able to catch me at work or at home. The automated telephone machine at work, and my regular answering machine at home, were filling up fast. For days now, I hadn't returned any phone calls. I didn't feel up to it. And I also felt that the new character I was portraying could care less about anyone, especially in the emotional state he was in. So I wanted to ignore them all.

In particular, for three consecutive days I ignored Tom, the manager. No doubt he wanted to speak to me about my drunken state, and stinking clothes from last week when I saw Mary in the office. Each day the message got louder and nastier, and much more demanding. The last message was threatening me with my job if I didn't call him right back. That message was from yesterday.

Tom was steaming mad. Good for him, let him bust! I thought. I could just visualize him, with the top of his head as red as a beet. Then, as he fumed about me, his ears would be all red. Especially after the third day of no return calls. He should've been a sergeant in the Marines. He would've been perfect. Especially the way he screams when he gets mad, just like he screamed on my answering machine. "You better call me back-sonny, if you know what's good for you!"

213

"I'll call him back now, but in my new character," I said, as I dialed the phone. "Yeah, give me Somi!" I said nastily, to Mary when she answered the phone.

"Who may I say is calling?" She asked, trying to sound sweet.

"It's Granstino, Mary!"

"Oh, uh, hold on, he's been looking for you!"

"Hey Granstino," Tom soon bellowed, "where the hell are you? You're supposed to be sick with the flu!"

"I am sick, I'm sick of you. You're always bothering me! Why don't you get a job with the Russian army and leave me alone!"

"Listen here sonny boy, do you realize who you're talking to?"

"Yeah some fat slob who's always throwing his weight around!" I said, in an obnoxious drunken voice, nastier than I'd ever been.

"Hey listen buddy, have you been drinking, Frankie? You sound like you've been drinking."

"Somi, I told you that I was sick last week. What do you need a telegram?"

"Mister Granstino, you're already on thin ice. Watch what you say, and my name is mister Somi to you."

"OK, mister Somi to you. I'm sick. Leave me alone, you fat jerk!"

"That's it buster, if I don't have a doctor's note in this office, in three days, you're fired!"

"Aw, stuff it. Go fire yourself. Do the whole world a favor!" I said, as I slammed the phone down so hard, the vibration hurt my hand.

It was now 12:00 noon on Tuesday. It had been one week of intense planning, surveillance, and character acting. I had been running all over the place. Feeling exhausted, but with a sense of urgency pushing me, I forged ahead. I had to get out of the apartment, in case Mad Dog Somi came looking for me. After that phone call he just might, his head must be bright red now, I hope he doesn't have a stroke.

The character acting had to continue, no matter whose feelings I hurt. Even if I made some enemies. It had to be understood that I temporarily lost my mind, and I became suicidal. It wasn't young Frank Granstino screaming, but some very troubled young man who needed psychiatric help.

The next person on my list was Tony Vongemi. He was the real reason I was going through all this torture. If he was a normal man, I could just report him to the FBI and go on with my life. But Vongemi was so powerful a force, that even the FBI, one of the government's most sacred, and safe protectors would be totally suspect. Even the FBI can be infiltrated with guys like the Vongemis, one of this countries most powerful crime families.

Once again, I put on my putrid clothes, the stagnant disgusting ones I've been using all along. I had to admit the smell was even turning my stomach. The raunchy smell was similar to a mixture of rotten garbage, soaked with stale Scotch. I don't know why, but after fifteen minutes, the smell didn't bother me. Maybe my senses turned themselves off. I don't know, but I sure was happy when the smell lessened!

Chapter Forty Nine

The time was nearing 1:00 o'clock, as I haphazardly parked the car half-on the sidewalk and half on the end parking spot. I was in the parking lot at Tony's restaurant and I just didn't care anymore.

I was already in character, as I very noisily entered the restaurant. The first person I saw was someone new. I yelled, "Where's Tony?"

The guy walked right up to me, and very nicely asked, "Who wants to know?"

"Tell him Frank Granstino, and be quick about it!" I snapped.

"Wait here please," he said, as he quickly walked off.

"This guy must be brand new." I said, "He's being too nice." The first one out to greet me was Benny.

"What do you want you big gorilla!" I yelled.

"Sit down and shut up!" he screamed.

"No, you shut up!"

He quickly raised his arm to hit me with the back of his hand, when Tony entered the room and shouted, "Benny, no!" As Benny looked at Tony in disgust he slowly lowered his hand, while at the same time looking me straight in the eyes, with a fierce stare.

The other guy was with Tony, as he stepped next to Benny I couldn't believe it. This guy was even bigger and heavier than Benny. His head was the size of a large basketball, and his arms were the size of my legs. He must've been seven foot tall, because Tony looked like a midget next to him, and Tony was a pretty big guy himself.

"Tony, how are you?" I asked, as I reached out my hand to shake his hand. As we shook hands he pulled me closer to him, and said, "I'm fine Frankie. Have you been drinking again?"

"Who, me?" I said.

"Leave us alone!" he said, as he raised his hand to Benny. The two goons moved away to the side of the room.

I asked, "So, Tony, where's Carlo? And who's the new gorilla?"

"Carlo had an unfortunate accident, he's no longer with us, Frankie," he said, sounding sad.

"Oh, he got another job. Where did he go?"

"No, Frankie, no. Carlo's dead! He died two days ago!"

"Oh, Tony!" I said, as sympathetically as possible. "I'm so sorry, Tony!"

"Thanks, Frankie," he said, I know you liked him."

"Yes, Tony, he was good people!"

"Tony, let's have a few drinks, and go find those two girls again!"

"No!" he said sternly, "You're not drinking anything but coffee!" he shouted, while waving his hand. Frankie, you've got to straighten yourself out. You stink! When was the last time you took a shower?"

"Yesterday," I said, with as straight a face as I could.

It was about an hour later when I got ready to leave. Howie, the bigger gorilla made sure I drank the whole pot of coffee down.

Tony sent Benny off somewhere, before we got into another fight. Then Tony disappeared into his office until it was time for me to leave. When Howie finally felt that I'd sobered up, he ran to get Tony.

After a few minutes Tony and Howie returned. Tony, not wanting to get too close to me, looked me up and down for what seemed to be a solid minute.

"Are you alright Frankie? Can you drive?"

"Yeah," I said running over to him, "Let's go get the girls," I shouted as loud as I could, while at the same time slapping him on the back. Once I was in character, I was capable of anything.

I made believe that I didn't notice the rage building up in Tony's eyes, as he screamed, "Get out of here, now! You embarrass me!" As he turned to leave he said, "And don't come back here again until I call for you!"

"You got it, pal!" I said, as I trotted out the door.

Not until I was well on my way home, did I crack a big smile on my face, as I said outloud, "I can't believe that I'm still alive, I just slapped a mob boss!"

My mission today was a success, I managed to convince Tony that good old Frankie was no longer around. The new Frankie was insane, out of control and a drunk. Tony had to be thinking that I finally lost my marbles.

The digital clock on the car's dashboard read 3:01 when I reached my house. I was starving, but I didn't want to go to a restaurant, especially smelling as bad as I did. I fixed myself a peanut butter sandwich, using the fresh loaf of bread I'd purchased the day before.

The phone rang. I let my answering machine pick it up, but I listened to see who it was. After the beep I heard, "Frank it's Paul. Are you there? Frank pick it up. Ok, Frank I...

"Paul I'm here," I said, sounding tired.

"Oh Frank, I just wanted to see how you were feeling, buddy. How are you doing?"

"Oh, I'm alright," I said, "just feeling very tired. The bronchitis is knocking me out!"

"Frankie, I thought you had the flu, didn't you?"

"Yes I, yeah, I-did. But then I got bronchitis. A bad case of it too."

"So you're still laid-up then, I wanted to get together!"

"No, that's no good, I'm exhausted and what I have is extremely contagious. In fact I'm going to lie down again, right now. Thanks for calling."

"Whoa, wait a minute. Why are you are rushing me off, Frankie?"

"I'm just really tired, OK, I'll talk to you again!"

"Yeah, okay, if you ever return my calls. Ok, feel better buddy. See you later Frank."

"Bye" Knowing how unfriendly I was to Paul was bothering me. It really hurt, keeping such a distance. It hurt even more, not showing my true feelings. But I knew in my heart that I had to stay away. I had to cut off my outward feelings toward everyone I loved. Everyone including Paul And it was taking its toll emotionally.

219

The next thing I had to do, was call my mother. There was no way that I could see her now, not in the state I was pretending to be in. And I know that If I went to see her, she'd see right through me. She always could. One look into my eyes would tell her just what I was thinking and doing, just like when I was a child.

No, I had to call her on the phone. I had to say my good byes, but in my own way. After all, I couldn't say good-bye forever to my mother in person. Not without falling to pieces right in front of her. I had to hide behind the telephone. Some place where my mother couldn't see my eyes. I waited till the evening, until I got my nerve up to call her. After half a bottle of dry Chablis, which I needed to take the edge off, I was finally ready.

"Hi, Mom, it's me, Frankie."

"Oh Frankie, how are you feeling? And why didn't you return my calls?"

"Ma, I've been sick with the flu and then bronchitis. So I haven't been taking anyone's calls. I'm just feeling a little better, and strong enough to call you now."

"Oh, Frankie, do you need anything? Do you want me to come over to take care of you?"

"No, Ma, I can take care of myself. I've been doing it for years now, remember?"

"Frankie, is there something wrong? You sound different?"

"No Mom, I'm just tired and under the weather, that's all!"

"Frankie you sound troubled. Have you been eating? I can drop off some fresh lasagna, Ok?"

"No, Ma, I'm fine. I've been eating well. In fact I even ordered baked ziti tonight, from Dino's Pizzeria. I just had it delivered. And no, nothing's bothering me."

"Frankie, you sound sad. What are you sad about? I'm your mother, Frankie don't try to keep a secret!"

"Ma, alright, I've been feeling a little down lately, but I think that it's because I've been sick."

"Ok, Frankie, as long as you think that everything is under control."

"Don't worry Mom, I'm all right, I'll call you again in a couple of days."

"Ok, Frankie, remember that no matter what happens, that your mother will always love you."

"Ok Mom, and I'll always love you too, bye!"

With tears in my eyes, I filled my glass full with the white wine I'd been drinking earlier. In the next hour I managed to finish off the bottle. By nine - thirty, I'd fallen asleep. I was exhausted from both the wine and the nervous energy working on my mind. No matter how many times I convinced myself, I knew that I'd never get over having to end my life as I knew it, and play dead. Forcing my family and friends to live with it for the rest of their lives. The guilt was really working on me.

Maybe it was the wine, or maybe just the endless torture I was putting myself through. But I slept like a baby. In fact, it was one of the most restful night's sleep I could ever remember having. My mind had been totally exhausted. I had cried myself to sleep Tuesday night, with the visualization of my funeral, and the impact that my death would have on my mother, and the rest of my family and loved ones.

The sun shining through the blinds told me it was time to get up. One glance at the clock radio next to me, told me it was 8:30 am on Wednesday. Surprisingly, I didn't feel energized. Even with more than ten hours of sleep, I still felt that I needed more rest. Then I realized that the depression gave me the urge to sleep more than usual. But still, I had to try to work through it.

After showering and shaving, I took off for the local diner. For the past few days, I had a craving for bacon and eggs, along with a side order of pancakes. Sure, it was another sign of my nervous energy at work, but I didn't care. All I knew was, right now, I was starving, and I needed a lot of food real fast. The newspaper, as usual, was right outside my front door.

As I entered the diner, I had my paper tucked neatly under my arm. My waitress this morning was Phyllis. Phyllis was always pleasant she actually brightened up the day for me, and probably everyone else she waited on. After I placed my order, I could swear that Phyllis ran to the kitchen, just like she was going to cook it all herself.

Phyllis was tall and slender, maybe five foot seven and 115 pounds. She was probably thin from all the running she did, back and forth to the kitchen.

As I looked at Phyllis, I guessed her age to be around thirty - six. She was so nice and sweet to all the customers, that if the food was bad no one would ever want to tell her. What I liked most about her service, was you never had to ask her for more coffee. She was always there with a refill before you needed one. After half a cup of hot coffee, I opened up the Daily News to read a little bit.

As I was flipping through the pages, I stopped abruptly. There it was. As if someone had shouted at me. The name and headline, both caught my eye. The article on page two read: "Mob figure, Vongemi, arrested in gangland slaying says he was framed"

Lifting up the paper, closer to my eyes, I couldn't wait to read the story. It read: "Bobby "The Bull Dog" Vongemi was arrested late last night, and charged with the murder of one of his Family associates, a small time mob player, Carlo "Hammer Head" Hanni age 29. Carlo leaves behind a wife and three children."

The story went on to state that Carlo got the nickname "Hammer Head" because he used to play semi-pro football and supposedly he had a hard head. The story stated how nice a person Carlo had been. Not once, did it mention that Carlo snapped peoples' necks, and broke their legs. Or that Carlo probably rubbed out his fair share of people while carrying out the orders of the Vongemi Family.

Bobby Vongemi claimed that someone set him up for a fall. The News stated that an anonymous informant called the authorities, and tipped them off as to where they could find the body. Also, Bobby "the Bull Dog" was responsible for the hit. It was definitely a "hit," as the News put it, because of the way Carlo was killed.

The medical examiner's findings reported that, "The victim was shot with a high caliber shotgun through his mouth." In other words someone stuck the gun in Carlo's mouth and pulled the trigger, which blew the back of Carlo's head clear off. "A classic mob-style killing," was the way the medical examiner described it.

"Great!" I said, as my food was put on the table, "I'm ready to throw up, and I didn't even eat yet!"

"Are you feeling all right, you look awful pale?" Phyllis asked.

"Oh I'm alright, I guess I'm just hungry," I said as I dug into my food.

As I ate my breakfast, I suddenly wasn't as hungry as I thought I was. I read the rest of the story. The News went on to say, "the reason the mob kills someone, by putting the gun in their mouth and blowing their head off, is because they turned into a rat. Once someone turns on the mob by talking too much, the hit is put out on them."

As I put the paper down and continued to eat, I wondered, if Bobby "the Bull Dog" Vongemi would get out of jail, or at least get out on bail, and then beat the rap. Nothing ever sticks to the Vongemis. My real concern, was whether or not my name had been brought to light as a possible snitch.

My conclusion was this, if I was a target before, I'd surely be a bigger target now. Anyone who wasn't an actual insider, an associate, would be under close scrutiny. Now, I'd definitely be under suspicion. Mostly by Tony, who was well aware that I knew far too much.

After finishing my breakfast, I left a two dollar tip for Phyllis. She was always so sweet to me. I knew I'd miss her too. I thought about the other regulars I would miss, and how we get used to the same people like a habit.

Chapter Fifty

After breakfast I headed to the west side of Manhattan again. I needed to drive around, even though I didn't have my putrid, Scotch-soaked clothes on. I still felt the urgency to cruise the city for a body. Maybe I just needed to keep myself busy or maybe I'd get lucky, but I had to keep moving in the right direction.

The temperature was no better than the last few weeks. It was five degrees, with a wind chill factor of minus 17, and once again the sun was hiding behind the clouds. It dawned on me that I'd left my police scanner at the house. I couldn't go to the city without my little spy box, so I circled around the block and headed home. It was only five minutes away. I'd grab the radio, change my clothes, then head for the city.

As soon as I drove down my block, I noticed something unusual. Parked right in front of my apartment was a big black Cadillac. I stopped abruptly. From a distance, I assessed the situation. The car appeared to be a late model Fleetwood.

There was no doubt about it, this was a Tony Vongemi car. Even though I'd never seen this particular car at Tony's before, I knew it held goons-in-waiting. And I wasn't going to bite. In fact, I promptly backed up the block, until I hit the first cross street I could turn up. "I better get out of here fast!" I said to myself.

Maybe Tony just wanted to talk, or maybe he wanted more. Especially with his brother's recent arrest. I hoped he didn't think that I had anything to do with Bobby's arrest. Maybe this was the car that slammed into Paul the other night. There was no damage, but that was probably fixed the same night by some crooked body shop the Vongemis use as a front.

Time was running out and I felt edgy. Something was about to happen. I was sure of it. My plan would have to be carried out sooner than I expected. Or else, someone would be carrying me out in a body bag.

I stepped hard on the gas which promptly accelerated the car quickly off my block. As I headed for the city, my mind drifted to the suitable body I desperately needed. My work was cut out for me. I'd have to scour the area once again to locate a potential clone.

It was cold but I didn't feel it, as I walked the same general area I had walked a number of times before. It appeared that even more boxes were around than the last time I was here. More homeless people. And more black men than before. As I walked and looked around through the area, no one looked at me twice. Maybe I looked like a detective, but none of the homeless people seemed concerned with my presence. Maybe they were too frozen to worry about anything but staying alive.

This time I took down some notes, such as the exact location of certain homeless huts. Also, I took notes on what kind of liquor was near certain homeless peoples' areas. Still walking and writing I gave names this time to particular men. Also, I was making notes about them along with a star system. The best matches received a mark of four stars. The least likely ones would receive a single star.

I knew that I needed help, so I had purchased a couple of pints of cheap liquor and some cigarettes. My plan was to find someone who could lead me in the right direction, point out the worst off of the homeless men.

I lucked out. I found an old black man named Maurice, who must have been seventy five, but looked ninety. His eyes lit right up when I gave him two pints and the cigarettes. It was like I had found a friend for life.

Maurice told me about certain sick men. Some had full-blown HIV. Some had lung cancer, many had liver disease. I told him that I wanted to help only the ones that were sick. That I would provide food to the worst ones through a Meals On Wheels program.

Maurice was eager to help, as he drank and smoked his reward.

There was a guy I named Sammy who got three stars. Sammy had Aids. The notes I made under Sammy's name were: "appears to be of Spanish decent, but somewhat light in complexion. His hair was not perfectly straight, but not exactly curly either. Sammy's teeth were white, but one top tooth was missing. Sammy isn't perfect for my plan, but would do in a pinch."

Then there was Joey G.. Joey was a real good match, Sammy wasn't bad, but Sammy was about thirty three years old. Joey was about twenty five and much better for my plan. Maurice informed me that Joey had brain cancer.

As Maurice put it: "This guy's dead already. He was given only months to live a couple of months ago. He's been trying to drown the cancer and pain with as much alcohol as he could find."

Joey looked like a mix, he could pass for Italian or Indian. His hair was brown and full. Joey, as I noted, seemed to be a mix of Spanish and Italian. His teeth were all there; white and straight.

Joey's height was approximately five foot ten, his weight about 165 pounds, just right for my clone. His appearance, of course, was filthy. Maurice told me that his addiction seemed to be only alcohol. Cheap alcohol and a lot of it. He probably wasn't on drugs, most of the homeless weren't. It was just too expensive, even if it was the way many of them ended up here. Empty bottles of cheap liquor were strewn around Joey's area.

This stuff must've tasted like turpentine, because the place sure smelled like it. Joey was the best bet so far, in my numerous visits. Only he scored four stars. and was close to death.

There were many black men to choose from, but they just wouldn't do, no matter how many floors they fell.

Then there were many men that were about my age and height, but who had absolutely no teeth in their mouths. Or, were just totally destroyed, in both body and mind. Many of them looked like they were close to death, which would've been good for me, but they were just so shriveled up, like old stale prunes. I could never have passed them off as me.

No, Joey G. was my man, I told myself. I had seen him here before in the same exact spot. It was his own private space. The box he lived in was a well-worn General Electric refrigerator box. He called it home. To have an actual refrigerator box as a shelter-in this area was a rarity. Most of the other homeless people had pieces of cardboard or wood. There were only few that had an entire intact box.

Joey was my choice. Especially with the brain cancer. I didn't think I could find a better match, at least not in this field of despair. Joey was the best one, but would he die quickly enough for me? Time was running out. I needed a body, but more importantly, I needed one quickly. Especially now, with Vongemi's men waiting outside my door. They weren't there to bring me flowers.

Tony probably wanted to see me, and he wanted an urgent meeting. So urgent, that he didn't ask for one by phone. No, this was one of those command performances. The kind of requests you just can't refuse. My memory of Tony's last command performance was still vivid in my mind.

Tony didn't understand no, or I can't. He was used to getting what he wanted. Look at Carlo! I never really liked him but I never thought that Tony would eliminate him. Carlo, I thought was Tony's right-hand man. This confirmed my understanding of the Vongemi Family. No one was indispensable, not with these mugs. Especially me: "Frank Granstino, the little two-bit insurance jerk!"

If he can wipe out people in his own Family circle, as easily and nonchalantly as he does, how much would my rubout bother him? I was convinced that I was in big trouble. Maybe even sooner than later. My life wasn't worth a nickel, not in this town. Not with Mad Man Vongemi around, along with his brother, Bobby the Bull Dog.

My problem still remained, how do I get the body I needed right now? How did I get a dead Joey G? I needed some cooperation. A dead body would cooperate real nice, but Joey was still alive. Would he die in time for me?

As time slowly ticked away, my sense of desperation grew. At this moment I was so desperate, I felt like running. Although I knew this wasn't the answer to my problem. Tony's men were waiting outside my door for me. And Bobby the Bull Dog was looking for revenge against anyone he felt was a rat. My nerves were definitely more on edge than usual.

With all the pressure, all the activity lately, I don't think I'd have a problem with killing someone right now. Someone to take my place at the top of the World Trade Center. When your life is in danger, it's amazing how you can rationalize just about anything away. Even killing someone else. My life had just begun, I had a full and long life ahead of me. Joey G. and his homeless friends had used their lives up years ago. Now they were merely existing, serving no purpose, just waiting for the candle of life to burn out.

I have so much I want to do, so many places I want to see. I want to experience life to the fullest. It wasn't my fault that I was in the wrong place at the wrong time. I was just trying to sell insurance.

Time was flying, it was already 1:00 o'clock in the afternoon. My surveillance of the west side area was a success. My notes were thorough and conclusive. In the few short visits to the area, my conclusion was simple. The area was pretty stable and there were no real surprises. The players all seemed very much alike. All lost souls, with no real life. They all seemed to be waiting for an end to their torture, their despair, their misery.

Maybe I was just seeing what I wanted to. I don't know. But I did know one thing, Joey G. fit the bill the best. It's sad, but somehow I wished Joey was dead already, and from what Maurice told me, Joey wanted it to end.

The music was playing loud and clear. And I knew that I'd have to face that music today. Tony wasn't a bad dream. He wouldn't go away. Each and every morning, when I opened my eyes, Tony Vongemi was there. More importantly, my problem was still there. At least the worst nightmare ultimately would end.

Tony must've still have his goons waiting for me. I knew that I'd have to go home sooner or later. But right now, I wanted it to be later. Much later. After all, what was it that Tony wanted this time. My heart couldn't take much more of these command performances. How much more stress could a person take? My nerves were already shot.

Chapter Fifty One

All the worrying, all the thinking made me very thirsty. I headed over to my current watering hole, The Broadway Pub and Grill. They were always open, I thought, as I made sure to park my car down the street.

As I entered the bar I saw good old Charlie the same bartender I've had for my last few visits. My clothing this time was much different than the other times I'd been here. I'd dressed differently, not knowing I was going to the city. My clothes were much better. I had dark brown corduroy pants, a nice wool shirt, and a heavy black wool coat. All the other times I wanted to look and smell like an alcoholic.

As I walked up to the bar, Charlie jumped to action. As he wiped the bar with his rag, he put a coaster in front of me and said, "Nice to see you again, fella, what'll be?"

"Hi Charlie, I'm working today so just give me a white wine please."

"You got it pal!"

Charlie looked much more red in the face than usual. He was definitely an Irishman. I imagined that he must also indulge in the drink, especially being in the bar business. He was also overweight, and probably had high blood pressure. As Charlie put the glass of wine in front of me, he said, "So what kind of work are you in?"

"Oh, I sell life insurance Charlie, in fact, I have an appointment later."

"Oh, that sounds like an interesting line of work. You deal with the public every day just like me. You're in a people business. Do you like it?"

"Yes, very much," I said, as I drank down half a glass of wine rather quickly. I should've told him to just bring me the bottle of wine. Charlie was a genuinely nice guy, but I had to back off.

I only wish that I could talk to someone about my problems. But I knew that I couldn't. There was no intelligent way to include anyone else in my mess, not even just in conversation.

As soon as I finished the rest of my wine, right on cue Charlie was there. "Hit it again Charlie," I said.

"You bet," he said.

I could tell things were slow, Charlie was dying for anything to do.

"Cold enough for you?" Charlie asked.

"It's cold enough to kill someone!" I said.

"I hear you, my friend!" Charlie said, with a grin.

It was a little after 4:00 o'clock when I walked outside into the ice cold air. The sun was hiding behind some clouds, so it felt even colder then before. The buzzing inside my head, confirmed my count of five glasses of wine. I didn't care. It didn't even bother me that I was going to drive the car feeling this way. If I was lucky I'd hit a tree straight on. Lately, I'd been feeling like a coward, unable to fix things like a man.

The walk up the street seemed to sober me right up. It's amazing what sub freezing weather will do to you. Even if you're feeling sleepy it'll snap you right out of it. Strangely enough, walking slowly made me think of the people that walked to their execution. It felt the same to me, as I thought of what was waiting for me outside my front door.

The drive home was longer than usual. With my mind racing, I was in no real hurry to get back to Vongemi's tough guys. But I toughened up. What's the worst that could happen to me? I asked myself. Could they kill me? Maybe. Then again Tony may just be lonely and want to talk. Oh yeah, right! Who are you kidding! I said in answer to myself.

As I caught a glimpse of myself in the rearview mirror, there was a sparkle in my eyes, and a smile on my face. Why should I be cautious? Quickly I parked, without looking around me. Whatever was about to happen would happen without me looking. As I got out of my car, I heard the sound of car doors slamming. The sound was from across the street.

Nonchalantly, I glanced across the street, reminding myself that I wasn't supposed to know someone was waiting for me. I saw two men running toward me, away from their dark blue Lincoln Continental. Those clowns from this morning must have gotten tired, I thought. Unless they went away, and came back

232

again. Whatever the case was I wasn't going to be rattled. I'd face them and see it through, no matter how bad it was. My father would be proud of me.

"Yo, Frankie, wait, we want to talk to you!"

Turning abruptly, I saw Benny and that new guy, Howie. Howie was huge, even standing next to Benny, who was himself six foot two. Benny yelled, "Where the hell you been?"

"What are you - my mother?" I replied.

Howie was smiling at me, I hoped he didn't get mad.

"How are you Howie?"

"Great Frankie!"

Benny snapped at me, "We've been waiting all day for you Frankie. The boss wants to see you. I hope you haven't been drinking Frankie!"

"Benny, leave me alone, I'm busy!"

"I'll leave you alone, with a broken neck if you don't get in the car right now and come with us!"

"Ok Benny, hold onto your shorts!" I said as I walked toward my apartment.

"Where are you going Frankie. Are you deaf!" Benny shouted.

"Benny, I have to go to the bathroom!"

"What? You must be kidding! We wait here all day for you, so you can go to the bathroom. Get your stinking ass in the car!"

Benny was a convincing type of guy, especially when he glared at you with those piercing dark brown eyes. And especially when you can tell that Benny was dying to break somebody's neck.

"All right! I'll get in the car Benny. Calm down," I said. Benny just smiled that weird, sadistic little smile, as if to say: "I knew you would!"

No one spoke a word during the short ride to the restaurant. The palms of my hands were sweating. Trying to be inconspicuous I wiped them twice on my pants legs. The car ride felt like the last ride a prisoner gets on his way to the electric chair.

As we pulled into the parking lot of Tony's restaurant, I was feeling a lot calmer. If this was it for me, then I'd face it like a man. When we got out of the car, Benny immediately rushed over to me. He grabbed me by the wrist and held tight, as if to keep me from running away. It hurt, so I promptly pushed him hard from the side, and broke free from his hold. Benny got that glaring look in his eyes as he quickly regained his balance. He shot a punch at me so fast I didn't see it coming. It hit me right in the center of my chest. So unexpected was it, that it knocked the wind out of me, I lost my breath and couldn't catch it for at least 20 seconds. This guy was tough. After all I'm only a skinny little guy.

As he grabbed my arm this time, Benny said, "What are you - a wise guy?"

Still not able to breathe, all I could do was smile, while trying very hard to show I wasn't intimidated by him. Taking little gasps of air in slowly, finally took my mind off my present situation. I had a hard enough time just breathing.

When we walked through the front door of the restaurant, I immediately saw Tony. He was sitting all by himself at the bar. All I could think was, Great, a drunk mobster. I still couldn't breathe. Tony looked like he was already wasted.

Benny shouted: "Boss, I'm back!"

Tony looked over in our direction and said, "In the back room!"

Even though I was walking, Benny kept pushing me along a little faster. My breathing was starting to improve. Benny roughly pushed me down into a chair, at the round table that Tony liked to use. Howie and Benny took their usual spots, one on each side of the doorway. It was five minutes before Tony entered the room. He was carrying a large pot of coffee. Feeling relieved, I was so glad it wasn't the cigars again. I happily flexed the fingers on both of my hands a few times.

"Hi, Tony," I said, as cheerfully as I could under the circumstances.

"Oh, hi Frankie. How you been?"

"Great, Tony, how about you?"

"I've been better, Frankie, but I'll survive."

Tony looked pale, and he sounded a little sad. He smelled of alcohol and looked like he had about five too many.

"Frankie, have some espresso, it's fresh," he said, as he poured out two full cups.

He looked at Benny, raised his hand and said nothing. But Benny ran off, and in thirty seconds he returned with a full bottle of sambuca for the coffee.

As Tony slowly stirred the liquor into his coffee, he stared at me, looking right into my eyes. I acted as if I had nothing at all to hide. But I was shaking on the inside with a knot in my stomach the size of a melon. So I stared right back into his eyes.

Tony kept staring as he asked: "Are you ratting us out, Frankie?"

Looking him square in the eyes, I said, "No, Tony, not at all!"

He kept stirring his espresso, as if he were waiting for the next question to come out of the coffee.

"Frankie, someone has been talking to the Feds about the Family and it's been suggested that it's you!"

Feeling that I must do something here to convince him of my innocence, I quickly jumped up and said, "You've got to be kidding! Is that all my friendship means to you?"

I shouted at Tony, as if he were a small child. Benny came racing over from his position, fist cocked, ready to strike, but Tony just raised his arm which backed off Benny.

"Sit down Frankie. I trust you. My brother, though has his doubts. But you just remember one thing," he said as he picked up the large coffee pot. "You're just like this coffee pot. When you're good, you're great. But when you leak, then you're worthless!"

With that statement, Tony got a nasty look on his face and flung the coffee pot against the wall 10 feet away. The crashing sound of the pot, and the coffee dripping down the beautiful paneled wall seemed to shake only me up; because Benny and Howie both remained as still as statues.

I knew that Tony wasn't wrapped too tight to begin with, but this guy was truly dangerous. Not only to me, but to everyone including himself.

"Tony, I'm your friend! That's the reason I stay loyal. You don't have to worry about me!"

235

"I know that, Frankie," Tony said. "But just you remember, Benny over there is just dying to break someone's neck. You know he takes great pride in snapping the neck with just one quick yank," Tony said, while demonstrating with his hands in the air.

Tony then got up, and gave me a hug, this time he kissed me on the right cheek. He screamed for Howie to get me something to eat. All I could do was smile. Even though I felt like throwing up, my stomach was still knotted up, and felt like a brick was in it.

All I wanted was to get out of there, and be anywhere far away from this madman and his faithful sick sidekick Benny.

There was no choice, I had to eat with Tony. I dared not say a negative word. We ate filet mignon and salad. For some strange reason, Tony felt like celebrating, so he ordered a couple of bottles of expensive champagne. Trying to numb the fear I was feeling, I drank two glasses down very quickly. In the mood I was in, I felt like guzzling the entire bottle.

Tony was drinking heavily. He already was pretty loaded when I had seen him at the bar earlier. Tony started moving closer to me as the night wore on. Every time I tried to leave, he stopped me. Now, unbelievably, he wanted to tell me more mob family secrets.

Every time Tony drank too much, he talked and when he talked, he really talked. He'd tell you anything you wanted to know. Tonight was no different; he practically admitted to everything, including fixing all the death claims and beating the insurance company out of millions of dollars.

"Tony, please don't tell me any more, I don't want to know, Tony."

"Shut-up Frankie and listen. Don't interrupt me!"

Maybe Tony thought that he was giving his confession in church, but he wouldn't stop spilling his guts. He went on to admit, that the Capici Funeral Home was run by the mob, and Augie "The Fish" Planantone ran it for the Mafia. He also bragged that Augie could make anyone up in such a way, that they'd look like anyone he wanted them to. And that was precisely how they'd fool insurance companies into thinking someone was dead. Maybe Tony's been doing this insurance scam for years, I thought.

With a big smile on his face, Tony said, "We really beat the insurance companies out of millions, didn't we, Frankie?"

"I didn't do anything, Tony, I just sold the policies!"

"Don't worry about the insurance companies, Frankie, they've got billions of dollars. They won't miss a few million."

"You used me, Tony, I feel like a fool!"

"Frankie, let me explain something to you. You were our way into a multi-billion dollar company. If we didn't connect with you we would've made a different connection into a different company. Don't feel used. Feel chosen. We only choose the best of the best, Frankie. You were able to help strengthen our Family. You should feel good about that!"

"Well, Tony, I never thought about it like that before," I said, trying not to get him too excited. Even though I knew the real score. I didn't want Tony to know what I was really thinking. It was 11:00 pm before Tony, feeling too tired to talk, allowed me to go home, but not before shooting off his mouth about the mob businesses he was instrumental in running.

Maybe Tony was confident in his belief that I dared not talk to the authorities. Maybe that's why he allowed me to know that Carlo, his right hand man, was killed off because he talked too much. Tony knew that I wasn't a tough guy. I wasn't a mug, and I didn't go around looking for a fight. He also knew that Frankie was just a good Italian boy with a little more smarts than the average Joe.

Talking to the Feds, was like signing your own death certificate. Tony knew that I fully understood this fact. He was comfortable with my cowardness. Perhaps that's why Tony started bragging about all the killings, all the blackmailing of different people and fraudulent claims against insurance companies.

He knew I was too smart to rat on the mob. "Or was I?" His brother, Bobby had his doubts. I guess Tony would have his doubts too, if he landed behind bars because of someone ratting him out.

My suspicions all along were correct. It was only a matter of time before I outlived my usefulness. As soon as Tony felt that it was time to quit putting in phony claims, I'd be eliminated, just like Carlo.

My suspicions of the Vongemi Family were all correct. The biggest suspicion was that I would soon become food for the fish in the ocean. The only question was, how soon? How much more time had I bought myself?

It's funny, but a man destined to die starts to lose his fear of most things. I had slowly become fearless during the last few months. So consumed, with possibly getting whacked, I no longer feared Benny. I no longer feared talking back to Tony, and telling him exactly what I thought. Maybe I was losing my mind.

As I reached my apartment, it was late, but I was still alive. Feeling totally drained and exhausted, I settled into my favorite recliner. The stress-filled day had drained all the energy from my mind and body.

As I sat and stared into my living room, my mind was consumed with my plan of escape. All the details of my plan were running through my mind non-stop, colliding, one thought against the other. I was obsessed with the urgency of my escape, as I quickly drifted off into a paralyzing sleep.

Chapter Fifty Two

"Thursday morning, already!" I said, as I twisted and turned. First it was at 4:00 am, then at 5:00 and again at 7:00. It was hopeless. I knew that I couldn't fall back to sleep again. My mind was racing with all the things I had to do. There wasn't going to be any peace. How could there be?

Fully convinced that my life was in immediate danger, I was finally determined to act on my suicide plan today. It was taking too long waiting for an acceptable body. So I'd just have to take the closest matching body I could.

My answering machine was loaded with messages. Frantic messages. People begging me to return their calls. I had three messages from my friend Paul alone, each one sounding more desperate than the one before. My mother, my sister, even Alicia, the spy.

There were so many things that I needed to do and only one day left to do them all. There was no point in shaving, after all I was going to be in my drunken bum act today. There was one last desperate message from Tom Somi, the manager. He now resorted to cursing me out on the message he left. Tom surprisingly, didn't fire me. But demanded that: "I show up at 9:00 am today, or you'll be in deep trouble, buster." He dared not fire me. I was the number one producer in the agency. How could he ever explain that to the home office-brass? But all I could picture as he screamed, was the beet red color of his face.

My suicide letter was short and to the point. I explained that I'd felt too lonely without Lisa and too pressured in my work. That I wanted to join my father. Also, how I'd given up on mankind, its selfishness and lack of respect. The suicide letters would be left in three places. I'd leave one at work, one at home, and one at the suicide scene in the city. Of course, only after the body was set up on the roof, in place to fall, would I put out all the letters.

There were still supplies to pick up and a bag to pack. A shopping bag would have to do. There would be a clean set of clothes needed for me, as I'd switch my present clothes with my body double, just before I left him on the roof of the World Trade Center. Just in case it was needed, I also packed all kinds of hygiene gear: razors, shave cream, a nail clipper, wash cloth, a towel and a bottle of water. The two liter soda bottle would do nicely. I knew that I'd have to clean the dead body up before I left it on the roof. I've never been as dirty as some of those homeless men.

Various other things were needed as well. Including a second set of sneakers, some socks, underwear, Q-tips, etcetera. There would be only one shot at getting this right. If I screwed it up I'd be dead.

Over the past two years I'd saved up an enormous amount of cash. Most of it coming from the last nine months.

Carefully, I ripped the strapping tape off from the underside of my bathroom vanity top. This had been my emergency hiding place for years. After all, who'd ever think of looking for money under the bathroom sink, taped closely to where the sink is connected to the Formica top?

Taped under the sink was in excess of a hundred thousand dollars in cash, mostly in hundred dollar bills. That's enough cash to start my life over, I thought. That hundred thousand dollars was to be Federal Expressed to my new identity at the Hotel Royale in Barava. Not wanting to show too much money, I had spread it out over a few bank accounts, then withdrawn it all, months ago when I knew there was trouble.

The money should get there sometime after I arrive, maybe the next day. There was no rush, I had my whole life ahead of me. I kept only three thousand dollars, just in case I needed money on my trip. I dared not carry a hundred grand in cash. Not in New York, and not anywhere near Vongemi and the Mafia.

With so many things to do, I had to make some notes. There were airline tickets to remember to take. I must also remember my leather gloves. There were other items like strapping tape, and tools, such as screwdrivers. Also, I'd need rope, and a utility knife. My list included various fireworks, such as blockbusters; those very large firecrackers.

It took me twenty minutes more to pack various other things, such as: alarm clock, plastic drop cloth, and a Rough Neck 30 gallon garbage can, with heavy-duty wheels on the bottom.

After I loaded the ice cooler into the car, I felt that I was as prepared as I needed to be. Whatever I was missing, I'd merely purchase. My plan had been worked out for months now. Although it might change slightly somewhere along the way, I was pretty confident that I could pull it off.

The goal of course was to convince the world, but more specifically, Tony Vongemi, that I was dead. That I was out of the way. No longer a threat to him or the Vongemi Mafia Family. Once Tony was secure in the knowledge that Frank Granstino, could never talk, never tell anyone of the Vongemi secrets, killings and fraud, then and only then would I be able to live close to a normal life.

The air was dry, the temperature extremely cold, as I hit the outside morning wind. It was even colder today than some of the other January mornings. The wind chill factor was minus thirty degrees.

As I pulled into the parking lot of the Right Choice Diner, I thought for a Thursday morning, this place looked empty. This was the day. This is what I'd been worrying about for months now. Sleepless nights, anxiety attacks and a burning stomach. It all came down to today. One last day, one last chance to fix it all. This very important day, maybe even my last. I was confident that I could execute the plan, but then I was always a confident person, even right up until I failed at something.

My favorite restaurant for breakfast was the Right Choice. Phyllis, of course was my favorite waitress, always friendly, everyday. As usual, she was smiling with enthusiasm.

As soon as I sat down, Phyllis came right over, and with her big smile, she said; "Hi ya sexy!"

All I did was smile, back at her. I wasn't in a very playful mood, just totally consumed with the difficult task at hand. "Phyllis bring me that Hungry Man Platter and some decaf please."

"Ok, big boy, you must be really hungry today!" she said, as she left.

It wasn't hunger, it was more like starvation that I was feeling. My nervous energy was making my stomach churn up acid, making me feel like I hadn't eaten in a week. When my food came, there were pancakes, eggs, bacon and a pork chop. I ate the whole thing. With a full stomach, I was ready for the busy and demanding day I had planned.

As I sat in my car, it suddenly dawned on me: this was no longer a plan on paper but reality. My suicide plan would have to be carried out in its entirety. I'd have to be safely aboard a jetliner on my way to Barava, for it to be called a success.

The most troubling part of my day, the thing that really hit home as I sat in my car, was that today I'd have to end someone's life. My plan had to be modified. I had run out of time and options. Because there were no dead bodies, drastic measures had to be taken. I knew that for this plan to work, I'd have to take a man's life. Joe the homeless man, the closest body double I had come across. He'd have to die, now, not in a weeks or months. He would have to die in my place, so that I may live.

No matter how many times I told myself that Joe's life had really ended years ago when he checked out of society, or how convinced I was that Joe would definitely be dead in weeks due to his brain cancer, or that there was no life for him, only torture and pain. It still hurt me. No matter how sick, how close to death, or how much pain he was in, how could I take this man's life away from him? Who did I think I was? God was the only one who should be making these choices. There are Doctors of Death that end terminal patient's lives. But I'm no doctor. Just someone who wants to live.

Still, no matter how sick my stomach felt at that moment, I knew that it was Joe, or it was me. My time had run out. All my options had disappeared. My choice was clear. I knew exactly what had to be done, and I knew how to do it. I knew that I had no other way out unless I wanted to be a hunted man for the rest of my life. Too scared to flip on the light switches in my house, too scared to start my car and scared to death just to walk around the next corner.

No, Tony had helped me make my mind up. He convinced me that I was better off dead. But I never figured I'd actually have to kill another man. Maybe I was no better than Tony, or Benny, who both enjoyed killing someone by snapping their neck. Maybe I had become cold blooded. But at this point I knew that there was no turning back. This was my only ticket to freedom, my only way out, and the train was about to leave the station.

Chapter Fifty Three

There were various other things that I still had to do. My notebook told me that I needed to pick up dry ice. My calculations called for three cubic feet of dry ice. The ice would have to be kept in one of my Styrofoam coolers.

Knowing how scarce dry ice was, I had to go to the yellow pages of the telephone directory to find the closest store. Luckily there were a few places in the Sheepshead Bay area, due to all the fishing done in that area.

All of my elaborate ideas started to take form. The many pieces were fitting together like a jigsaw puzzle. Slowly and painstakingly my dream for a new life, a new liberty, was starting to look like a little more than just a dream.

There were sleeping pills that I'd also packed away. There was an important need for sleeping pills. The sleeping pills were from a prescription, two years ago, when I'd undergone an operation for a deviated septum.

The sleeping pills would come in especially helpful. I'd need something to help do the job of a gun. Killing a person never entered my mind before my association with Tony. I'm a simple man, an easy going guy that lets everything roll off his back. Never before have I started trouble and I never encourage trouble. Somehow, luckily, I manage to talk my way out of trouble if it should start.

Unfortunately, there'd be no talking my way out of the Mafia link I was connected to. There was no easy way to bow out of the Mafia. They just don't understand that someone would want to distance themselves from the mob, and start a brand new life, somewhere far away.

If a mob person wanted out, the Mafia would be glad to oblige them, by sending them into the hereafter. As long as the person was dead and the threat of ratting out against the mob was nonexistent, then and only then would the mob be satisfied. I knew all too well that slogan, "Dead men don't talk."

Could I shoot Joe the homeless man? Not a chance. I could never shoot anyone. I'd probably freeze with the gun in my hand aimed and ready, but unable to move. But I could, and I had all intentions of poisoning him with an overdose of sleeping pills mixed in his liquor. After all, if I had to kill someone, if this was my only way out, and there weren't many options, then Joe's terminal life for mine was acceptable to me.

It sounded cold, heartless. Even as the words passed through my brain: Joe's life for mine. It also was, in my heart, my only way out of the mob. After all, if I were dead in their minds, then the Vongemi Family would finally let me go.

I could kill Joe, at least I could in my own way. He wouldn't feel a thing, I kept convincing myself. I tried to convince myself that I was helping him go before the worst of the cancer consumed him.

It took fifteen minutes for me to carefully open the sleeping pill capsules. Once opened I emptied them each onto a piece of white looseleaf paper. The prescription on the bottle of pills, stated to take just one. So I figured that five pills, coupled with the effect of the high alcohol content of liquor, would take Joe quickly up to meet his maker.

Carefully, I tapped the creased paper using it as a funnel and aiming the deadly dosage of powder into a bottle of liquor I had previously opened. The sleeping pills were now mixed thoroughly in the liquor. The liquor I chose to be the means to this murder, was Ouzo, the potent Greek liquor. Ouzo has close to a hundred percent alcohol content.

Joe wouldn't know what hit him. The Ouzo would knock him out and the sleeping pills would finish him off.

"The quicker the better!" I said.

Earlier in the morning I had stopped by my office at Financial Life. No one was in because it was too early. Just as I planned, I put a suicide note in the top center drawer of my desk. I also placed in the same drawer two matchbooks from the Broadway Pub and Grill. The matches were important because they would connect me to the bar. Once the police questioned the bartender, Charlie, they'd find out just how messed up I was before my death.

Charlie, I was sure, would tell the authorities that Frank Granstino was very sad. That he appeared to be at the end of his

246

rope, and was lost with nowhere to turn. If my acting was good then Charlie would tell everyone, that he wasn't surprised that Frank committed suicide.

If I'd been right in my calculated behavior pattern, then it should be no real shock to many people. Take Tom Somi - he'd just shake his head yes, like he had it figured out all along. Then there was Paul Luggi, my friend, the guy that I'd been avoiding. The guy who'd been begging me to get together with him. Paul was going to be devastated. He'd blame himself. Paul would say for the rest of his life, that he could've saved me.

My mother will take it very hard. No matter what anyone tells her, somehow she'll blame herself. No matter what I put in a letter. No matter how anyone tries to explain away my actions or my good deeds, my mother, will think that she failed terribly in my upbringing. Mothers are just this way. It breaks my heart each time I think about my mother's future agony.

Candice will be devastated too. We have no other siblings. We were so close growing up - best friends. We still are. This will be a terrible shock to Candice to lose her only brother, so early in his life.

To think that I'll be remembered as an alcoholic, a man with deep seated emotional and psychological problems, a man who desperately needed mental therapy, but never received any help. I'll be remembered as a sad individual, a pathetic soul, who couldn't be saved. Someone who killed himself to end his problems. Someone who took the cowards way out.

Sure it bothered me! But at least I'd still be alive to regret some of my actions. Instead of a dead hero, remembered for heroics. A martyr who was trying to outsmart the mob. No, I'd rather be stupid in attitude and be alive, than so smart that I got myself killed by the Mafia.

Everything was playing out the way I planned it. My only concern was getting through the day, getting to the last lap of the race safely. To the part where I was comfortably on the plane, and on my way to the beautiful and safe island resort of Barava.

As I sat still resting, before I continued with the monumental task before me, I thought. With all the trouble I was in over the last few months and all of my dealings with Tony and the mob...

With all the pressure I felt, all the depression and tension, not once did I ever consider actually committing suicide.

There are so many things I still wanted to do. So many goals and dreams that I had. My life was in its beginnings. The way I look at it, my adult life was like a little baby just yearning to grow up, enthusiastic with life, not scared to try anything, and not afraid of anyone or anything.

If my plan should fail and I was caught by the mob before my escape, then I know exactly how I want to be remembered. I want the world to know, that Frank Granstino believed in God, and loved life to the fullest. That he was filled with the highest level of enthusiasm around and that he was a positive and uplifting type of person. Always trying to help someone else improve their life, as I had always strived to improve mine.

Chapter Fifty Four

As time slowly ticked away, my stomach felt like it was tightening up, just a little more with each passing minute. Sure I was nervous, just the thought of what I had to do, raced endlessly rambling through my brain. My mind was working in overdrive.

The tension level was never so high as it was at this moment. Could I handle it? I had no choice. I had to carry on now, or lay down and simply wait to die!

The wandering of my mind was abruptly interrupted by the ringing of the telephone. The answering machine picked up the call. After the beep, I heard, "Hey Granstino, Oh, Frankie, it's Tony, pick up."

"Not on your life!" I said out loud to the empty room.

"Frankie, as soon as you get this message drop by the restaurant. My brother Bobby just got out of jail and wants to ask you a couple of questions."

"Yeah, right! Sure, and I'll bring a grenade so you can stick it down my pants!" I shouted.

The message was over and there was no reason to play it back. My suspicion was correct all along: my life wasn't worth anything. I was a marked man. A dead man. Just the time of my death was the only remaining question.

The Vongemi Family weren't going to let me continue to walk, talk, or to breathe. Maybe it was Bobby "the Bull Dog," or maybe Tony. But really it was unimportant who wanted me dead. The time had finally come to disappear. It was only a matter of time now, and I was as prepared as I possibly could be. It was finally show time, I had to go through with my suicide plan. I had to give them the body they so desperately wanted.

Within two minutes of the phone call I was out of the house and driving down the street. Vongemi's men, no doubt were on their way to my house now. They'd be looking to kill me, or bring me to Vongemi for my last command performance.

They won't get their way this time! I thought, with a new found conviction in my voice. Never before was I so determined to carry out a plan of action, as I was with this one.

For a change I was finally more annoyed than I have ever been. The Vongemis thought they could do anything they wanted. They thought they could kill and maim - at will, and intimidate the whole world. Well not Frank Granstino. They weren't taking my life away.

At this particular moment I felt as if I could snap Tony Vongemi's neck with my own bare hands. That's as mad as I felt. Although I knew I couldn't get away with it and I'd be dead as soon as they caught up to me. Still I felt proud in a way that I finally stood up for my own life instead of whimping out at the sight of danger.

I was feeling both proud and sad. Proud, that I finally toughened up, but sad that I'd lowered myself down to taking another person's life. I felt though, that there was no other way out. The guilt was working on my already over worked subconscious mind, much like the annoying sound of the dripping faucet.

Within the next twenty four hours, I was preparing to kill an innocent man, all because he didn't die on his own soon enough. One day I'd have to answer for that sin. But today, it was kill or be killed.

The adrenaline was pumping feverishly. I felt this strange surging sensation within my body. Almost out of control, yet so powerful. I felt like I could do anything at the moment. What a strange, yet exhilarating feeling!

While I drove I reviewed this mornings activities one last time. The Ouzo was packed, the cordless electric razor was in the duffle bag, I also packed a wash cloth, and a nail clipper. I even remembered some of my cologne, which I put in a little travel bottle, making sure to leave the actual bottle in my medicine cabinet. It was important to maintain the status quo. No one should be the wiser. After all, it was supposed to be a suicide.

The suicide letters were all in place, at home, at the job, and one in the car, which would be planted at the scene of the crime. As I thought about the content of the letters, I wondered if my family would figure out that for the last few months I wasn't acting like myself. That I was depressed, over the apparent loss of a girlfriend, the frustration and pressure of life, and the stress of a demanding sales position.

Okay, I had the Broadway Pub's matches planted at work, at home, and in the car. I also planned to put a matchbook in the pants pocket of the dead body. I had a couple of latex gloves in my pockets, so I wouldn't leave any fingerprints by mistake along the way; I'd definitely need those gloves later. The latex gloves were skin tight and easy to work with.

My planning was meticulous. I tried to plan down to the smallest detail, trying to perform and maneuver the perfect con. Trying my best to fake out the mob. There surely had to be something I forgot to do, but I couldn't remember. Anyway, I knew I could pull it off no matter what obstacles I encountered. My duffel bag contained the extra clothes I'd need, and the extra pair of walking shoes.

Since my family knew my taste in shoes and clothes, I knew that the body found at the foot of the World Trade Center had to be dressed accordingly, especially, if I wanted to pass off the body as Frank Granstino. Someone would have to identify the body, and if my calculations were right - nothing would be recognizable. Except for the clothing, and of course, any personal effects left on the body.

There was certain jewelry which I'd transpose over to the dead body. I'd put my gold bracelet and tigers eye gold ring on the body. These were additional identifying characteristics the body would have. There should be no trouble at all in giving the dead body the identity of Frank Granstino.

My wallet also would be found at the scene of the suicide. I wouldn't need anything that proved I was Frank Granstino. Especially not after the so-called suicide of myself. Everything had to be left behind. My new identity had to be my only identity. Frank Granstino was dead. It was time to move on.

As I was driving along, my mind wandered, as it usually does. For the past two days all I kept thinking about were the women. First, Lisa DeVoe, my old girlfriend, and then Alicia. Good old Alicia, Tony's spy. The girl I fell in love with during my vacation. After a short while I figured out that I was set up.

251

Still I missed the interaction, that special feeling I got when she looked into my eyes. Alicia was a beautiful woman.

There was a terrible emptiness inside. If I wasn't in such deep trouble with the mob, I'm sure I would've tried to get back with Lisa. I was never so lonely as I was these last two months. Especially since I was avoiding everyone I usually socialize with. My friends, my family, my co-workers at the job, even all of my clients - I totally ignored them all. I was fully aware of the term "love deprivation," the lack of any love being shown to another. I understood what I was feeling, I knew it was self-imposed but I didn't have to like it.

How I longed for just one more night of passionate love with Alicia no matter how phony it might be. I needed interaction, I needed human response again. A person can't stay away from other humans too long. But I was fully aware that I had to stay alert. I had to push these feelings and thoughts out of my mind. There was just one more day I had to get through. One more day. Another day wasn't too long to endure.

This was the most important day of my life. After today, Frank Granstino would be dead, and Mario Taini, my new identity would be born. Once I was settled as Mario Taini on the small island in the Cayman Islands, I'd finally be able to start my life over again.

The blue Honda Accord that abruptly cut me off, snapped me right back to reality. "You're not in the Cayman Islands. At least not yet," I told myself. I was still in the Big Apple, and driving my car. There was no daydreaming allowed. Not in New York. As I rolled down the drivers side window, I told myself: I have to stay awake and concentrate on my driving. All I needed now was a car accident. That would really destroy my whole suicide scam.

The miles piled on, as I ran errands and picked up odds and ends needed for my plan. The dry ice filled half of the ice chest in the trunk of the car. While I was there I picked up various extra tools, just in case I ran into unforeseen obstacles along the way. There was extra rope, chain, screws, bolts and nuts - anything that hit my eye in the hardware store.

I purposely stopped at the gas station to get a full tank of gas. The suicide must appear to be a sudden act, a desperate out-of-control thing. It must appear that I had no intention of ending my life, at least not on the day that I filled the car with a full tank of gas.

Chapter Fifty Five

I set out for the city. The weather had suddenly turned cloudy and colder than it had earlier in the day. The once visible sun was now well hidden under thick black clouds. The wind was blowing twenty miles per hour, but combined with the frigid arctic air the wind chill felt brutal.

My mind focused on Joe, and how I had to kill him. Then I realized, I was like a man fighting a grizzly bear, I'd do anything to survive.

Rationalizing that it was only a matter months before Joe's liquor-ravaged body failed, I told myself: Better him than me! My guilt level wasn't too high, but I wondered how I'd feel after I actually killed a man.

Along with the garbage pail I bought, I also purchased a high beam flashlight, and chloroform. I was as prepared as I could be, for the battle of my life.

The Broadway Pub and Grill was pretty empty, considering the time of day it was. This would be my last appearance at the historic, old rustic bar. My attitude would be exactly the same as every other time. My plan was to drink heavily, at least in appearance. My drink of choice, as always, would be Scotch whiskey. Of course, I wouldn't be swallowing much of it. But the way I was feeling lately, I just might let one shot slip down my throat.

As I entered the bar, I observed only two other patrons. They were older men, both were nursing beers. No doubt they had nothing better to do with their day, and were in need of a little conversation. As soon as the big Irishman, Charlie, saw me he got all excited and rushed right over.

"Hey, how've you been there, fella?"

"Fine Charlie, and yourself?"

"Great! What are you in the mood for?"

"The usual Charlie, with a chaser."

"You got it my friend, a Johnnie Walker Black with a Heineken chaser, coming right up."

Charlie was the fastest bartender I'd ever met. It seemed like only seconds before he was back with the drinks.

"So, what do you think about those Knicks, are they hot, or what?" he said with a big wide grin.

"Great, Charlie," I said. Sounding flat, and not wanting to get into a whole conversation. After all, this was the day I was supposed to be at the lowest point of my entire life. The day I was to commit the highest form of sin; the sin of suicide.

If I gave one-word answers then Charlie wouldn't be able to accurately read my true inner feelings, or my emotional state of being. Charlie would just assume that I was depressed.

As Charlie went to refill one of the other patron's beer mug, I quickly leaned down and spit my shot of scotch on the floor. "One down, seven more to go," I said to myself. I drank down some of the beer, mostly to get that nasty scotch taste out of my mouth. I'd need to show Charlie much more drinking today. Today was the day I'd drink myself silly.

Charlie, the pro that he is, was right on the ball. He caught my empty shot glass and ran right over. In the wink of an eye he was back with fresh drinks.

"So how have you been feeling lately?"

"Not too bad, just very tired," I said, in a monotonous voice, sounding as down as I could.

"I hear you," he said, with a sympathetic voice. Bartenders like psychologists, are great listeners. A good bartender will allow the drinking, troubled, patron to vent.

I wasn't going to bite. Charlie wasn't going to get inside my head. Not now. Not today.

"Anything I can help with?" he said softly, sounding like a priest would sound.

"No, I don't feel like talking about it, I'm here to forget, Charlie!"

"I hear you fella," he said, while nodding his head in understanding. Charlie finally backed off, and picked up his conversation again with the old man across the bar. "So how do you like those Knicks?" he asked the old man who was already half-crocked.

It took two and a half hours for Charlie to bring me seven Scotches and four beer chasers. I made a few trips to the bathroom to spit the shots out in the sink. I don't believe anyone was wise to my act.

I was getting a slight buzz in my head. Maybe it was the four beers, or maybe the residual effect of all the Scotch. Whatever it was, it felt good. It helped me forget all my concerns and worries, at least for the time being.

My tip for Charlie was the same as all the other visits, I left a five dollar bill under the empty mug of beer. My mission for the Broadway Pub and Grill was accomplished. I don't think that a professional actor could've done a more convincing job.

My acting was superb in my attempt to portray a depressed helpless man, someone who was probably a danger to himself, as well as others around him.

My plan was to leave the bar with a bang, a final curtain call, something to remember me by. On the way out, I purposely caught my right foot on the leg of a bar stool. Not only did the bar stool go flying, slamming into the floor with a loud bang, I too went flying for about five feet. Crashing heavily to the floor, with a big thud and hitting my head on the floor.

Everyone that was within shouting distance ran immediately to my aid. I acted as if I were temporarily knocked unconscious, even though I was completely unhurt. Charlie rushed over and anxiously asked, "Are you all right! Are you bleeding anywhere? How do you feel?"

Looking around the room, I stared at the celebrity photos hanging on the wall. Looking at each one for a second or two, just for effect.

"Oh, I'm fine, I think," I said, as I swayed from side to side trying to sit up. "I just hit my head a little!"

With the help of a person on each side, I tried to stand up.

"Do you think you can make it buddy?" Charlie said cautiously.

"Of course I can!" I shouted, as I pushed everyone out of my way. "Just leave me alone!" I said, as I left the bar and entered into the frigid late afternoon air.

The air outside was extremely cold, not even a dry cold, but a moist, wet kind of cold that stung the skin more than usual. The buzz in my head was completely gone, as soon as I hit the air.

As I walked the four blocks to where I'd parked my car, I couldn't help but feel proud. With a big smile on my face I shouted, "All right!"

There was no doubt in my mind, that if Charlie was questioned by the police, as to what he thought about Frank Granstino; the guy in the bar, Charlie would no doubt say, "What a poor soul that fella was. I should've known that he'd kill himself. I'm not surprised he took his own life."

My task now was fairly simple, go downtown and get the body I needed so desperately. Joe, the terminally ill, homeless man hopefully would already be unconscious. Maybe dead. He was the best match available. And besides, he stayed for weeks in the same spot, so I was fairly sure of his body.

Joe was a predictable man. He was trying to drown his pain. The pain he felt in life and from his cancer. Almost any type of alcohol would do. I needed to convince Joe to drink an entire bottle or two of the potent Ouzo. I didn't think there would be a problem. I'd bought enough to kill a moose and that was without the tranquilizer substance I mixed in. There's no way that Joe will be standing after that deadly mixture, I said to myself.

Time was ticking away, as the day quickly progressed. It was always that way when you've got so much to accomplish. With pen and paper in hand, I grabbed a bite to eat.

The food joint was no more than a glorified diner in an office building. How bad could it be? I thought, as I cautiously entered the diner, looking carefully around.

The hamburger wasn't too bad. But I did wonder if there really was any meat in it. It tasted a little funky. Maybe it was me, after all that liquor that I swished around in my mouth a little earlier.

The list I wrote while I ate included everything I had to do, leading right up to the moment of leaving the body on the roof. The preparation of the body, and the movement from the shelter to the top of the World Trade Center. There were different obstacles I knew that I'd be encountering, so I had to be mentally prepared to face almost anything. As I played it all out in my mind I was scared. But I didn't dwell on it. I knew that constant worrying would only drain me of all the energy I needed to see this plan through to its conclusion.

My new life was only a day away. A life free and clear from any future threat of the mob. If I failed, if I got caught killing another man, then I too was as good as dead.

There wasn't a prison in existence that could keep anyone safe from the mob. Not if they wanted to get to you. Even the prison guards were bought off. There was no failing. There would be only one shot at pulling this complex scam off. Would Tony Vongemi, who knew me so well, fall for this suicide scam? Or would he see through it, like a sheer white negligee on a woman standing in the moonlight?

There I go again, my mind keeps drifting back to the thing I most desired at the moment. A gorgeous woman in a nice safe place. I focused on my list as I sat in the diner writing, reviewing, and refining the plan. Then I thought of my mother, and it inspired me. I'd do this for my mother. My mother gave birth to me, I wouldn't give up my precious life to anyone, especially Tony.

As I sipped my third cup of coffee, I wished that it was alcohol. Anything that would make the guilt lessen. But there was no cure-all, no drug, no alcohol, no easy answer. Only one plan, one chance for a new life. Just maybe, with time, the guilt would at least lessen.

I knew the toll the past few months had on me. The stress was tremendous, the fear unbearable. I never thought that I could think, no less, act out certain terrible deeds. But the fear of losing my life had driven me to the point of no return.

It was time to move out, get the operation off the ground. Time to conquer the demons. I cleared my head. The time for reminiscing was over. No time to feel sad, but time to act. Maybe it was the coffee, or the fact that I was in the diner for more than an hour. But it felt even colder outside now. The wind had picked up. It felt like twenty mile an hour winds. The temperature had dropped and it was now just simply brutal.

Chapter Fifty Six

By six o'clock it was already dark. It was the perfect time to move my plan forward and drop off the bottles of the Ouzo. If my calculations were correct, Joe would try to polish it all off. An alcoholic doesn't know the words: tomorrow, or moderation. Joe wouldn't share the booze; he'd drink until he passed out. The three bottles I'd leave would only remind him of Christmas time. He'd just think that it was his lucky day.

My liquor should finish him off, or at least knock him out first. Then I'd carry my plan out. My only question was how long it'd take to finish him off. The west side was always quiet, especially after six o'clock. It was especially quiet in the homeless section where the poorest of the city lived.

Walking through the homeless area I looked for Joe. I looked for Maurice. The place was quiet. As I feared, Joe wasn't at his cardboard sleeping spot, so I placed the three bottles of Ouzo near the mounds of cardboard that he used as a mattress.

At least Joe would be a happy man, if only for a few hours. My only fear was that Joe might stop drinking too soon. He had to drink enough for the alcohol mixture to work.

After dropping off the bottles of Ouzo for Joe to drink, I took off. I needed time for the concoction to take its toll. I felt like I was baking a cake. I'd mixed all the ingredients together and put the cake in the oven. Now I had to be patient and let it bake properly.

With extra time on my hands, I thought it'd be an excellent opportunity to visit another local bar. That also would attest to my drinking and depressing behavior on this last day of Frank Granstino. I'd also make sure to pocket a book of matches from this bar as well, which would lead the authorities back to it for questioning. It would piece together very nicely the last hour of Frank Granstino's life.

As I drove down West 33rd street, I chose at random a place called, Gingers. It was a nice little place, with a white brick exterior, and many small paned windows. Over the doorway hung a big sign, showing a beautiful blond haired woman and underneath it was the name, Gingers, painted in fancy script.

When I entered the bar, I immediately spotted the woman known as Ginger. Ginger was a bleached blond woman. I estimated to be in her late fifties, with large breasts. Ginger must've been a knockout in her day, but clearly the lines and wrinkles of time were taking their toll. She had a midsection spread, no doubt from all the drinks that the old men were buying her. I could tell that Ginger was fighting time, and time was clearly winning. I tried to squint slightly as I looked at her, hoping to picture her thirty years ago.

As I waited to be served, I carefully observed the bar along with the woman it was named after. Ginger still must look like a goddess to the old men that drink a few, especially with her large breasts, and the way she exposed her cleavage.

I'd made it a point to stagger through the door. After an hour, I'd spit out several drinks, I appeared a little more drunk with each drink. There were matchbooks on the bar, showing the name and Ginger with her famous cleavage. Very nonchalantly, I slipped the matches in my pocket.

Playing the role of a drunk was becoming easier for me. I basically exaggerated the clumsiness. I made sure to hit my head on the way out.

With a cracking sound, I purposely hit my head on the doorway, just hard enough for everyone to see and hear. Emphasizing it even more with a well placed moan. As I staggered through the doorway, I kept talking to myself and yelling at no one in particular. My goal here was to be remembered and I am sure that I'll be after that performance. Ginger would surely take note. Bartenders always noted who drank too much, then stored the person's face, so they didn't sell them too much alcohol on their next visit.

As I drove back to the homeless section, I made it a point to park as close as I could to the makeshift cardboard shelters. The waterfront was only fifty yards away, straight in front of me. As I looked out over the water, ships could be seen in the distance. I couldn't help but think that the most beautiful view from

Manhattan Island was had by the homeless people, the people who didn't have a dime to their name.

It was pitch black outside, as I sat in my car waiting, watching, not wanting to be seen yet. I'd let the liquor take its toll on Joe, as long as he was at his personal shelter area. The police scanner I had sitting in the car was bringing in little news.

It was a slow weekday night, in the Big Apple. No crime, no accident and especially no bodies to be found. My plan was the only answer. It was the only way I could find a body.

It was so cold out that I had to keep wiping the inside of my windshield from the fog that kept building up. With the heater on and the engine running, I kept my driver's side window slightly open.

Waiting patiently I killed another hour in the car. I didn't want to rush right out to look at Joe. After all, I had the whole evening. There was no rush, as long as I reached my ultimate goal. Feeling a little squeamish, I stayed in the car for a little longer. It was still quite chilly even with the car's heater on.

At 10:00pm, I could wait no longer. It was time. I just had to look and see if Joe was dead. Like a chef opening the oven door, to see if his prize roast was cooked to perfection. Was Joe there? Was he still drinking? Or was he not biting at the bait? Perhaps he was suspicious of the foreign liquor? There were no guarantees in this plan of mine. But there were no other plans, no other brilliant ways out. This was the plan for all the marbles.

It was so cold, that my face was stinging, even with the pull over hat and mask I had on. It was so dark, that as I walked, I shined a penlight flashlight on the ground. I didn't want to disturb any of the homeless, or possibly trip over anyone. As I got to Joe's area, I noticed an empty bottle of my Ouzo lying on its side. Joe must be here! I thought, because no one else would invade his territory. It was a well known rule in the homeless world that no one moved in on another person's shelter, not until they were dead, or they left.

Joe was definitely there. I inched slowly closer, not wanting to make any sound. My breathing had almost stopped completely. I could feel my bones creak, I was moving very slow. As I got almost on top of Joe's cardboard box, I saw a second bottle of Ouzo, empty, and on its side. Shining my flashlight on the bottle, I looked carefully for any liquid, thinking that maybe the bottle might've tipped over. Not a chance. Every drop was missing. It could mean only one thing: Joe was dead, drunk, or he had a lead-lined stomach.

As I inched even closer, I could actually hear my heart pounding harder than it ever had before. There he was! Joe was flat on his face. I was happy, then quickly sad. My assumption was Joe was dead. The two bottles of Ouzo should've killed him. Not to mention the sleeping pill mixture.

As I observed further, there was no movement, not even a flinch... Not a breath, nothing. I knew what the real test was, but I was very reluctant to do it. I wasn't ashamed to admit it - I was down right scared!

While still staring at the lifeless body of Joe the homeless man, I thought: Two bottles of Ouzo would kill a moose! There was no breathing. He has to be dead! I had to get moving. There was still plenty of work to do. "Snap out of it, don't be scared now!" I said to myself.

Joe's body was lying on its left side, but Joe's face was flat on the floor of his cardboard shed. After about five minutes of staring, I got up enough courage to push the body with my right foot. The lifeless body moved from its side and flipped over on its back. Still, there was no movement, no breathing. Joe was dead, as dead as anyone I ever saw, and there haven't been too many.

As I backed the car ever so slowly, up to Joe's box, I made sure not to cause a commotion. The body, which was on its back, would not be too easy to move. I knew this and was prepared. I opened up the rear passenger side door. The body was only five feet away. Still scared, I bit down hard on my lip, as I reached out grabbing the body at the armpits, while dragging and lifting at the same time.

It took me approximately three minutes to lift the body into the car. My stomach was churning up pure acid, and I felt like throwing up, but I continued. Feeling half frozen from the winter chill, I laid the body clear across the rear seat of the car. How fortunate I was, that Joe's body didn't weigh more than 160 pounds. With the car still running, and the heater on high, I eased it out of the area.

No one saw me and there was no movement in the entire area. Maybe it was the coldness of the night, but I didn't see another person the whole time I was there. Looking into the back seat, I kept waiting for movement of some kind. Again, there was no stomach movement, no movement of his eyelids. Half of my mission was complete. For the first time, I realized that I was shaking life a leaf.

With the body now in the back seat of my car, I needed a deserted, dark area, to complete my work on the body. After driving three blocks, I found an empty parking lot. There were no cars, no lights, no activity. This lot was perfect for what I needed. Again, I looked closely at Joe. He was still dead. I kept wondering if he'd sit straight up and say, hello.

Chapter Fifty Seven

It took a few minutes to get up enough courage, but the most motivating force I had, was the crystal clear visualization of my own mob style execution. Every time I pictured myself being shot in the back of my head, by one of Tony's mugs, it encouraged me to forge ahead with my plan. It motivated me to do all the things I so despised doing.

With my courage raised to an all time high, I climbed in the back seat with Joe. The car was still running, the heat was blasting away on high, and the window was slightly open. Between Joe and myself, the car reeked of rancid alcohol. It was a disgusting odor that would turn anyone's stomach. Even though I was very close to throwing up, I continued forward, as quickly as I could.

Never before had I touched a dead man's body. I tried to tell myself that the body wasn't real. That it was a only a dummy. But at the moment, I was the one who felt like a dummy. After all, I was the one who was about to undress a dead man. And to think, I am the same guy who used to be embarrassed in gym class, when we all had to change our clothes.

Joe's body was cold. All the limbs were lifeless, dead weight. The skin of a dead person feels like leather, cool and a little rough in texture. The feelings I felt, as I touched this dead man were indescribable. My body shook with fear, as I started to change all of Joe's clothes into the spare set of mine.

This dead body could be me, if I didn't act as fast as I did, I thought. It still could be me, if I screw this plan up! The thought scared the heck out of me. My lips were all chewed from all the biting I was doing to them. My nerves were shot, but I knew there was no turning back now.

First, I took off all of Joe's old clothes, and cleaned his body. Then, I put all of my fresh clothes back on the body. Next I performed personal hygiene on the dead body. Things such as cutting and cleaning all of the finger and toenails, and trimming the hair. Lastly, I applied some of my own cologne.

Right down to the smallest detail, I tried to remember everything. During this whole process, I don't think I breathed through my nose even once. By the time I was finished cleaning him up, he looked and smelled good.

All of my personal identification, including my wallet, driver's licence, credit cards and pictures, were placed into Joe's pockets. Then, I added the matchbooks from both of the bars that I had gone to, and the handwritten suicide letter. Even down to the walking shoes, Joe was now wearing all of my clothes and carrying my personal effects. I had turned Joe G. into a clone of Frank Granstino.

After all my efforts, Joe resembled me enough to get by. Who would be able to tell the difference once he fell some 110 stories straight into concrete? All I could picture was a watermelon being dropped, and the splatter that'd occur. No one would ever recognize the face of anyone that fell that far.

With the clothes replaced, and the body cleaned up, my plan was moving along nicely. The acid in my stomach was burning hot, churning like a volcano. The stress level was intense. There was no way I could take an antacid, because I knew for sure at this time, that it would cause me to vomit. The thought entered my mind, What have you done! But I pushed it right out of my mind and continued.

My next big obstacle would be getting Joe's body up to the top of the World Trade Center, one hundred ten stories up from the concrete finish line.

In the pitch black of the empty parking lot, I loaded the body into the Rough Neck garbage can in the trunk. Then, with the strapping tape, I taped the cover of the plastic garbage can shut, with the body securely inside.

Now, with the body secure inside the garbage can and in the trunk of the car, I was ready to roll. Looking carefully around, I had to make sure that no one was on to me. I couldn't risk any witnesses at all. This wasn't a game, this was for real. Everything I did, or didn't do, was of utmost importance. Any mistake, even a slight one, could spell disaster. A mistake now could blow my cover, and expose the true identity of the body I was using. My life, was the prize I was working towards.

For five minutes, there was no one within sight. As I eased the car, ever so slowly from the parking lot, rolling forward I made sure not to put on the headlights until I was at least one block down the road.

After a block and a half I turned the headlights on. Carefully, I made sure to follow every driving safety rule, and keep my speed at exactly 25 miles per hour. If I were to be stopped by the police now, I'd be sunk. There would be no talking my way out of that one. Not when I knew that a dead man was sitting in the trunk of my car.

It was 1:48 am when I reached the World Trade Center area. As I drove around the general vicinity for almost ten minutes, I visually took everything in. There was no activity, no people. It was as dead as Joe was, which was no surprise to me for 2:00 am, during the week. After parking the car, I walked the perimeter of One World Trade Center. There was no need to get impatient. Not at this point, not after working so hard on the plan, I assured myself.

Once again, no people, no outside security guards, nothing but darkness and quiet. The silence was scary. Still I waited, I looked and I listened. Total silence. I could hear and feel my heart pounding at a feverish pace. Maybe I was scared that I'd get caught, or maybe the day had finally caught up with me. In any event, my nerves were on edge, as I stared at the huge skyscraper in front of me.

The World Trade Center area looked like a ghosttown to me, it was eerie in a strange way. So silent, that it felt as if at any second, someone would jump up and yell, Boo!. The silence scared me. The height of the building also scared me, as I wondered whether or not I could get to the roof.

First, I looked at the top of the building, 110 stories high. Then I looked over to my car, waiting, resting silently, holding quietly onto our secret that lay in the trunk.

Time was ticking away, and the pounding of my heart seemed to keep track of the seconds ticking away. It was time to move, but every time my body said Go, my mind said, No!. My fear was, that after all the strategic planning, I'd get caught and the whole deal would blow up in my face.

Just as I got my nerve up to move toward my car to get the body, I caught a glimpse of what appeared to be a full sized black car, about 200 yards down the street. Suddenly, I stopped. I made believe that I was walking in the opposite direction, just out for a stroll. When I turned around at the corner to look, the car was nowhere in sight. Total silence, once again. How strange it felt to be in this part of the city, with all this silence and only my conscience.

This time I got up enough courage to walk back to the car. As I quickly got in, I started it up and blasted the heat. It was frigid outside. No one in their right mind was outside in this weather. And I knew that I had to be the only idiot with a dead man in my trunk. What was my next move? I thought, as I moved the car slowly around the corner.

As I eased the car past the building, I quickly stopped. There was a service entrance, a small door toward the rear of the left side of the building. This was my way into the building.

My adrenaline was rushing once again, as I pulled the car away from the building and parked down the street. Time slowly moved on. My dilemma now was how to open the door, the solid steel service door, that was locked.

I've got it! I thought. I'll use a trick that I used when I was a teenager, back in junior high school. It worked then, so I know that it will work now. In fact I have all the material needed right in my trunk, along with the body. I just needed to work out the exact details in my mind, before I jumped right into it. Think Frank, think! Do it right!

The problem I faced was the service door was locked from the inside. I had to get the door opened, then keep it unlocked for future use. A previous time, I'd done a similar thing on a supply room door that was in the basement of my junior high school. From the trunk of the car, I took a piece of aluminum and the nylon strapping tape.

As I looked up and then down the block the entire area was desolate. Feeling paranoid, I didn't want to blow the entire operation on any impulsive moves or carelessness. Feeling secure that no one was in sight, I walked cautiously up to the service door, making sure no one was around.

Once I was at the doorway, I took out my piece of aluminium and bent it until it was approximately six inches by four inches. Then I located the strike plate on the jamb of the doorway, it was approximately four feet off the ground. At this point, I taped the aluminum onto the outside jamb of the doorway lengthwise. Leaving the four inch side overlapping the outside of the door, just over the outside of the lock.

Once the door was opened from the inside the piece of aluminum would snap past the opened door. It would then press against the inside dead bolt, of the edge of the door, and remain stuck between the jamb and the dead bolt; keeping the dead bolt from locking into the strike plate of the jamb.

As soon as I accomplished this simple task, I could then gain entry into the building. All I needed now was for someone to open the door just once. I needed a diversion.

Finally, with my little strip of aluminum in place, I was ready to proceed forward with my plan. Carefully I unloaded the large garbage can from the trunk. I loaded it onto the sidewalk, less than 50 yards away from the service door entrance I was using. I planned to keep the body outside the building, hidden in the garbage can until I could gain access to the building.

With Joe's body now close enough to the service entrance of the building, and my aluminum strip in place, next to the lock on the door, I was ready to proceed with my plan.

Chapter Fifty Eight

There was a pay phone located at the corner of the block. My plan was to call 911 and report that a bomb was set to go off in five minutes. As I started to dial the phone, I stopped abruptly. For a moment I was in a daze.

With adrenaline pumping, my heart racing and my skin stinging from the cold, I stopped to reflect for a moment. I couldn't believe all the things I'd already done, and what I was about to do. Killing another human being, and calling in bomb threats. Was I going crazy? Look at all the laws I was breaking, just to save my own life! If I ever got caught, I'd be locked up in prison for many years.

One thing for sure - if I didn't pull off this elaborate suicide scheme, then my life would be worthless. There was no way the Vongemis would allow me to live long. Especially with all the incriminating evidence I had against the Family.

Was my life really worth killing another human being, and then throwing him off the top of a building? Looking to the heavens above, I prayed: Forgive me, Lord, for my sins. With all these doubts running through my mind, I was positive about one thing: my tremendous will to live. My not wanting to die would force me to do anything imaginable.

Was it morally right? Were all the things I'd done and were about to do-acceptable? Or should I just give up my life, and leave the world alone? As I looked back at the pay phone, I knew I had to continue forward with my plan.

If I ran away now without providing a body that showed the mob that I was dead, the Vongemis could threaten or use my family as hostages. It would force me to surrender myself to them for ultimate execution.

No, this was the only way out. I had to continue forward with the plan I structured so meticulously. I want to live! No matter what I have to do. I'm no hero, I am only an average man!

Feeling secure once again, I punched 911 into the phone. Then quickly I set my mind into action. The foreign accent I'd use, my tone of voice, my demeanor. When the 911 dispatcher answered, I said, "Take this down, so there'll be no mistake. There'll be an explosion in exactly five minutes at number One World Trade Center. It'll be major, so don't hesitate." My Iranian like accent was clear and distinct. "Well done!" I said, after I slammed the phone down. I think I missed my calling.

I quickly got back to my car, and gathered a small box of supplies. Immediately I set off two blockbuster explosives near the base of the building. The sound was deafening, as if a portion of the building had just blown up. My thinking was this: whoever was still in the building would now be running for their lives. It should only be two minutes till everyone evacuated the building.

Hiding by the corner of the building, I waited. It was only one minute before three men and one woman, all security personnel, came running out the service entrance. They kept running around to the front of the building and then across the street. Everyone would take this bomb threat very seriously, especially after the infamous bombing a few years ago in the same building.

I waited only one minute more, before grabbing my box and running up to the garbage can that held Joe's body. Placing the box on top of the lid of the can, I grabbed the handle and rolled the pail to the service entrance. No one else had come running out of the building. It was safe to assume that there was no one else in the building. I had my vinyl gloves, and woolen face mask on, anyway.

Being on the safe side I reached for the door. My piece of aluminum, had, as planned, wrapped itself around the inside of the door after it had been opened, which stopped the dead bolt from locking into the jamb of the door. With the dead bolt held snug against the aluminum, all I had to do now was just pull the door open.

With a piece of duct tape I taped the dead bolt tightly into the lock of the door, so it couldn't lock again. Quickly, I set off another blockbuster, right inside the service entrance. Much the same way that a soldier, in combat would clear the way in order to proceed forward into a new area. I didn't want to deal with anyone. And with the power of a quarter of a stick of dynamite, these blockbusters did their job, making enough noise so that everyone heard.

As I went to the service elevator, rolling the garbage pail with Joe in it was easy. Once I loaded the elevator with the body-filled pail, I set off three smoke bombs, right near the service entrance.

Then, I quickly pushed the top floor button of the elevator. The elevator was moving fast as it whizzed through all the floors, to the 44th. I then walked 20 feet to the Promenade elevator, which took me to the top. I lit off three more smoke bombs and threw them behind me as I ran down the hallway to the stairway that led to the roof.

Moving quickly, I rolled Joe and my box of dry ice along the roof, right to the edge, overlooking the street below. I laid the pail on its edge and knelt down.

Moving as quickly as I could, I knew that I was racing against the clock. In no more than three minutes, I should be back outside the building. Anything more could force me to run straight into the arms of the police.

As I planned for, there was a ledge that ran all along the edge of the top of the building. The ledge was one and a half feet wide. I placed Joe's body onto the ledge, lengthwise. The concrete ledge was angled slightly, pitched outward away from the building. Moving the body, just right, I positioned it so most of the weight was leaning over the outer ledge.

Toward the outside ledge, and under the body I placed chunks of dry ice. When the ice melted, the weight of the body leaning toward the outside ledge combined with the pitch of the ledge angled downward would force the body off the ledge and down some 110 stories. The body then would come to an abrupt concrete landing on the street below.

Running back to the elevator, I now had about ninety seconds left in my preset deadline. Only ninety seconds to get out of the building and make a getaway. The elevator seemed even faster on the way down to the main floor. It made my stomach slightly queazy from the speed.

Once I was back at the service entrance, I quickly set off five more smoke bombs and blockbusters. But this time I set them off on a delayed timer system. One was set to go off in five minutes, the next one was set to go off in fifteen minutes.

I was right on schedule, as I prepared to exit the building, along with my box and the empty garbage pail. Carefully, I looked out of the service entrance doorway. No one was in sight. The police hadn't arrived yet and there were no bystanders, no witnesses.

I quickly ditched the garbage pail, at the first building I saw. The cardboard box and other items I threw in a building's Dumpster. I discarded the surgical vinyl gloves and mask down the first sewer I saw. Everything was moving at lightning fast speed. I was fully aware that an extra thirty seconds could be disastrous.

On the way out of the building I had tore off the duct tape, the strapping tape and the piece of aluminum. They also were all discarded down the sewer, along with all the tools I had carried with me for the job. The last thing I had to do was take a small duffel bag out of my car. I had left my keys in the ignition. After all, I did supposedly commit suicide, and anyone that commits suicide doesn't lock their car and take the keys.

By the time I heard the first explosion, I was on my way down the steps of the subway station. I had reached the train platform before I heard the sirens from above. In less than three minutes the N train was pulling into the station.

What timing, what luck, everything was going perfect, too perfect. I thought, as I started to carefully analyze my performance of the day.

There was only a handful of people on the train heading back to Brooklyn. I dared not leave for the airport from Manhattan. I had to stick to my systematic plan. This wasn't the time to take any short-cuts.

It was a long, but soothing ride on the IRT "N" train, back to Brooklyn. The gentle swaying and vibration of the train was calming. The soft rumbling of the train made me contemplate the day. The worst was over, I thought, as I reflected happily over the whole escapade. It felt like I'd just run a marathon, I was exhausted, but elated.

Feeling proud at how my plan had unfolded, I first reflected on how brilliant it was. Of how I came up with the idea to take battery operated clocks, and expose the dials along with the hour and minute hands. Then, with the clock exposed, I tied a long fuse to the minute hand, and positioned the clock's minute hand just inches away from lit butane cigarette lighters. The lighter, which I'd forced into the lighted position, and set on very low, remained lit. This way in five and fifteen minutes the minute hands of the clock would carry the fuse precisely to the flame of the two cigarette lighters, lighting the fuses and setting off all the fireworks.

So much effort. So much worry. All the planning and thinking that went into this elaborate plan. Sitting there-motionless, I was exhausted, not from the physical exertion, but from the mental effort and its affect. I was ten minutes away from home, when I thought about Joe. The man I willingly sacrificed. It was the most selfish act of my life, so far. I lowered my head and said two prayers. One for Joe, and a special prayer for me; not to be forgiven, just to be understood. Just then, Tony Vongemi popped into my mind, his voice, his face and his tough goons. Again my stomach was in knots. Each and every time I thought of this weasel, I got sick.

There were no words for the anger I felt towards Tony. I wished that it was him I could've pushed off the building. But that would only make things worse. You cannot kill a mob boss. You can't even spit in his direction and live to talk about it. There was no beating the mob. I knew that. The best I could hope for was to fool them into thinking I was dead.

What I did tonight was the only way out. It brought tears to my eyes, as I thought about my family. It finally hit me hard. I felt as if someone really close to me had died.

I was sad. Sad, because it was me. I had just died this evening. Frank Granstino was no more. The name and the person had both come to an end. No longer would I ever hear my name. No one would recognize me where I was going. I would no longer see a familiar face, nor hear a familiar voice.

My family and my friends had all died along with me. No longer would I be able to hold or speak to them again. Tonight

277

my life had changed for good. Once again I reminded myself that this was my only way out, my only chance to live. At one time I thought that my escape would give me life, but at the moment I felt like a ghost. Someone non-existent, with no life, no family, and no purpose. I was glad the train car I was in had no other passengers, as the tears ran down my face.

Chapter Fifty Nine

Once I reached Brooklyn, with my duffel bag in hand, I quickly took a bus to the Bushwick section. I didn't want to be seen by anyone that knew me. In Bushwick no one knows anything. No one sees anyone. I got off the bus at a business section of Bushwick, right where I saw a car service. From there I took a taxi to Kennedy Airport.

Since I purchased my airline ticket with an open date, all I had to do was check in, and wait as a stand-by ticket holder. After everyone boards the plane, the flight attendants do a head count. If there are any seats still available then the stand-by ticket holders are called in order of their arrival. They're offered seating aboard the plane, instead of waiting for the next outgoing flight.

For four-thirty in the morning, Kennedy Airport was still surprisingly busy. There were many people trying to travel to many different destinations in time for business meetings.

I had to wait almost two hours before my name came over the loudspeaker. "TWA Flight 413 to Barava, paging Mr. Mario Taini." It took me five full seconds to realize that they were calling me, with my new name. How foreign that new name sounded. But I'd hit pay dirt. My stand-by ticket made it on the first flight out to Barava.

We were only ten minutes away from takeoff. I stowed my duffel bag in the overhead compartment. Then I adjusted my air vents, fastened my seat belt and looked wearily at the safety video.

Feeling exhausted, I couldn't wait to take off so I could go to sleep. My eyes were starting to close, even with all the commotion going on in the plane. Flying was never something I looked forward to, but I tolerated it only to get to new and exciting places.

Ten minutes passed and we still hadn't moved. Ten more minutes passed very slowly and still no movement. The captain came over the loud speaker and said, "Ladies and gentlemen, we have a slight delay ahead of us, so please be patient. We should be taking off in no more than 20 minutes."

Great! twenty more minutes, I thought, as I started to get restless from all the waiting.

With nothing else to do, I reviewed in my mind my new home. What would Barava be like? From all I'd read about the Cayman Islands it sounded beautiful. The crystal clear beaches, the palm trees swaying in the trade winds, and the nice people. Also, the weather was supposed to be fantastic. Gentle warm breezes, and clean air, normally everything a person could want. I wondered though, about my adjustment.

From my window seat in the ninth row of coach, I could hear the door of the plane sliding open. The stewardess was standing at the doorway speaking to someone who appeared to be in upper management. My interest was peaked, my nerves just about shot. I really wanted to get off the ground and on my way. The last thing I needed was more delay. It must be a celebrity, boarding late, I told myself, now feeling slightly annoyed and tired.

As I looked on with growing concern, I could see that the man boarding the plane was dressed in a black suit and tie, and speaking very low. While at the same time he started looking over the rows of passengers. When he looked my way I turned my attention to the window on my right. I began staring out the window, not wanting to look his way. Just hoping that he'd finish his business and leave quickly.

The talking continued for what seemed like hours. The passengers started to wonder, as the combined sound of low chatter started to pick up. There was an older woman seated next to me, on my left. The flight attendant came over to her and asked the woman to follow her into the first class section. She explained that since they had the extra seat, she was the one chosen to receive the free first class upgrade. Evidently, the woman was very happy as she followed the attendant through the curtain and into first class.

After approximately one minute, the man at the door proceeded to my row. He sat down in the older woman's empty seat. Now I was really worried.

The humming from the jet engines stopped, although I knew that they were ready to roar. Out of the corner of my eye I could get a general idea of what he looked like. The word hefty came to mind. About five eleven, dark hair, and on the large side. I dared not look. It didn't take more than five seconds before I felt something pushed into my ribs. Now I had to look.

There he was, smiling, this Italian guy in a suit. As I looked down, I saw a Magnum 45, I remember seeing them from television.

"It's the end of the road for you buddy!" he said, as he kept grinning a sick looking grin.

"Who are you anyway?" I asked, suspiciously.

"I'm Detective Moori, NYPD, and you've got to come downtown with me!"

"Your not a detective, and I'm not going with you!" I said angrily," knowing it was Vongemis executioner. With that, the creep grabbed the back of my shirt, dug the gun deeper into my ribs, and yanked my body closer.

"I'll kill you here, right now!" he screamed in my ear.

There was a loud bang. Then nothing, total silence. Suddenly I felt wet. No engine humming, no gun. Slowly I opened my eyes. I saw my bed, my dresser, my room. All at once I realized that it was a terrible dream. As my eyes focused on the alarm clock that hadn't gone off, The time showed 6:20 in the morning.

My body was drenched with perspiration. The day was just beginning. I never killed Joe, I never went to the World Trade Center. It was all a nightmare. The whole day and escape mission had been a dream. I looked around, the Ouzo and all of my tools for the suicide job were waiting patiently for me.

It was then that I heard the cause of the noise. A city sanitation truck was collecting garbage. With it's screeching brakes, the truck, no doubt back-fired, making the noise that brought me back to reality. Still half asleep I reviewed my dream. It was a full detail of the plan that I still had to carry out. As I slowly got out of bed, I realized just how smooth the operation went in my dream. I wondered: could I carry this mission out so flawlessly-for real, later on today?

281

With my head aching from lack of sleep, I headed toward the bathroom, for a hot shower. I stopped and looked at the liquor, the gloves, the pills, the tape and tools. Was I ready? I guessed I was as ready as I possibly could be.

As I entered the hot water of the shower stall, I realized that I had so much still to do today, that nothing had actually happened yet. My Thursday had actually just begun.

It was when my hair was full of shampoo that I heard the door bell ringing three times. Quickly I rinsed and jumped out, putting a towel around, covering my front and back. Again three rings of the bell. "All right! I hear you!" I yelled, rushing to the door. At this point I didn't care who the hell it was.

"Yeah, who is it? I yelled.

"Open the door Frankie, we've got to talk to you!" I heard from the other side of the door.

"Hold the boat!" I said, while fixing my towel. As I slowly opened the door, not knowing what to expect. I peeked out, "Yeah, what is it!"

"I catch you at a bad time?" he asked, with a smile.

"Kinda," I said a little bothered.

Standing tall outside my door was man of about fifty, dressed in a dark grey pinstripe suit. Was he a detective, or a hit man? Continuing to look him over, I said, "What's up?"

He looked me over, looked at my towel, and smiled. A full ten seconds passed, before he casually slipped a gold FBI badge with picture identification in front of me.

My heart sank, my breathing stopped for almost five seconds and a nauseous feeling came over me. All I could do was stare at the large FBI logo on the badge. Its as if the world had come to an end. I heard nothing.

Immediately - I became dizzy, almost passing out. Then my eyes slowly moved to the name: Robert Brennen, assistant director, FBI. I recognized the name, Brennen, from the newspapers, connected somehow with the Vongemi case.

The man said nothing for a full five seconds, which seemed to me like an eternity allowing the seriousness of the problem to sink in.

Then he spoke.

"Mario Taini, or should I call you by your real name - Frank Granstino?"

As I looked at his face and into his eyes, I knew that I was in big trouble. I said nothing. I just felt like I had died.

"Frank, we know what you've been planning, and why you were doing it."

All I could do was look into Mr. Brennen's eyes. They were brown. For the first time ever, I saw the details of another man's eyes with all the different hues of the iris. I knew full well that it was all over. There was nothing I could say, nothing I could do. The only thing I felt like doing was crying. I knew Brennen was the real McCoy. There was just that certain air of authority about him.

"Frank, I know how you feel. You feel like your world has just come to an end. We know about your involvement with Tony Vongemi and his organization. We know it all. We've been watching you very carefully and we're here to protect you. But Frank, we'll need your full cooperation. In order to protect you, we need you to help-us-help-you!"

"Mr Brennen," I said, "With all that I've been involved in, you want to help me and protect me?"

"Yes, Frank. You see we have been following you and watching the Vongemi Family very closely. We even followed your every move, in planning your suicide mission."

"But I was planning to kill a man."

"Yes, but we were watching you very closely, and we would've stopped you. We know why you feel you've no place to turn. We're here to help you. Please don't try to fight us, Frankie. Frank, we need you to come to FBI headquarters in Manhattan so we can discuss this case with you."

"You mean you're going to help me with the Vongemi Family Mr. Brennen?"

"We're in full control. We'll explain it all to you, once we're downtown. Now, let's get some clothes on you and get you out of here, so no one's the wiser."

I was dazed, as if I was still dreaming. Mr. Brennen patiently waited, until I put some jeans and a shirt on. Then we quickly left the apartment. Once we were on the street I was led to, and into a black sedan. Now, as I thought back, I remembered seeing this car several times before. These guys were good, I never once suspected the FBI was involved.

It took us thirty-five minutes to get into midtown Manhattan. Traffic was nonexistent. It was nearly seven o'clock in the morning - too early for the big daily rush. My mind was racing while trying to understand exactly what had transpired in the last several months.

When the car came to a stop, we were somewhere on Broadway in midtown Manhattan. Feeling half dazed now, I didn't know what number on Broadway we'd stopped at, but it was a big old brick building. At this point it didn't matter; I already felt that I'd been beaten. That I had failed in my plan.

So this was FBI Headquarters. I had never thought about the FBI, before today and I only knew about them from what I had seen in the movies for many years.

Once we entered the building, there were several FBI agents to escort us through the building. Security was extremely tight. These guys didn't play around. We took the elevator to the twenty second floor.

Along with our escorts, there was Mr. Brennen, and Mr. Hughes, who was an associate of Brennen's. They stood straight; almost at attention. FBI agents reminded me of Marines. As the elevator sped by the floors neither Brennen or Hughes looked at me, nor said a word. During the car ride from the airport to now, not one word. Maybe they were allowing the severity of the situation to sink in.

As soon as we entered the FBI office, Mr. Brennen quickly ushered me past the secretaries, past the office suites and into a large conference room. The room had a big, long, cherry wood table with thirty burgundy leather chairs all lined up around it. It was quite impressive. The conference room was furnished as if it were in the White House. I imagined all the high level meetings that must've taken place here, all the discussions of the most wanted criminals in the world, and the elaborate plans of how to capture them.

Mr. Brennen pulled out a chair on the right side of the table for me to sit in. He sat in the chair on my left, and Mr. Hughes sat on my right. Mr. Hughes was a stocky man in his late forties. He had thinning gray hair and beady eyes.

Mr. Brennen on the other hand, looked much more on the friendly side. He was a thin man, about fifty years old, with short brown hair and friendly brown eyes. When he spoke he had a soft, but firm commanding voice confirming his management position with the FBI. One could tell that Mr. Brennen was pulling all the strings.

"Frankie, let me start by telling you what we know," Mr. Brennen began, "We know that you're a good person, you come from a good family and, Frankie, we know you have a clean background. We also know that you unknowingly got involved with a major Mafia Family. According to our records, you sold insurance to clients that were supplied by Tony Vongemi, a kingpin of the Vongemi Crime Family, and some of these clients died. We know, Frankie, that millions of dollars in fraudulent claims were submitted to the insurance company. We know that some of those people were killed by the Vongemi Family, and some were sent to Italy and are in hiding. We've been watching the Vongemis, very closely, for a long time now."

"Mr. Brennen, if you knew all of this, then why did you allow me to go on all this time. All this self torture. Why didn't you step in to help me?"

"We had to be certain of your motives. We needed to compile enough evidence without tipping off the Vongemi Family. Frankie, we have you on film coming out of the restaurant the night that Sam 'Willie The Gambler' was killed in Tony's illegal gambling parlor. We had to make sure that you weren't recruited into the Family."

I didn't answer, I couldn't, so I just stared at him.

"Frankie, we know it all!" Brennen said, with a cocky tone in his voice.

"Yes, Mr. Brennen I remember it all. It's all etched carefully into my brain. But I don't understand why the FBI didn't stop me earlier in my plans to throw someone off the top of the World Trade Center."

"It's very simple Frankie. We knew precisely your every move. When you were home, we were watching you. When you went out, we followed you, and we even had someone look through your apartment, seeing what your next move might be."

"We even had miniature surveillance cameras set up in your apartment," Hughes added.

"So you guys were the ones with the listening devices, not the Mob?"

"We had your whole place wired, but the Mob also may have had a bug or two," Hughes said. "Our men swept your place clean of all bugs yesterday,"

"That's a lovely thought, I'm so glad I'm not some pervert," I said with a smile. "But what about the gas leak that almost killed me?"

Hughes shook his head as he said, "We missed that one Frankie, I'm sorry to say! By the time we realized what happened, you were already in the apartment"

"Well I'm just relieved it's all over, now. I'm not sure whether I could've carried out my plan today. I feel very close to the breaking point," I said, while shaking my head.

"We're well aware, Frankie," Brennen said, "it's been torture for us, just watching what you've been going through. But we knew you could hold up till now."

Chapter Sixty

Mr. Brennen had coffee brought in for all of us. As he took a sip, he continued: "Frankie, once we'd established that you were an innocent outsider and that you'd gotten sucked into and used by the Family, we started to document evidence against the Vongemis. We also were carefully and meticulously surveying their every move; waiting patiently for the day that they'd take you out."

"Tell me about it Mr. Brennen, I've been scared silly for at least three months now, praying and planning."

"Frankie, we know full well. We could read your plan. We could tell exactly what your next move would be. You didn't know it, but we were right on the scene and would've stopped any hit ordered against you. But to be honest Frankie, we thought that your suicide plan was brilliant!

"You guys saw it? How?"

"At the FBI, we're masters at surveillance." Brennen said. "We knew your plan as well as you did. We had to. This way we could step in at the precise moment we did. From the moment of planning your new identity, we knew that you were onto something good. All we had to do was watch that you didn't blow the plan and start an all out Family war, which of course we weren't prepared for."

"Mr Brennen, I'm sure you can appreciate and understand why I'm reluctant, and scared to talk to you now. And why I never came to you before."

"Of course we do. Your family would've been sitting ducks, even if you were in the Witness Protection Program. But it's all different now. Frankie, trust me. You have nothing to fear now, as long as you cooperate."

"All right, but I'm nervous. The Mafia doesn't play tunes I know how to dance to."

"Allow us to explain our plan, and show you all the dirt we have on the Vongemis," Hughes said, "Frank, just work with us - ok?"

"All right, I'll do my part. Anything you guys want. I'm totally exhausted mentally,"

"Your plan, which we photocopied was quite good, Frankie," Brennen said, with a friendly smile. "Your plan of access into the World Trade Center, and the way you were going to carry out your little trick of delayed ignition with your little bombs - terrific. But we especially liked the dry ice idea. Although we honestly don't know how long it might have taken before the body weight shifted enough to push it over the edge. We give you an A for effort, just in the meticulous planning you did, the drawings and all, Frankie. We were there all the way. Actually we were quite proud of you in driving determination to succeed."

"Mr Brennen, I'm sorry for my actions, and intentions, but I felt that there was no other way out. My back was against the wall! I was at the end of my rope. It was pretend to be dead or be killed for sure. Now what do I do? The Vongemi Family will surely find out about the failure of my plan, the FBI, and me."

"But Frankie, your plan did succeed! With the agency's help, we'll allow your plan to be played out to a tee."

"But the body, Mr. Brennen?"

"Oh there was a body Frankie, just as you planned it."

"Now I'm thoroughly confused, you guys really have to help me here!"

"You see Frankie, as we're speaking, our best FBI agents are carrying out your plan, just as you planned. But in a much more professional manner. We have a body all ready to go. A John Doe, who'd been on ice for some time. So there is in fact a body." Brennen said.

"You see," Hughes said, "the John Doe body, blood and all, will be doctored up to look like it'd fallen from the roof. All your paperwork will be carefully planted on the body to ultimately be found. The only difference was, because of your planned phone call of a bomb scare, we changed it to a call to the FBI. Which in turn, now has complete jurisdiction and control of the entire investigation and crime scene. Including the investigation of the suicide of one Frank J. Granstino,"

"Frankie, what most people don't realize, is, we have, at the FBI, unlimited resources and phenomenal technology. We can do almost anything. We're state-of-the-art. It would blow your mind. We can show you around later, son," Brennen said, reassuringly.

"Now, within the next half hour," he continued to explain, "our FBI cosmetologist will come in here to take a mold of your face, along with pictures and samples of your hair. He'll then will take the mold and make a latex skin mask of your face, and fit our John Doe body with a Frank Granstino face. Then a wig will be professionally made to match exactly to your hair color, texture and shape.

"Believe it or not our body will be an exact clone of Frank Granstino. Even your own mother wouldn't be able to see a difference! We'll explain that FBI people were able to work on the body, so that the top half of the casket can be left open at the funeral parlor."

"You guys are truly amazing!"

"Yes Frankie, we are. There are many things that we can do, that the public will never see on TV. Of course you know that many things are top secret. But we're very capable of doing the impossible. So this, quite honestly is a piece of cake for us."

"So Mr. Brennen, you're going to take whatever body you have on hand, and try to make it look like me?"

With that, Mr. Hughes cut right in, "Son, you don't realize it, so listen up. We're good! We can even make a black man look exactly like you. Trust us, we have even made exact clones of the President of the United States. We send these clones to places we're suspicious about. Before the President himself arrives, in case of any assassination attempts."

"So then what happens to me?" I asked.

Hughes replied, "Well son, if you work with us and if you listen to the advice we give you, we'll arrange to send you anywhere you want.

"By the way, Frankie, Barava, in the Cayman Islands, was a fine choice. We found that anywhere there is an out of the way tropical island, that one would be quite safe in that environment and they also would be far safer, for longer periods of time.

"We also firmly believe that the Vongemi Family will buy our story hook, line and sinker. Oh, and you can also be sure that they'll most definitely be at the wake, and at the funeral. They may even tap your family's phone lines. But, as long as you remain far away from New York, and you stay dead to all who know you, you'll be just fine," he said as he winked at me.

"Are you sure Mr. Hughes? Are you certain that no one in your agency will sell me out to the Vongemis?"

"Frankie," Brennen interrupted, "let me assure you that the three of us here, are the only people alive, that will know where you are. And that you're, still alive. No one will ever have access to this information. We've been waiting too long to nail Tony Vongemi and his brother, Bobby 'The Bull Dog' to the cross. I've personally taken full control of this case. I'll be in on every decision affecting you and the case. You can be sure that everything will be done by the book. We won't let anyone else in on any of the details."

"Mr. Brennen, your word is all I need. I'll do whatever you want me to do, except testify. I won't look at Tony Vongemi again!"

"You won't have to Frankie," Brennen said calmly. "Trust me. I know what personal torture you've been going through these last few months. I wouldn't wish that torture on my enemies. But you can be confident in the fact that we have enough evidence on the Vongemi Family to lock them all up for a very long time. Frankie, listen to this," Brennen continued, as he took a small micro-tape player and hit the play button.

I listened carefully, as I heard; "You played with the books, Louie, didn't you?"

"No! Tony, no way Tony! I wouldn't, Tony, please listen! Tony, please listen to me... no!   Not my fingers. No, Tony, please, I swear, anything!"

Then I heard the loud clipping sound of Louie G's finger being clipped off.

"Yes, I remember that Mr. Brennen. I can't believe that you have recordings of all this stuff. I can still see Louie, the jeweler screaming with tears running down his face, as he was begging Tony not to chop his finger off."

"You would be amazed at all the things we have on video and audio tape of the Vongemi Family, including carrying bodies out of the back entrance of the restaurant. We even have evidence of that charade, with the football goal post through Willie 'The Ears', the informant, after he was killed by orders from Bobby 'The Bull Dog'; listen to this," he said.

As I listened I heard a tough sounding character say, "Waste him. That Willie 'the ears' will finally get what he deserves, nobody rats on the Vongemis, Tony, nobody. And I want that Granto insurance agent deep sixed too."

"His name is Frank Granstino, Bobby, and we're fixing to waste him in a few weeks. We were just scaring him into keeping his silence about all our business. Just give us a few weeks, until we can put in a couple of mil, more in claims."

Brennen shut the tape player, as he just looked into my eyes. "Yes, Frank, we have them all on tape. They were planning on killing you real soon. You were right to run when you did. Any more of a delay would've been deadly. There's no doubt; starting next week they would've kept you under round- the-clock surveillance. We also have him on tape ordering other hits. We just want some additional evidence from you, on tape, before we convict them all, Frankie."

"What do I have to do? I'm exhausted. But I'll do anything to lock those creeps up for good!"

"It's simple," Hughes said, "just put on tape and in writing, certain facts and dates as you remember them, and whatever you were told that would help us."

"Do you mean things like monthly shake downs on local businesses, the collection fees, and all the protection money?"

"That's exactly what we want, Frankie," Brennen said. "But we want it all in your own words, as if you mailed us all the information before you committed suicide."

Chapter Sixty One

After Brennen and Hughes excused themselves and left me alone with a tape recorder and some notes to jog my memory, I thought for awhile. My mind drifted to my father, and how I felt that somehow, someway he had looked after me. If my father was here right now, he'd be proud of me, mostly because of my belief in myself, and my will to live. I've always wanted him to be proud of me, somehow I knew he was.

It took me approximately an hour, to first document all the information I'd collected in my head on the Vongemi Family. First, rough drafts, then finally the finished taped copy. It included all the things Tony had told me, all the details he let slip every time he started to drink. All the inside information that I never wanted to hear. All the secrets that Tony was certain I'd never have the nerve to repeat to anyone.

Tony's boldness, his confidence, was commendable, but very foolish in a way. Because one of the few things that I learned from hanging around the mob was, you can never ever trust anyone in that business. No matter how much you intimidate people. You never know when someone will start singing. People will talk for many different reasons, even when their life was at stake.

I wouldn't be around, but I'd pay to see Tony Vongemis face as all the charges were read out loud in court. There was no doubt that he'd have that sarcastic grin on his face, as if he wasn't worried about all the charges against him, although he'd be silently calculating all the years he'd have to spend behind bars, for each charge he was convicted on.

Bobby "The Bull Dog" Vongemi on the other hand, wouldn't be smiling. He'd be looking to strangle the closest person to him. God help his lawyer, if Bobby was convicted.

Mr. Brennen was notified by Mr. Hughes as soon as I completed my tape recording and the written documentation of my dealings with Tony Vongemi.

He glanced quickly at the written report, "Excellent, this is perfect, Frankie."

"It's all that I can remember at this time, Mr. Brennen. What happens now?"

"Well, let's see, your complete accounting is right here. We dated it on the day you were to have killed yourself. So there's no more for you to report, because you'd be dead."

"Thanks, Mr. Brennen, I feel like I've already died!"

"We'll change your appearance until you reach your final destination. Just to be on the safe side of course. There's no reason to risk having anyone recognize you. Once you're at your final destination, you should change your appearance slightly. I'd suggest a mustache and sideburns, just enough to take on a different look. You'd be amazed at the difference it'll make in your appearance.

"We'll also give you a new identity. Or if you so wish you can keep the name you have chosen. In any event, your new name will be able to be traced back to a long family history. Your fingerprints also will be able to be traced back to that new identity. Frankie, I promise you we'll cover all the bases, even down to a family photo album. Your old photos will be kept in a safe deposit box, as well as all the other personal effects from your former life. Anytime you wish to review these items you can and you should, but they must all be returned, for your own safety."

"Should I look for a job when I get down there, or not take the risk in working?" I asked.

"No, Frankie, we'll arrange a job for you. But for the first three months, I want you to get accustomed to the land, and to the people. I want you to settle in. Then you can let me know what line of work you wish to take on and we'll arrange it for you."

"I always wanted to make Dunkin Donuts," I joked, with a big grin on my face.

"Keep in mind that you shouldn't contact our agency, under any circumstances. We'll stay in touch with you on a weekly basis. You should only speak to Mr. Hughes or myself. If you have an emergency, there's a private beeper number that can be accessed through a remote 800 number. Then the message will be forwarded directly to me. Frankie, you're never to use your old name again, and you must purchase all new clothes in Barava when you arrive. Do you understand?"

"Yes Mr. Brennen, I understand. I said, taking it all in. "But, Mr. Brennen, what about my family?" I asked.

"You do realize, Frankie, as sad as it may sound, your family is basically history. There can be no contact in any form with them. We'll send you a video every six months, showing some of their activities. Of course filmed without their knowledge. God forbid anyone should pass away, we'll send you video footage of whatever we can safely film. You must keep it all in the safety deposit box."

"When will I be leaving for Barava?"

"I think we'll have you take a nap for a couple of hours, in a secure room right here. Then we'll have our cosmetologist give you a new face made of latex, just for your trip to Barava. Once you reach the airport there, just go into the bathroom, remove the thin latex mask and wash your face. Your flight from JFK Airport will be in five hours."

Mr. Hughes chimed in, "Frankie, you'll be flying first class. There'll be much less chance of any encounter in the first class section."

Feeling troubled, I asked, "Mr. Brennen, how bad will my death be on my family? This thought has been bothering me for some time now."

"Well, Frankie, there's no question that it all will be a tremendous shock to your family. A suicide always is. The family members may go through periods of guilt. Feeling like they should've known that something was wrong with you. They'll feel that, somehow, they should have prevented it all.

"We will be able to help them - more than regular suicide families, because our agency is in charge of the investigation. We'll send all family members some of our best psychologists. Frankie, I promise you, that these professionals will work with your family as long as they need them. You have my personal guarantee on this matter. I'll make sure that the best support will be there for your family. Trust me, this is the best you can hope for now, Frankie."

"Mr. Brennen, is it possible that Tony Vongemi will ever find me?"

"No, because the Vongemi brothers will be behind bars so long, they will never see the light of day again. Keep in mind that tax evasion has put more Mafia bosses behind bars than any other convicted crime. Then add to this all the hits that each one of them have ordered. And then, we'll also have all the Family goons that'll turn states evidence to save their own necks. We have so much on the Vongemis that we'll dismantle the entire Vongemi Mafia Family within one year.

"Frankie, what usually happens in these types of situations, is when we dismantle the Vongemi Family, the strongest Mafia Family actually becomes stronger. They step in and absorb most of the Vongemi business assets.

"Then, the Vongemis immediate surviving Family that are not in prison are taken care of financially, forever, by the much more powerful Mafia family, although no member of the Vongemi Family can stay in the Mafia link. Organized crime is actually glad to have the Vongemi Family out of the way. They know how much attention was being paid to all of organized crime due to the tactics of the Vongemis for the past few years.

"Now that the Vongemis are out of the way, the remaining Families can get back to normal again. Although they'll operate on somewhat of a smaller scale, there'll be no immediate threat from the FBI. You see, Frankie, we don't have the resources to clean up the entire organized crime business. We can only dent its armor and they know it. But we do the best we can."

"The whole Mafia scene was making me sick to my stomach, Mr. Brennen. The shooting in the back room, the cutting off of the jeweler's finger, splattering blood all over. The nonchalant way that Tony would have someone killed. The way that they killed Willie 'The Ears' Shoteri, by impaling him on the upright of the goal post. It's a nasty business, I don't know how anyone could do it."

"It's easy son!" Hughes said. "It always starts out small time. Little things that are asked of a new recruit. Most guys are wanna-be's. They hang around with Mafia-made men so long that sooner or later they're recruited. These new thugs are totally unaware in the beginning that they're working for the mob. By the time they realize it, and the chores become more gruesome, they can't get out. And at that point, they know better than to try to get out. The Mafia is big business, and at that point they've reached the point of no return!"

"I have a question, Mr. Brennen. If I was supposed to have mailed the letter and tape recording of the Vongemi details yesterday, how can you say you received them before my death?"

"Oh, that one's easy Frankie. We have people in the post office that will stamp any date we request on the envelope that you already addressed to us," Brennen boasted.

"Don't you worry son, it's all been worked out," added Hughes.

"You guys really do think of everything!" I said in amazement. "Will my family find out about my confession to your agency before my suicide death?"

"Yes, Frankie, but only after the evidence is introduced in court. We then will explain to them, that one of your last actions before your death, was to fix the Vongemis who were out to kill you. We'll also explain how you were unknowingly suckered into the Vongemi crime syndicate, and used in their illegal operations.

"When we're done, you'll look like a hero to all who know you. Although, you do realize, that this won't happen until the trial has been ongoing for some time. It may take up to two years before the case goes to trial. So, from now to then, no one except the Vongemis will have the slightest clue as to why you self destructed and took your own life."

"I realize, Mr. Brennen, that I have no control over any of those details. But I now feel much better knowing that you guys are on my side," I said, as I reached out to shake both of their hands, while fighting back tears of happiness.

"Oh, one last thing. Do you guys have anything on a beautiful girl named Alicia, the girl who was spying for Tony?"

Hughes looked puzzled, then he looked at Brennen. Brennen looked my way and said, "Frankie, we have nothing on anyone named Alicia. We have many beautiful women connected intimately to the Vongemi clan. Unless we missed something"

"You got a crush of one of Tony's girlfriends son? Some kind of power-sex, thrill thing?"

"No, not at all, Mr. Hughes. Just forget it. I just thought that..."

"Just keep thinking one thing Frankie, you're a very lucky young man." Hughes said, "Be happy with that, try to make a new life for yourself, ok?"

"Yes sir! I really am lucky. I'm so glad to be alive, and so glad to move on and get this weight lifted from my brain. Thank you once again for you help"

I was finally confident in their total support and in their assurance of setting the record straight with my family, but especially because I knew that Mr. Brennen would ultimately assure my mother.

I always wanted my mother to know that her only son was a success. She always had such high expectations of me. I never wanted to let her down, and after the record is set straight she'd feel much better about my passing.

Now I was feeling totally spent. Mr. Brennen allowed me to sleep for two hours. It was the most restful sleep I could remember having in many months. Maybe I slept great because I was exhausted. Or maybe because my mind was at ease, and not racing two hundred miles per hour. But for the first time in many months, I felt totally safe.

By the time I had awakened, the agency had a whole meal set up for me in the conference room. It felt like a celebration. There was a dinner of turkey, stuffing and all the vegetables, and of course, cranberry sauce. You can't forget the cranberry sauce! I thought.

While I ate, as if I was just let out of prison, Marvin, the cosmetologist was preparing me for my latex travel face. These guys were just like the guys in the movies. Everyone was an expert!

Marvin was a friendly sort of fellow. He liked to talk about himself a lot. Although, I felt that he just might be a woman in a man's body. He had many female tendencies, but he was excellent at what he did best. He could make anyone look different. I just couldn't look at him, because he was wearing eye makeup and blush. He appeared to be about five foot six, and maybe 130 pounds. He looked forty five with longish salt and pepper hair.

By the time Marvin was done, I didn't recognize my face. As the finishing touches were applied, with the blue contacts and new hair style, with a wig, I couldn't believe my eyes. I liked my new look so much that I had only wished that I could look like this forever. Marvin made me look very handsome. I even wondered if the flight attendants would make passes at me during the flight. What a clear head I had. After all I had just been through, my mind was back to women. My nerves must be calming down, I was thinking about beautiful women again!

Chapter Sixty Two

The flight to the Cayman Islands was fabulous. The FBI drove me to the airport in a black Lincoln limousine. As they promised, I was sitting in first class. This time, there was no delay. I was allowed to board the flight five minutes before we took off. Just before I could buckle my seat belt, Crystal, the blonde haired flight attendant, in my section ran over to me with a glass of fine champagne.

"What a way to go," I said, as I slowly savored the champagne. I hadn't felt this good in many months. Maybe because it was finally behind me, all the tension and Mafia pressure. My life would be free once again.

Crystal smiled at me with a sparkle in her eyes, as she handed me a pillow and a blanket. "Sir, are you comfortable?" I quickly looked around, before I realized that she was talking to me.

"Oh, I'm very comfortable, thank you!" I said, smiling my best smile. I wondered if she liked the new me, or was she just being friendly to everyone in first class.

My new face must have something to do with it, I thought as I smiled. Men are far too easy. All it takes is an innocent, friendly smile from a beautiful woman, and men start to see stars, as their heads get big with all the extra hot air. What suckers we men are when it comes to attractive women.

It was champagne and lobster all the way to Barava. Flying first class was like flying in a living room. It felt as though my seat were as big as a large recliner, and the leather seat was even more comfortable than even my old recliner at home. Leaning back, I listened to some soft classical music, on my complimentary headphone set.

I continued to sip the fine champagne. "Dying never felt so good," I said, softly to myself. Half of the seats in the first class section were empty. Even though I had never flown in first class before, I still could imagine how much extra it must have cost.

My emotions ran from immense satisfaction, in still being alive and away from the Vongemi's, to a complete feeling of emptiness and hopelessness. I've never felt such extreme intermittent changes of emotions. There was a sense of loss, as if my family had all suddenly died. I knew that this was to be expected, but it didn't make me feel any better. Still I knew that I'd have to work myself through it all. There was no other way out, I kept convincing myself. I was so thankful to still be alive. The soft humming of the engines put me into a sound sleep.

The sound of the landing gear being lowered abruptly woke me out of a much needed sleep. We were only minutes away from landing. Only minutes away from the beginning of a new and exciting life, in a brand new land. My heart was pounding at the thought of this new adventure in my life.

Money wasn't a problem. I now had plenty of money, which I'd been able to accumulate over the past several months. The FBI had also wired some money ahead for me. As Mr. Brennen explained to me, it was customary for the agency to start a Witness Protection Client off with fifty thousand dollars in cash as soon as they were relocated. He went on to explain that this always calmed the fears of the witness, as they changed their entire life and identity.

Once we landed, I headed straight for the men's room in the airport, as I was instructed. Once I was in one of the toilet stalls, I slowly tore off my latex fake face and removed my wig and blue contact lenses. The latex was making my face sweat, but for the most part it was comfortable. The guys at the bureau know how to do faces well. Now it was back to the old face that had gotten me this far in life. But now, I was Mario Taini, I chose to keep the new name that I had come up with.

The agency was nice enough to quickly print up all documents with my new identity on them. Including a birth Certificate, New York State drivers license, and credit cards that could actually be traceable to a Mario Taini. I don't know how they did it, but the FBI was truly amazing. Looking at them carefully, I couldn't see any difference between these documents and the real ones I'd once possessed.

Also, the agency changed my hotel. They now had me booked into the Barava Hilton Ocean Front Resort. A four star resort complex.

The hotel was a soothing pink color, located right on the beach front. All of the rooms had a balcony overlooking the beautiful blue ocean. My room was on the second floor. I figured that the FBI didn't want it on their conscious if I decided to jump off of the balcony. That had to be why they put me on a low floor. It didn't bother me. After all, this was a new life, a new Mario Taini. The old person was dead. I didn't even want to think of my old name, or my old problems.

The mini-suite, as they called it, appeared big to me. Almost as if it were two rooms converted into one. Perhaps the agency arranged this type of room, knowing that I would be staying in the hotel for three months, before I was scheduled to move permanently into a new apartment. In any event, it was great! It was just as I pictured it in my mind. I knew that I'd love Barava. The water was blue, the sand was pure white and they say that the sun was always shining here. All of this, of course, along with the beautiful women in Barava, make for a true paradise. Things could be far worse. I could easily have been shot. I guess I could live with this.

Mr. Brennen and the FBI wouldn't allow me to bring any of my clothes. So I had to purchase some new clothes in the hotel shops. One of the first items on my list was a bathing suit. I had to have a bathing suit right away, especially with the sun shinning so brightly. The temperature was 89 degrees at 11:15 am. The hotel listed the temperature yesterday at a high of 95 degrees, and there'd been no rain for the last two weeks.

It was 11:45am by the time I reached the hotel pool area. The pool was huge, not just long, but shaped different than any pool I've ever seen. The center jutted out on both sides almost like an intersection of a main street and then rounded off at each end. From a distance in the air the pool must look like a star. In the center of the pool, there appeared to be a fountain from which water shot straight up in the air ten feet, then spread out into a shower type of spray.

The entire lounge area around the pool was huge, maybe five times larger than the other resorts I'd seen. By the sides of the pool there were numerous lounge chairs set up. I set a chair up for myself on the left side of the pool, not too far from the center.

303

There was bar service at poolside. So of course, I got right into the spirit and ordered a Heineken beer. Never too early for a Heineken, I thought, as I sipped the iced cold beer. As I watched the various activities in the pool, the laughing, the diving, the sun bathing, and the families all having fun, my mind started wandering, and wondering. First, I thought of my mother, then my sister Candice, my niece, and my father.

Then my mind focused on the mob. On my hatred of Tony Vongemi, his brother, Carlo and Benny and of all that they stood for. I remembered and felt very sad about the dead people, and how many the Vongemi Family had killed.

As I sat in the beautiful tropical sunshine, I thought of all my associates at Financial Life. I remembered my good friend Paul, and all the wonderful memories I'd always have. I thought of Alicia, and wondered what she'd think of my death. I wondered if it would even matter at all to her. Maybe she did feel something for me? Or, was it all just an act on her part?

Then I thought of all I'd left behind, and would never see again. Brooklyn would only be a pleasant memory now. My life was new and it was here in Barava now. I'd been born again, with a new chance to live. A new hope to achieve my dreams.

I stopped thinking. I looked straight up to the blue and cloudless sky and said, "Thank you God! Thank you for a new day, a new life!" Then I smiled, raised my hand up high, and looked at the blonde blue-eyed waitress. Then feeling great about my new life, I said, "I'll have another Heineken, please!"

Out of the corner of my eye, to my right, a great pair of legs came into view. Lying on my back, comfortably, in the chaise lounge, I tried not to look too conspicuous. As my eyes slowly moved upward, a bright pink bikini suit told me, this place truly was paradise.

Ever so slowly, my eyes took in more, I almost flipped out of the lounge chair as I heard, "Hi Mario, missed me?"

I looked up in amazement, "Alicia?"

"No, it's Susan now," she said. "Don't worry, Mario, Brennen knows, he put me in the Witness Protection Program too. It's a long story and we'll have plenty of time. I'm here to stay, if you'll have me?"

"Have you? I'd have you right now! You mean you're..."

"That's right, I was always undercover. Brennen had me infiltrate the Vongemi Family years ago. Tony thought I was spying for him, but in actuality, I've been with the FBI for ten years. One day, I'll tell you stories that will curl your hair!"

"So all along, even on our vacation, you were with the FBI?" I asked, still in a state of shock.

"It's been a few years, now. But with the latest Vongemi mess, Brennen believes I deserve out. The Vongemi convictions will be big-time. Besides, I told Brennen that I fell in love with some Italian-Stallion, from Brooklyn."

"You mean on Paradise Island, your feelings toward me were real?" I asked.

"Right from the first smile. You see, I had an edge, I had your full background, pictures, videos, story, before I even met you. Right from the beginning, there was a strong attraction. Especially, when I knew you were in trouble with the Vongemis," she said.

"It feels like a dream, I can't believe you're actually here! I said, with tears of joy in my eyes. "I've missed you so much!"

"We have so much to catch up on. Aren't you going to tell me how much you missed me?" She asked, with a smile.

"Alicia, eh-Susan, I, of course I..."

"Shut-up already, and kiss me, you mug!" Our kiss lasted for five full minutes, I thought I would need oxygen. But the best part was - this was only the beginning.

* The End *

About The Author

John Paul Carinci has been a successful business owner for 25 years. Currently, he is President of Carinci Insurance Agency Inc., with over 250 brokers. John, is also an author, songwriter, and poet. He is the C.E.O. of Better Off Dead Productions Inc., a movie production company. John has had numerous poems, and a short story published.

As a writer, some of John's works include; "Better Off Dead," "Second Chance," "Be Different," "Exchange of Life," and "A Gift From Above."

John, is also co-writer of the screenplay: "Better Off Dead," which was adapted from his novel, and due to be in production in the winter of 2001.